DEADWOOD AND BEYOND

DEADWOOD AND BEYOND

KIP MEYERHOFF

iUniverse®

DEADWOOD AND BEYOND

iUniverse books may be ordered through booksellers or by contacting:

iUniverse
1663 Liberty Drive
Bloomington, IN 47403
www.iuniverse.com
1-800-Authors (1-800-288-4677)

ISBN: 978-1-5320-2761-1 (sc)
ISBN: 978-1-5320-2762-8 (hc)
ISBN: 978-1-5320-2763-5 (e)

Library of Congress Control Number: 2017911750

Print information available on the last page.

iUniverse rev. date: 10/05/2017

There's no telling what's coming
through the door next.

Contents

Prologue

Boston gangster Whitey Bulger was long feared by his fellow criminals because every one of them with a working brain knew that to cross Whitey could get you killed. So those caught with their pants down did the time, refusing to rat on Whitey and his crew. Well, most of them anyway. Some gave it up to the feds with a promise of a new life in the witness protection program.

Ironically, Bulger was a snitch himself who traded information about his rivals in exchange for a certain amount of protection from law enforcement. This corruption eventually led to Bulger becoming one of the first gangsters to penetrate the FBI's informant rolls. Unfortunately, he wouldn't be the last.

John Smiley, known in his previous life as John "Smiling Jack" Cochran, felt secure in the new life provided for him by the witness protection program. He didn't think that day would be his last. He had plans. He was in control. That morning, he'd tipped his barber five bucks for a little off the sides and a squared-up back. He joked with the manicurist about maybe a bright red on his left pinkie instead of the clear. His mood was high because he had a date that night with Cindy, the hot cocktail waitress from work. The next day, a Harley ride to Sturgis, maybe with Cindy hanging onto his waist. Next month, he had a two-week vacation coming, a trip to Seattle in the works. In spite of being two thousand miles from his Long Island home, life was good.

Like most in the life, Jack spent considerable effort suppressing thoughts of his own demise. Women and booze were his choices to keep his mind busy, and dealing cards provided him the wherewithal to indulge both. He'd learned to do card tricks as a kid, and after serving a two-year stretch in Attica honing his skills, he'd become an accomplished card cheat for the outfit. They used him to fleece many a mark in crooked games set up to do just that. In one such game, the mark caught on to Jack's bottom dealing and called him on it. Jack just smiled and stuck a knife in the guy's heart.

Impressed with Jack's decisiveness, the boys let him do a couple of contract hits in Far Rockaway and another in the Bronx. With the addition of button man to his card-shark résumé, Jack was a mob up-and-comer. Until he got caught.

Faced with a lifetime of doing card tricks for fellow Attica inmates, Jack became a rat for the feds. And who could have blamed him? But after a couple of Salerno family bosses were sent to federal prison, the mob's suspicions focused on Jack. Word on the street had it that a $10,000 contract was the reason for a botched attempt on Jack's life. So when Jack disappeared into the promised safety of witness protection, many wondered if Jack had paid the ultimate price for his treachery. Fish food? Cement barrel? Landfill? Speculation was rampant, but the bosses knew different. They had no doubt Jack was being protected by the feds. The mob would feel the pain when the feds netted forty-six La Cosa Nostra underlings in August 2016 mostly on info Jack had given to his FBI handlers.

Ensconced in maximum security, Slats Salerno and his second in charge, Dino Mendolia, were no longer able to safeguard their interests. Soon, the Salerno operation was in chaos. The Russians were moving into the Kennedy and LaGuardia Airports, MS-13 gangsters were pushing dope all the way from the Bronx to Montauk Point, new labor problems arose on the docks, and the garbage contracts in Nassau and Queens were expiring. Dino's cement business was also being threatened by unwanted competition. Worst of all, tribute payments from all the wannabe wise guys ceased with the guilty verdicts passed on Salerno and Mendolia.

A Salerno lieutenant, Vincenzo "Big Vinnie" Costello, ruled Suffolk County with an iron fist. No one dared a move against any Salerno interest in which Big Vinnie had a part. Great bodily injury or worse could ensue. When La Cosa Nostra appointed Costello caretaker of the whole Salerno operation, Vinnie vowed Smiling Jack would pay for his treachery. But truth be told, he was grateful to Cochran for his promotion. How else would he have moved up?

Fortunately for Cochran, all of Big Vinnie Costello's attention was required to restore order, thus moving Cochran way down his to-do list. Four Long Island counties saw an increase in their homicide and missing-person rates. Beating and gunshot victims kept emergency rooms busy, and arson fires and a few bombings increased overtime costs for emergency responders. Big

Vinnie's efforts had a positive impact on Long Island's economy, which President Trump took credit for.

It would take six months of guile, diplomacy, and muscle for Big Vinnie to complete his consolidation work. His reputation for violence grew with the territory he regained and controlled, and all the talent in Vinnie Costello's crew soon made him the mob's biggest moneymaker from Montauk to Staten Island. Big Vinnie decided it was time for Smiling Jack to get his due. And Vinnie knew that even his top enforcer, Sean "Soldier Boy" Mahan, could use a little help from a friend. Hello, Rollo Michaels.

Chapter 1

Dead in Deadwood

"Hey!" I shouted, reaching for my Walther.

Both men flinched, but the gunman managed to squeeze off a double tap, and the man I was following went down. The shooter swung the business end of his weapon toward me and fired twice more as I ducked between parked cars for cover. A woman screamed. I popped up over the trunk of a Buick and let go two of my own, and then the shooter was gone. I heard more screams. A man shouted, "Look out! He has a gun. Call the cops!"

I worked my way up the aisle, cautiously sneaking peeks over, under, and around the many parked vehicles. I heard a car alarm blaring from the floor below and the footfalls of people running from the parking structure. It seemed like it took forever to get where John Cochran lay between two cars. He looked up at me, fear in his eyes and blood spurting from a hole in his neck. I reached down to stem the flow.

"Older," he whispered between broken teeth as the last of his life seeped through my fingers.

The wail of approaching sirens soon drowned out the blaring horn and sharpened my focus as I stood over the lifeless body. The smile was gone from Smiling Jack's face, having been removed by the two bullets pumped into him only moments ago. I felt guilty about something but didn't know what. Jack was dead fifteen minutes after I had met him, and I was left there holding the bag.

I'd followed Cochran from the casino where he dealt cards to get a visual on his vehicle and maybe tail him to his residence. I was staying back so as not to spook him when up popped the shooter to take Jack's life and ruin my plans.

My name is Rollo Michaels. Though my ID says Roland Michaels, I prefer Rollo, but I've been called many other things—some nice, some not. But I usually answer no matter. I'm an ex-LAPD detective sergeant pensioned off because of a work-related injury. A couple of years of feeling sorry for myself killed a twelve-year marriage that had blessed me with a daughter and a son. Child support and alimony pretty much ate up my monthly disability checks. Periodic personal security gigs kept me in beer money, but even all the celebs in Los Angeles couldn't employ all the hired guns running around La-La Land. Mounting debt and indulging bad habits made finding steady employment a necessity.

Desperate, I teamed up with my divorce attorney and another retired cop to open a PI shop along LA's Miracle Mile. We were surprised by the number of clients who quickly signed on. We paid the rent, leased nice cars, and enjoyed the excesses that were both the best and the worst of Los Angeles.

Our team specialized in finding people, and one of the cases I was currently working had added about six thousand frequent-flier miles to my account. It was a long way from LA's Miracle Mile to the second floor of the Deadwood City Parking Garage, but there I stood, a dead man at my feet, a gun in one hand, and blood dripping from the other. I was sure the sheriff of Deadwood, South Dakota, would want to know what the hell was going on but no more than I did.

I heard footsteps coming up the ramp. "Freeze! Drop your weapon!" was a line I'd used on many occasions. I complied by dropping my Walther on the lifeless body at my feet. I sure as hell wasn't going to drop my best friend on the concrete.

The two deputies were pretty good at roughing me up, probably their first homicide. They weren't interested in what I had to say about the shooter; they were content with having me cuffed in the backseat of their cruiser, case solved. While we waited for the detectives, the crime scene was quickly becoming a tourist attraction.

The first person of authority to show up was right out of central casting—white Stetson, snakeskin cowboy boots, and pearl-handled Colt six-shooter riding low on his hip. His star said sheriff, and a thick handlebar mustache didn't hide his frown. He huddled with the two deputies whose heads kept nodding as his forefinger pounded their chests in cadence with the expletives I could read on his lips. Once they had established control of the crime scene, the detectives and coroner arrived to take over.

The detectives jerked me from the cruiser, bagged my hands, and turned me back over to the chastised deputies, who were then instructed about gunshot residue and blood-splatter evidence. I was put back in the car, that time more gently, and transported to the station. There, I was swabbed, strip-searched, and left in a holding cell with only my socks, my Hanes tagless T-shirt, and my boxers. A request for a phone call got me a scowl. *Hard guys these. Like I'm the reason the sheriff chewed your asses out.*

More than two hours passed before Sheriff Bullock showed up with one of his detectives. My bladder was about ready to cry uncle when they gave me a pair of paper slippers and an orange jumpsuit with PRISONER stenciled on the back. After a pit stop, I was taken to Bullock's office. The contents of my pockets were laid out on his desk. My retired LAPD ID, California private investigator license, and California driver's license were neatly fanned out for the sheriff's perusal. Noticeably missing were my Walther PPK and seven rounds of hollow-point ammo. I was directed to a chair in front of the desk by the escorting detective. The sheriff dismissed him with a "Thank you, Bubba."

"Coffee?" he asked as he poured a cup for himself. I nodded. He poured a second and placed it before me. “So, Michaels, what are you doing at the scene of our first homicide in over two years?”

“Doing my job finding a missing person,” I answered, wondering if he could hear my stomach rumble. “Where’s my Walther?”

“Booked into evidence. Tell me about your so-called job,” he said as he sat in his very big chair.

“Make more coffee. It could take a while.”

Chapter 2

Soldier's Story

You can run, but you can't hide especially if you're somebody like Smiling Jack Cochran and a stone killer named Sean "Soldier Boy" Mahan is coming for you. Those in the profession referred to Soldier as the Terminator and describe him as your worst nightmare.

Mahan was a veteran of the first Gulf War who returned home with a Bronze Star, Purple Heart, and the scars of war, mental and physical. But like many of his comrades, he was without the job skills necessary to ease back into civilian life.

He had joined the army right out of high school with his best friend, Richie Salerno, the only son of Slats Salerno, a high-ranking Brooklyn gangster. War changes all who are touched by it. Killing the Iraqi soldier whose bullet had ended his friend Richie's young life had changed Mahan's world forever.

A patriotic Slats gave Sean Mahan the Soldier Boy handle and a job of collecting for his loansharking operations. Soldier's size, scars, and reputation made him a very useful and proficient employee. Over time, Slats entrusted him with more and more of the heavy lifting required to grow the business. With Slats in the joint, Soldier's loyalties were pledged to his new boss, Big Vinnie Costello. Vinnie wished he had ten more just like Mahan.

Soldier Boy's experiences had taught him that things rarely went as planned. He had waited in the casino until the PI had braced Smiling Jack. He knew Jack always ran, so he went to the parking lot where Jack kept his car and set up his kill zone. He had acquired an old MP model .38 six-shot revolver for the job. The front sight had been removed so he could slide a plastic soda bottle over the barrel as a silencer. He stepped from between two parked cars as Jack put the key into his car door.

Soldier pointed the gun at the back of Jack's head and was squeezing the trigger when someone shouted, "Hey!" changing things in the blink of an eye. He and Jack flinched. That caused the first bullet to tear through Jack's neck instead of his head. The second shot caught Jack in the jaw and knocked him to the concrete.

Soldier turned toward the source of the shout and saw Big Vinnie's PI standing at the top of the ramp. He fired twice more to make the PI seek cover, his instructions having exempted the PI from harm. As he turned back to finish what he'd been sent to do, two more shots rang out. The one that hit him spun Soldier around and sent him over the rail to the lot below. He landed on the hood of a parked car, setting off its alarm to mix with the cacophony of screams and shouts.

He rolled from the hood to his feet and ran two blocks down an alley, throwing his revolver, hat, shades, wig and fake beard into a couple of the half-dozen Dumpsters lining the alley. His shoulder burned from his wound as blood began to seep through his jacket. He was not being followed, so he slowed to a walk and placed his handkerchief inside his jacket to soak it up. That it wasn't the first time he'd been shot allowed him to keep his cool. In fact, it was the third—Kuwait, Brooklyn, and now Deadwood. It came with the territory, a hazard of his chosen profession.

Soldier entered the backdoor of a bar and walked through to the street where he had parked. He was just getting into his rental when a sheriff's car came screaming by, emergency lights and siren assaulting his senses and adding more adrenaline to his system. He pulled slowly from the curb and drove away as bar patrons poured to the sidewalk to partake in the excitement.

Back in the safety of his hotel room, Soldier took out his traveling hospital. He flushed his wound with antiseptic Irish whiskey. The pain of using his Old Kilkenny for that purpose hurt as much as the wound did. Again, luck had been with him. The .38 slug had dug a quarter-inch furrow through two inches of skin on the outer part of his shoulder. He was glad the PI hadn't been carrying a weapon with a little more pop. He took a healthy swig from the bottle to calm his adrenaline and steady his hand. He threaded a needle and sewed up his gash, tying off and snipping a stitch, sipping some of the Old Kilkenny, and repeating seven more times.

He thought of his luck in Kuwait when he and his best friend, Richie Salerno, found themselves lost in the desert with their platoon sergeant, their Humvee mired in sand up to its axles. An Iraqi patrol stumbled upon them and opened fire, wounding Sarge and him but killing his friend Richie. Soldier killed three of the enemy and captured two. The rest dropped their weapons and fled. After his prisoners dug out the Humvee, Soldier had them lift his dead friend onto the vehicle. Soldier saw his dead friend's bulging eyes staring at him, turned to the prisoners, and shot them both dead. Sarge put him in for a medal.

He washed the blood from his arm, smeared on some antibiotic ointment, and covered the wound with gauze and tape. He thought of Brooklyn, collecting for a loan shark and the debtor's brother shooting him in the ass, forcing Soldier to forgo the money and kill both men. His boss, Slats Salerno, took him to Dr. Janet Arroyo, a Brooklyn veterinarian indebted to the Salerno operation. While the vet tended to the wound, Slats had his fun.

"Tell me, Doc, any brain damage?" Neither Soldier nor the doc found it funny. Undeterred, Slats pressed on jokingly threatening to take the lost revenue out of Soldier's pay. The rule "dead men can't pay" was a major tenet of the loan shark's code.

Satisfied with his handiwork, Soldier washed his hands and face, combed his hair, and put on a clean shirt. He bagged his bloody clothing along with the soiled washcloth and towel. Donning another jacket, he was good to go. Exiting the hotel out the back, he disposed of the dirty laundry in another Dumpster. Reinvigorated by the crisp night air, he drove back to the scene of the shooting. A crowd of gawkers had gathered and were milling around the entrance to the parking structure.

"What's all the excitement?" he asked an onlooker.

"Someone's been shot during a stickup," said a woman who filled out a "Welcome to Deadwood" T-shirt she was wearing under a pink hoodie.

"Cops arrested some dude, took him away in cuffs a couple hours ago. Coroner just pulled out a few minutes ago," said her male companion from under his "No Deadwood Here" cap.

Soldier crossed over the street to a vacant bus bench and made the call.

"It's done. Your PI buddy got himself arrested for it, but the only person he shot was me. Being nice can get a guy killed."

"You okay, right?"

"I'll make it, Big Man. I was thinking 'bout sticking around a few days, see the Badlands, see what happens with your buddy. Okay with you?"

"Yeah, sure. See the sights, but not too long. You got other work to do. Ciao." The call ended.

The FBI wiretap logged the call on 4/21/17 1847hrs.

Soldier Boy Mahan didn't have a clue it was a month into spring. He had little use for calendars; he tracked his time in yesterdays, todays, and tomorrows. His seasons were summer and winter; the nuances of spring and fall eluded him. That it was starting to snow in the hills of South Dakota said it was just another winter's night to him. Since Desert Storm, Soldier didn't feel the cold. In fact, he didn't feel much of anything except a lot of lonely.

The wind kicked up a bit and carried the sounds of laughter, clinking glasses, and cowboy music, sounds he knew could help with lonely. He entered the bar in hope of companionship not seeing the sign above the door, which read, "Historic Site—Number 10 Saloon Where Wild Bill Was Shot August 2, 1876."

Chapter 3

About Three Weeks Earlier

It was a rainy Monday morning, not unusual for March in LA. It seemed a winter of record rainfall had failed to appease the rain gods. Tired of floods, mudslides, and washed-out highways, Angelinos were hoping for a drier spring. We at Michaels & Associates were about halfway through the meeting our business manager, Linda, insisted we start each week with. I was attempting to explain the inexplicable—the discrepancies in my expense account voucher—while my partner, Clancy, stared out the window, probably counting the raindrops. I was saved by the bell indicating someone had entered the outer office. As managing partner, l hoped it was a new client or an old client with a new problem. Linda went to see.

Inspired by the rain beating on the windows, Clancy went to the men's room. Our IT guy, Nerd, remained absorbed in his laptop and iPhone; he was going from one device to the other like a freewheeling jazz percussionist. I used the break to continue treating my caffeine deficiency with more French roast.

Our other partner and in-house lawyer, Art, was in court on another contested divorce proceeding, his own. A self-described brilliant attorney, he knew not to represent himself. Unfortunately, he and his wife's lawyers had a history of knocking heads with each other on behalf of dozens of clients. Legal one-upmanship was a rough game played in all courtrooms. When his wife's lawyer hit us with a bunch of discovery motions seeking hidden assets and undisclosed income, we circled the wagons. They claimed my partner's tax returns didn't match our corporate profit-and-loss statement. Our refusal to produce the records was being argued by yet another attorney, one who owed us a favor.

I'd first met Arturo Salazar when a friend recommended him to handle my divorce. The divorce was painful for me but Art got me through it with his humor. Our shared enjoyment of gallows humor, well lubricated by similar drinking habits, made the pain tolerable. When I questioned why divorce cost so much, he replied, "Because it's worth it." I often wondered how selling my boat and pickup to pay him and my ex's attorney was worth it. And his telling me so didn't make signing the checks any easier. On top of her getting the condo in Palm Desert, our house in the Valley, and a two-year-old SUV, Art insisted the twelve hundred a month in child support and another four hundred in monthly spousal support was a legal victory. But when spousal support ended after the two-year court mandate, my ex took me back to court for more money, Art was there by my side, fighting for every dime. So after five years, I'm still only paying twelve hundred in child support. But Obamacare for the kids, costing our company medical another grand per month, became our fallback position. Although this also came out of my pocket, no kids of mine were going to not have health insurance. *Why do I dwell on this so much?*

Linda rescued me from an impending migraine and whisked me from the conference room to my office to meet a prospective client.

"Rollo, this is Robert Howser, a resident of Beverly Hills with a most interesting story," she said as he rose from the client chair to offer his hand.

"Mr. Michaels," he said as we shook hands, "thank you for taking time from your meeting to see me."

He was dressed in a long-sleeve pullover and khakis. Tasseled loafers and no socks completed his attempt at California casual. His transition lenses were light enough for me to see dark brown, almost black eyes. But his most striking feature was the absence of eye hair; no brows or lashes to clash with his obvious man wig.

"Please call me Rollo, and thank you for getting me out of there. Linda says you have an interesting story."

The handshaking over, I sat behind my desk.

"And I go by Bob," he said, sitting. "I must tell you, Rollo, I've hired private investigators before, but none of them was able to find an answer to my question."

"And what question is that, Bob?"

"Who am I?"

"You have amnesia?"

He shook his head and flashed a brief smile. I waited for more. After a deep breath, he obliged.

"I grew up on New York's Upper East Side. When I was thirteen, my mother died, and my father sent my brother, sister, and me off to a Connecticut boarding school. We visited Father on holidays and for a month during the summer. Now and then, he would call or surprise us with a visit. He'd send us an occasional card or letter with some spending money, but that was the extent of it.

"My brother went off to college after the first year, and my sister the year after that. My turn came two years later when I was accepted by MIT to study architecture. Father died shortly before my graduation in 1971. His estate was equally divided between the three of us. After graduation, I used my share to establish myself here in Los Angeles. I landed a job with an engineering firm. I eventually lost ties to my siblings."

Bob was tense, holding eye contact only for short intervals, looking out the windows, checking the walls, the floor, the ceiling. I raised my hand to stop him and asked Linda to bring us coffee. He opted for water. While we waited for Linda and our beverages of choice, I took to small talk—weather sucks, wife or kids, no and no. Linda was quick. That saved Bob from coming up with any more one-word answers. He unscrewed the cap from the Evian, took a swallow, and continued his narrative while I wondered where this was going and if he'd ever get there.

Bob told me that while growing up, he felt a stranger in his own house. Of particular note was a recurring dream that had stayed with him since childhood. In the dream, he saw himself as a little boy in a stroller pushed by a woman. He believed it was in a park. His father and another man took him away. He seemed to be reliving it as he told his story and described the woman's screams. He'd asked his father about his dream when he was about ten and was told it was just a foolish little boy's dream.

This struck a chord with me and my own recurring dreams and the hours I spent pondering their meaning.

Bob had his head bowed as if staring at his hands clasped on his lap. Or maybe his eyes were closed. I couldn't tell. But he went on. He spoke of a mother who treated him differently than she did his brother or sister; she'd showed him little attention or affection. But the father seemingly tried to make up for the mother's indifference.

I watched his mood and demeanor change when he raised his head to talk about sitting on his father's lap and being read stories, something his father didn't do with his siblings. His brother in particular resented that and took it out on him whenever the opportunity presented itself. But the sister would often intercede on Bob's behalf and threaten to report these incidents to their father. Thus, he was never close to his brother.

He had seen him for the last time at their father's funeral. After that, they never actually spoke again. When the brother was killed in a boating accident off Montauk Point in 1995, his sister cajoled him into going to the funeral for her sake.

As a result of attending the funeral, he reestablished a lukewarm relationship with his sister. Not much more than a note in a Christmas card or a birth announcement of another grandchild and a few phone calls over the years. The funeral was also where he was introduced to two nephews and three nieces he hadn't known existed. But what he remembered most about the funeral was that none of these relatives looked anything like him.

Bob reached down by his feet and lifted a large leather satchel I'd failed to notice during Linda's introductions. He removed two file folders and placed them on my desk. *Finally he's getting to it.*

He took another big breath and another drink from the water bottle, gathered himself, and went on.

"When I got back to Los Angeles, I hired a genealogist to reconstruct my family tree and a private investigator to locate any of my parents' family. These are their reports," he said, sliding the folders across my desk.

I picked them up. They were light.

"And these were of no value to you?"

"Thirty-five hundred that says my father's brother is my uncle."

My "I could have told you that for nothing" didn't get a smile from him.

"My father and uncle stepped off the boat in the early thirties, half a decade before the Nazis started killing all their relatives. My mother's maiden name was Schaefer. Her father entered the United States in the 1890s at Boston with a wave of Irish immigrants. My mother was born in Boston in 1929 to Isaac and Mariam Schaefer. Her mother's maiden name was not available, nor was there a record of her parents' marriage in Massachusetts. End of family tree." He gulped down some more water. "But," he said while reaching into his satchel for a third folder, "there is this."

Dramatically dropping the folder on my desk, he continued. "Late last year, I talked my sister into DNA testing after a friend told me how he was tracing his roots with the help of a company called Ancestry.com. This folder contains my DNA report and my sister's. Are you ready for this? Sis and I have the same father but different mothers. And that's not all. My mother is of African descent."

He took another long pull on the Evian. "But that's not what my New York birth certificate says." He shook his head, perspiration forming on his forehead, his wig slipping a bit as he reached back into his bag of tricks to produce folder number four. He put it on my desk.

Bob didn't look right. His eyes fluttered as he adjusted his wig. A tear ran from the corner of his eye. He used a handkerchief to wipe his face, returned it to his pocket, and took a few more deep breaths. He stared at the ceiling.

"Bob, are you okay?"

"No, I'm dying." He looked at me.

"What?" I jumped from my seat.

"Cancer," he whispered and choked up some. Another tear rolled. "They give me two, maybe three months. 'Discovered too late,' they said. I was too busy with this project of a lifetime to let a little pain get in the way. When I couldn't handle it anymore, I went to my doctor. A week later, I was checked into Cedars Hospital for a bunch of tests. Liver and lung spots deemed treatable, but more testing found more cancer. Finally, it got to my brain. Chemo and radiation couldn't stop it—maybe a year earlier. Anyway, I don't want to go to my grave not knowing the who, what, and why."

As Linda had our new client sign our boilerplate contract and pay our retainer, I perused the contents of his four folders. I'd need other documents besides the birth certificates of the three Howser children in the fourth folder. We could use the items that make up a family history such as death certificates, Social Security numbers, military service records, old correspondence, names, old address books, and phone numbers. I gave him a list.

"We'll need this ASAP. Just call it in," I said. Sure that he had recovered from the telling of his story, I sent him on his way. Architect Robert "Bob" Howser of Beverly Hills had a lot of work to do and not much time to do it.

Funny how a person's life can be changed in the blink of an eye. The recriminations brought on by the would haves, should haves, and could haves can haunt people for the rest of their days. Robert Howser was a successful architect in his mid-sixties when he had been diagnosed with brain cancer. His firm had just landed a mega high-rise project in downtown Los Angeles, and the groundbreaking was scheduled in six months. It was supposed to be his signature project, but when the doctors gave him their prognosis, Bob had decided he had better ways to spend his remaining days and had walked on the deal, selling out to a major building consortium.

It has to hurt when your purpose-driven life has taken you right to the very doorstep of all you'd hoped to achieve only to discover it wasn't what you really wanted. And probably never was. In this circus of life and death, it was time to bring in the clowns.

Chapter 4

Teamwork

Michaels & Associates consisted of a lawyer who had earned his bones as a federal prosecutor, two retired cops, and a young woman who held us all together. We also employed a techno-geek who possessed extra skills. We handled most cases as a team, and it was time for our techno-geek, whom I affectionately called Nerd, to start searching the Internet for clues.

Emanuel Jefferson Hemmings, who wished to be called Manny but wasn't except by Linda, claimed to be a descendant of the third president of the United States and insisted there was DNA evidence to prove it. None of us chose to challenge his assertion. If that was his choice, so be it. None of us was responsible for who our parents were.

Manny the Nerd was an imposing figure at six three, two hundred and forty, and his Afro, though out of style, made him look even bigger. Besides being big and holding a black belt in karate, he was also a gay member of the Hollywood street scene whose sexual preferences had gotten him tied up on the wrong side of a homicide investigation a few years back. I was instrumental in getting him off the hook when another case I was involved in netted the actual killer.

Manny was grateful, and when he asked, "Is there anything I can do for you, Mr. Michaels?" I was momentarily at a loss for words. *Is he hitting on me?*

"What do you do?" I said, feeling my ears turning red as soon as I asked.

"I'm into computers, can make them do many things, get past firewalls, break encryptions, read your mail, write programs, do searches. If it's out there, I can find it," he said, much to my relief.

"Need a job?"

"Yes. That mess you got me out of left me unemployed."

And so he came onboard making Michaels & Associates a better, much more professional outfit.

The fact that his work added tens of thousands to our bottom line didn't hurt either. That he could scare the shit out of people was a bonus that had come in handy on a number of occasions.

After Bob Howser left, Linda herded us back to the conference room to pick up where we'd left off. She allowed me to share the good news of the Howser case and the $2,500 retainer before having me attempt once again to explain my expense voucher.

"Save that bullshit for you and Linda to iron out. I'm still working this missing juvenile," Clancy said. His directness was always so endearing. "One of her girlfriends notified the mother that the missing daughter called last night from a Vegas pay phone. They talked for two minutes before some guy told her to get the fuck off the phone. Phone was at a truck stop. Mom and Dad jumped in the car and headed out full speed ahead. Around midnight, they met up with a Vegas PD unit at the truck stop where the call had been made. The coppers checked the security monitors, and sure enough, the daughter was seen on the phone and some black dude calling her away from the cubicle, probably Tremaine.

“The parents woke me up around two this morning unhappy about everything. They’re going to hang around for as long as it takes and want me there by tonight. I’m cutting out with Sylvia this afternoon. I need a front on some expense money.”

“Five hundred carry you for a couple of days?” Linda asked.

“How about a thou?”

“Take the five and go. Keep away from the tables,” I said, demonstrating once again why I got the big bucks around there.

The meeting was over. I dropped the four Howser folders on Nerd and told him to run with it while Linda finished handing out money to Clancy and wishing him luck.

Clancy’s case involved another person with mommy-daddy issues. Our celebrity client, star of a popular TV sitcom, had hired us to find his missing daughter, Chastity Morrow, presumed to have run away. The parents, so wrapped up in their own stuff, knew very little of their sixteen-year-old’s activities. When the girl was taken into custody for cocaine possession a few months back, they opted for grounding the kid. Two weeks later, while the parents were at a cast party at MGM, Hollywood vice popped her for solicitation on the Boulevard of Broken Dreams. A week after that, the kid packed up a light bag and skipped, leaving the parents clueless. A Hollywood detective working juvenile, who shall forever remain anonymous, referred the father to Clancy.

Grandfatherly, with years of experience working juvenile, Clancy Jackman was the perfect guy to find this girl, and we would put his wife, Sylvia, on the clock to help. Clancy had over seventy billable hours into this case, having ID'd the "boyfriend" as Alphonse Tremaine, a Hollywood street lowlife with a felony sheet for drugs and prostitution but only two misdemeanor convictions for solicitation and possession of paraphernalia. Pleading down was the only thing that kept the LA court system from imploding.

Clancy had been trolling the Boulevard nightly to spread out some snitch money and photos and call in some favors. Other than Tremaine, he'd come up with squat. But the new lead seemed genuine. The source said Tremaine hadn't been around for a couple of weeks. If true, the kid was in real trouble. My bet was the girl's use of drugs had gotten her hooked up with this pimp. He was turning her out at truck stops between the City of Angels and the City That Never Sleeps.

"I don't think a client will pay for more than one or two drinks let alone the five you have on this expense voucher. I'm surprised you didn't fall off the bar stool," Linda said, handing me back my expense voucher.

"Send him the bill anyhow. I had to sit there for over two hours. Two of those drinks were for a young lady helping with my cover. When I wasn't searching the depths of her eyes for a soul, I could look right over her shoulder to watch the client's CEO enjoying dinner with their rivals for a city contract. Those phone photos and video I got pretty much cinched the case. I should have had dinner and billed for that too."

I signed the form and gave it back. She took it without further argument.

"So how does our new client, Robert Howser, strike you?" she asked.

"You don't know the half of it. He has terminal cancer—two, three months to live. As he put it, 'At the most.' He walked on his dream project to find out who his mother was before he checks out. He became very emotional telling me about it. I think he's a very angry man. Not because he's dying but because he never truly made the effort to find out why he felt so different from his brother and sister. He always believed something was there, and it's been haunting him as long as he can remember. I think Bob's one of these people who bury themselves in their work to tamp down feelings of being different."

"Imagine that. Was he adopted?"

"Not according to the DNA tests he and his sister took. I guess she's really his half-sister."

For over two decades, DNA has been used to identify the guilty and free the innocent. As the cost of DNA testing came down, the masses made it a billion-dollar industry. DNA profiles were being used for medical screening, treatments, and tracing family roots. DNA databases of arrestees were growing throughout the country and supplementing fingerprint identifications. The feds and the DNA industry were lobbying Congress for universal testing. Imagine a world in which employers, insurance companies, a prospective mate all have access to your DNA profile. Pros and cons are being argued. But that didn't scare me as much as the thought of our government having the information. An Orwellian world in which government clowns decide who should breed, live, or die? DNA testing to purchase a firearm, a license to drive, travel to San Francisco? *Who sent in those clowns?*

Chapter 5

Linda's Friend

Tuesday morning, I arrived at Michaels & Associates twenty minutes early. My nose told me Linda must have already brewed coffee and laid out pastries. Nerd had the printer whirling, the stack of documents in the tray a half-inch thick and growing. He had a raspberry Danish clenched in his teeth as his fingers danced on his laptop's keyboard. I headed to the conference room to get my share.

"Mornin', boss," Nerd said after removing two-thirds of the Danish from his mouth. "I'm just finishing up with the summary. I want to go over it one more time before I lay it on you. Lot of stuff here. The people Mr. Howser hired in 2011 should have found a lot of this for him."

"Where's Linda?" I asked.

"Went to the bank and the PO box. Said she'd be back before you got in. Why so early?"

"Had to write up my report on the dead ironworker killed in that crane collapse over on Broadway," I said, pouring coffee while taking two French vanilla doughnuts from the tray. Multitasking to make America great again. *What happened to my maple glazed?*

"That was some scary shit. Seems these cranes are falling all over the country," he said.

Is he editing his synopsis while conversing with me? Amazing.

Ironworkers Local 433 had been keeping the lights burning in our operation for over four years. Well, actually, it was the law firm of Scott Mathew, LLC, who had hired us to investigate the worker-comp cases of Local 433 members. The rule around here was that their cases always came first.

The latest case involved the death of one of their foremen. Samuel Steele—and you can't make this stuff up—got knocked off the iron when a crane cable snapped during the placing of a girder on the sixteenth floor. It fell two stories and bounced off a floor plate as if it were a trampoline and sent Sam over the edge of the central shaft. He wound up being impaled on some rebar points ten feet down. The job was immediately shut down pending a CAL OSHA inspection. The inspection found the crane was unsafe and ordered it to cease operations, but there was still plenty of work the ironworkers could do until the crane problem was resolved. So the work continued as various investigations were underway. In an ironic twist, it had been Sam's responsibility to safety-rig the shaft to keep anyone from falling in. And if the rebar crew had been a little slower, the rebar wouldn't have been there a week before the scheduled cement pour and Samuel Steele would still be alive with maybe only a bruise or two.

Contributory negligence is one of the issues insurance companies hide behind. The crane company had already circled the wagons and denied me access to any of their employees. I didn't get the case until a week after the occurrence, which was a bad thing for our side. Between the present and the year or so before the deposition phase of the case, a lot could happen. The lawyers would be privy to the OSHA finding only after bureaucratic review, which wouldn't be anytime soon.

Only after identifying all the witnesses and getting statements from the on-scene ironworkers did I find out that Sam Steele had actually been engaged in erecting the safety barriers when the crane cable broke. A good mitigating circumstance for our side.

I was finishing up my Dear Scott cover letter when Linda entered my office.

"What's the occasion?" she jabbed.

"And good morning to you too. I assume you're making light of my devotion to duty and my concern for the well-being of our enterprise?"

"I think Manny stayed all night working on the Howser stuff for you. How does that measure up on your devotion scale?" she asked, going for the knockout.

"Makes me feel like a slacker, of course. Let me know if there's any word from our new client this morning," I said, seeking an end to the sparring.

"I doubt we'll hear from Mr. Howser until this afternoon. He told me yesterday that he had a doctor's appointment first thing this morning."

I asked her to please go over my report, make any needed corrections, and e-mail it to Scott's office on Ventura. Our recent "free" upgrade to Windows 10 was driving me crazy and causing me all kinds of grief, so I was sure the report I gave her would take an hour for her to fix. Manny had given us a primer on Microsoft's latest, and I was his worst pupil. Old dog, new trick was Linda's critique of my learning skills.

"Where's your expense report and billable hours tally sheet for this?" asked the Rules Keeper.

"Didn't fill them out yet."

"You're going to wish you had when you don't get a paycheck next Friday."

I went to the conference room and got a warm-up for my coffee and the sports page from the *LA Times*. The Dodgers were playing the hated Giants in Frisco tonight, and I wanted to know what time I had to be at my apartment to see the game on cable or if I should watch it at Home Plate, a police watering hole two miles away. It seemed I always wound up closing the place whenever I dropped in to catch a game.

While returning to my office through the outer office with my coffee refill, a very pretty lady entered our suite. That caused me to walk into the doorjamb and spill a third of my cup down my pants front and onto the floor.

"Shit!" I blurted too quickly to take it back. I turned to apologize to the ladies, who started laughing. Linda sprang into action.

"Don't move, while I get some paper towels," she said, heading to the credenza in the adjoining room. "You two get acquainted."

"Hello. I'm Ruth, Linda's friend from Phoenix," she said, stepping forward and offering her hand but withdrawing it when she realized my hands were occupied.

"Call me clumsy. Nice to meet you, Ruth."

"So Linda tells me you're also known as Rollo, right? Any other a.k.a. I should know about? Linda never mentioned the clumsy thing."

Her laughter prompted me to join in.

Linda started to blot the front of my slacks, thought better of that, took my cup, and handed me some towels. She switched to cleaning up the floor while telling me she wanted a raise. Her friend Ruth egged her on. "You go, girl! Equal pay for equal work. Gender bias!"

I retreated to my office blotting and walking at the same time. Good thing I hadn't been chewing gum too. I decided to air-dry my slacks and boxers using my desk to cover my nakedness. It wasn't long until Nerd came in, really making me uncomfortable. He placed his report and a stack of documentation on my desk next to the contents of my pants pockets I had also spread out to dry. He stared at my wet clothing draped over the back and arm of one of the two client chairs. He pointed and gestured a silent *What?*

"Coffee spill," I said, shaking my head to end further inquiry.

"I can run some more searches and try a few more things, but I think you got what you need there to move forward. I'm going home to get some sleep. Don't call unless it's life or death." He was gone. He'd left my office door open.

"Bob Howser on one for you," Linda shouted over the intercom as if I were comatose.

"We have an intercom so we don't have to shout," I shouted back. "Please close my door, will you?"

"Why? What are you hiding?" Ruth asked as she stuck her head in before covering her retreat with a door slam.

I picked up the phone. “Hello, Mr. Howser. How may I help you?”

“It’s Bob, remember? I have the information you requested.”

“Good work, Bob. I’ll turn you over to Linda. She’ll get it all entered into the case file.”

“I can drop it off. I’m on Wilshire having breakfast in Santa Monica. Got up this morning and took a walk on the beach wondering why it’s been thirty years between walks.”

“I thought you had a doctor’s appointment this morning.”

“I said, ‘Fuck it! What’s the use?’”

His dropping an f-bomb was probably long overdue.

“You know, Rollo, I can see the light at the end of the tunnel, and it really is a train coming. There’s nothing left for these doctors to tell me, so I’m not wasting any more time. You get it?”

“Yes, I get it. See you when you get here. Coffee’s always on.”

"That stuff you were drinking yesterday smelled pretty good. Doctors told me to limit my caffeine, and I, like an asshole, did. You believe it? See you in forty."

"Good. My pants should be dry by then," I said, thinking out loud again.

"What?" was all I heard him say as I placed the phone back in its base.

Chapter 6

Getting to Know You

I got the feeling Robert Howser realized he was left to face his impending demise alone. I wondered if he had had any close friends. He was a lifelong bachelor, no children, and estranged from his family for most of his adult life. Seems a career made a poor substitute for a life.

Unable to concentrate on the sports page, I started in on Nerd's report beginning with the financials. Bob's firm, RH Architectural Impressions, Inc., in Century City, had a 3A1 D&B rating. He owned a home in Beverly Hills, a strip mall in Calabasas, an office building in Ventura, and a storage facility on Sepulveda in the Valley. His credit score was in the high seven hundreds. He drove a Mercedes and a GMC pickup, both registered to one of his corporations, of which there were three. If money could fix what ailed him, Bob could have gotten well real quick with plenty of money left over for life's pleasures at his leisure.

"Mr. Howser here to see you," Linda announced on the intercom, heeding the no-shouting mandate.

"Be out in a minute," I said and released the button. I got dressed. I opted to go commando; the coffee-stained boxers triggering my mother's warning, "What if you wind up in the hospital wearing dirty underwear?"

Tucked, zippered, and buckled, I went out to greet Bob. He, Linda, and Ruth were enjoying a laugh that they quickly stifled when I walked in.

"The ladies were telling me of your accident. Burn anything?" he asked with a chuckle.

"Not much," I said, causing another eruption of laughter from the three. Feigning hurt feelings, I invited Bob to step into my office and told Linda, "Bring us some coffee since I can't be trusted to do it myself."

Bob was looking a lot different. He had replaced that god-awful wig with a black leather beret and the previous day's drab pullover with a pink silk golf shirt. He completed the new Bob look with pink socks and black slacks. His loafers and vest completed the black-leather theme head to toe. Best of all, his frown was gone, having been traded in for a rather engaging, natural, and unforced smile. Bob had it working.

He opened with an apology for making light of my coffee mishap. He claimed the girls' telling of it was most entertaining. I told him I was more embarrassed than hurt and then gave him my version of the cause of the incident.

"I was having some medical issues with heart palpitations and was told I had to cut back on the caffeine. My mistake had been in confiding that to Linda, who immediately went out and bought a couple of pounds of Starbucks decaf and served me a cup without mentioning the switch. Though it wasn't the worst, I spotted the difference right off the bat. When challenged, she copped citing the 'It's for your own good' plea.

"That led to negotiating a weaning process where she would start with a fifty-fifty blend of the new stuff and a dark-roasted Colombian. The plan was to get me to straight decaf in three months—half and half the first, two-thirds and one-third the second, and three-quarters and one-quarter the third month. I caved. After about a week, the mix was palatable, but I was drinking a hell of a lot more coffee. Linda noticed that near the end of month one because of the number of trips I was making to the john. Again, the 'Doing this for your own good' thing kicked in."

A light knock on the door stopped the telling. Ruth entered with a tray of coffee, sugar, and cream. "I didn't know how you take it, Bob. There's some cream and sugar, but I'm sorry to say no Sweet 'N Low. Anything else?"

"I'm good," Bob said. "Thank you, Ruth."

"Thanks," I said to her back as she left. *Why is she delivering the coffee and not Linda?* "Where was I?" I asked Bob before sipping some coffee. *My God, is this straight dark roast Colombian uncut by any decaf?*

"It's for your own good," Bob said.

"Oh, okay. So I come to work one morning during the first week of month two, and the credenza and coffee setup are gone from my office. Well, I'm a little hung over and overreact a little, some might say a lot. Yeah, a lot, causing

Linda to tell me to shove it. 'You want to die from caffeine and booze? Have at it. I'm out of here,' and out she goes.

"I'm bewildered and have no idea what's going on. Panicked, I chase after her, yelling 'Wait!' to the closing elevator doors. I take the stairs stumbling and almost falling a couple of times. I hit the lobby seconds before the elevator. It dings its arrival and the doors open." I pause for effect and shout, "No Linda! She's done a Houdini! I get in the elevator, push the four button, and as the doors close, I see Linda coming out the stairwell. I shout another 'Linda!' Too late."

Bob was laughing, my office door flew open, and Linda rushed in. Bob was holding his sides. Guffaws filled the room.

"What?" Linda shouted as Ruth ran in behind her.

"I was just telling Bob about the first time you quit."

"The first time?" Bob said.

Bob was hysterical, blotting tears with a hankie in one hand and holding his side with the other. Linda shrugged and held up three fingers. "Three?" he exclaimed. His face lit up in pink to match his shirt and socks. Linda nodded, and the girls left announcing they were going to lunch. *Is this story really that funny, Bob?*

Before going on with my story, we took our cups to the credenza in the conference room, where the coffee setup had resided for the past year.

Half a pot sat on the burner, and two pastries remained in the box—a maple-glazed French I swear hadn't been there two hours earlier and a cheese Danish. I pointed to the box. "Pick one." I poured the refills.

"I really shouldn't," he said halfheartedly.

"What, it's gonna kill ya?"

He laughed again and took the Danish, leaving me my favorite.

"And so what happened? How'd you get her back?" he pressed before taking a bite of his pastry.

"Well, the next day, the 'associates' part of Michaels & Associates raised hell with me threatening to blow it all up if I didn't get off my high horse and get her back here. When she wouldn't take my calls, I staked out her apartment. A dozen roses delivered with an 'I'm sorry' note and a 'Please call me' plea got her to respond. She called me on my cell. I was parked across from her place. The rest is obvious. Coffee is here on the credenza though not where I want it and definitely not how I prefer it. Don't tell, but I sneak downstairs to the little diner and get a double-shot espresso every morning just to get my heart started."

"And the second time she quit?"

"We made her a partner," I said, enjoying the telling.

"And the third?" he asked as some of his Danish came out with his laugh.

"I asked her to marry me."

"You two are married?"

He looked surprised even without eyebrows.

"No. She turned me down flat."

That made him laugh even more. It was a good laugh. I doubted it had been used that much in quite a while.

Chapter 7

My New BFF

Bob Howser was having a good day for sure. Chemo and radiation had made his life a living hell, but once the treatments stopped, he immediately started feeling better. By resigning himself to his fate, he regained the energy to seek the answers that had eluded him. He said he was sure I was the one who would lead him to them. By telling him a little about me, I hoped he would tell me more about himself. Clues to who we are sometimes get buried in us, held prisoner by the fear of the pain they might cause if our psyche ever released them. It was Bob's turn to talk and mine to listen.

I gave him a cue. "Tell me about growing up in Manhattan. I grew up on the Island."

"We had a beautiful home, Gothic style, three stories, built around the turn of the century. A lot of wood on the inside, stone on the outside. Even had gargoyles. My brother had named them

Curly, Larry, and Moe after the Three Stooges. He named the fourth one Bobby after me, saying I was a clown like the Stooges. There was also a cellar, but I never went down there because he told me that's where the monsters lived. When I was about six, the bastard locked me down there and left. My father found me sleeping at the bottom of the stairs covered in coal dust and cobwebs. He wailed on my brother pretty good, but I was to pay for that too." His smile was gone. We both sipped coffee.

"Was he always a prick?"

Bob nodded. "It wasn't all bad, believe me. We had a housekeeper-cook who treated me kindly when my brother wasn't around." His smile returned.

"What is it?"

"My father. We had a secret I'm pretty sure he took to his grave, and you'll be the first person I've ever mentioned this to. From the time I was five until the time Father died, every time Ringling Brothers Circus came to town, we'd sneak off to see it. He cautioned me never to tell anyone, especially my brother, sister, and mother.

"The trip to the circus was always the best day of my year. We'd get the best seats right up close, the tightrope walkers, the flying trapeze acts right above us. But my favorite part was the animals, the lions and tigers, the elephants and horses, especially the horses. One of the ladies who rode the horses would come over to talk to us, let me touch her horse, introduce us to the clowns.

"One year, she took us back to pet the elephants. Another year, I got to feed a lion. Yet another time, I was given a ride in the clown car. They pulled their little car right up to where we sat, and four clowns got out. The tallest one lifted me over the rail, put me in their tiny car. The three little clowns got in with me and took off, the tall one giving chase around the ring. Then out the tent we go to deliver me to the horse lady. I was with her long enough to get a little antsy, afraid I was missing the show. She gave me a big hug and a kiss on the cheek, and back to Father I was delivered on the back of her horse. People cheered. Father shouted, 'I was starting to worry!' and she asked, 'How does it feel?' She rode off standing on the back of her horse.

"When we'd come home from the Greatest Show on Earth, Mother always wanted to know where we'd been all afternoon and what we'd eaten to spoil our dinner. They never knew."

He stared at something I couldn't see, savoring the memory.

"That's a great story, Bob," I said to bring him back. "You know, you light up when telling it. Maybe you should spend more time on the good stuff and less remembering the crap. Your dad sounded like a good guy. Your brother is no longer with us. What about your sister?" I asked, getting up to pour out the dregs in my cup. "Like more coffee?"

"Let's go downstairs and try out the espresso. I'll buy," he said.

"That will make it taste even better."

And we left, passing the girls returning from lunch.

Linda's "You'll be back before I quit for the day?" was a statement, not a question.

"You quitting again?"

Bob just couldn't help himself. He laughed all the way to the elevator.

Bob and I talked for another hour and a half long after the espresso was gone and the sugar drained from the bottom of my cup and the slip of lemon peel chewed and swallowed. I told him of failed marriages, police work, and how I couldn't get them to fit together. He told of his sister and how he didn't feel he could burden her with his problems. He confided that he had avoided relationships for fear of failure. He had rented a few women over the years, but his sexual experiences had often been marred with fears of failure too. I watched his moods swing during our talk and wondered if medication might have been in order.

"My psychiatrist says I'm suicidal," I told him, "and I tell her she's full of shit, and she asks, 'How else do you explain X, Y and Z?' and I tell her it's all part of the job and the services I perform."

"You see a shrink?" he asked with a double blink and a stare.

"Yes. Had to in order to get my concealed weapon permit reinstated," I said, pulling my pant leg up to show him my ankle holster. "Listen—this is what I think you should do tonight. Sit down and think some more about your childhood. Try sticking to the good stuff. Write down what you remember. Note the parts where you get stuck and any of the big gaps in time. You have a brain tumor that could start taking away your memories, so let's get this stuff down in writing."

"What good will that do?"

His tone made it sound as if he didn't like the idea.

"To find some leads, clues to answers. I'd like to call my shrink and ask her to see you. I just know she can help dig some of it out. What do you say?"

"I don't know, Rollo. You sure about this?"

"Yes, Bob. Without her, I would have eaten my gun a long time ago." I hoped I was exaggerating. I handed him her business card. "I'll give her a call this afternoon and have you take my next appointment."

Chapter 8

Hiring Help

I got back to the office and found our legal staff back from jousting with opposing counsel in divorce court. Art looked fried, and he smelled of gin and vermouth, obviously guilty of having doubled up on his normal, two-martini lunch. Thea Warren, clear of eye and speech, had obviously not been drinking. The day's hearing, at which Thea was representing Michaels & Associates, was about quashing a discovery motion demanding to see all our financials to expose Art's hiding of assets from his wife. I often wondered if divorce attorneys engaged in these maneuvers to help each other jack up their billable hours.

"We kind of won," Thea said.

"Kind of? Not what I was hoping for," I said as she and Art followed me into my office.

"The judge split the baby. We have to give them all of Art's remuneration info including the value of his car lease and any other perks plus a certified P&L statement from your accountant," she said. "Everything else is off limits to Mrs. Salazar."

"Tell Linda, and she'll contact Shady Numbers Accounting, get you what you need," I said, but that got me only a blank stare. "Thanks for the favor, Thea. You did a lot for the little bit we pay you."

"Linda's already made the call to Stan Newman's office. He said he'd drop off what we need in the morning. We're square, Rollo, till next time."

She was gone leaving me with a half-drunk partner who was probably thinking of getting a full load on.

"Where did you drink your lunch, Art?"

That got me the one-finger salute, something he couldn't slur.

"Got to catch up on some work in my office," he said.

That was probably a cover to catch a snooze. As soon as he left my office, in marched Linda.

"Can we talk now?"

That was not really a request.

My "Where's your friend Ruth?" didn't knock her off course.

"Sitting at her desk."

"She has a desk?"

"That's what we need to talk about. I hired her," she said, emphasizing the *I*.

"To do what may *I* ask?" That was to show her she wasn't the only one who could emphasize a pronoun.

"She has all the secretarial skills, she's smart, computer literate, and I'm convinced she can put up with all the bull rap you guys throw around."

That seemed rational to me, if we could afford it.

"You mentioned her desk. We don't have a 'her' desk," I said, sniffing a whiff of opportunity in the air.

"Right. I set her up with Manny's desk until we get another. Then we could squeeze him into the conference room."

"Tell you what. Move the credenza back into my office. That way, nobody gets squeezed," I said, laying my proffer on the desk. "Do I get to interview her?"

"What for? You're getting your damn coffeepot back in your office."

She smiled, knowing too well how I played the game.

"Mr. Michaels, there's a man for you on line two who keeps calling me sweetheart. He says he's your uncle Vincenzo. He laughed when I told him I'd check if you were available," a cheerful Ruth announced over the intercom.

"Pretty good, huh?" Linda asked on the way out.

I thanked Ruth and let Vincenzo Costello do two minutes penance while I wondered what I'd have to do for him. He wasn't my uncle or related to me in any other way. He was Big Vinnie, a.k.a. Vinnie C, whose father had been a business associate of my father's. When my dad's world was being brought down by the DA, the Costellos stepped in to pull his bacon out of the fire. Dad said he owed their family everything. I had managed to keep that from all my employers through the years both in LA and the feds.

When my father passed—it seemed like just the other day, not six years ago—the Costello family again stepped in to give him a good send-off by picking up the tab for the whole shebang. The folks at the crematorium got a little pissed when a couple of bottles of booze exploded with Dad's remains. When they started to make a fuss, Vinnie gave them the look, and that was the end of it. He would call to request we do a "small favor" for him from time to time. The favors never amounted to breaking a law, at least not knowingly. At worst, maybe a bending of the rules might have been required, but nothing that kept me awake at night. I'd bill him by the hour as I would any other client, and he'd pay in cash—no muss, no fuss, no record, *not* like any other client.

"Uncle, how ya' doin'? Been a while," I said, adding a little New York accentuation. He responded with a short rant about keeping him on hold, but then he got down to it.

"I need a favor. Friend of mine will be stopping in to see you next week. She has a problem I think you can help her with."

"What kind of problem?"

"I'll let her tell you 'bout it."

"What's her name?"

"Hey! Whatsamaddayou? Ciao, nipote mio," he said before hanging up.

He once told me, "Don't say too much. You never know who's listening."

The FBI wiretap logged the call on 04/06/17 1848hrs.

My guess was I'd find out who and what next week. Usually, the so-called favors I did for Vinnie paid well, and with a new hire, we could use the work. Art Salazar's divorce case had taken him out of the income-producing category, leaving Clancy and me to handle the cases. We also provided process service for a couple of law firms, mostly the hard-to-serve stuff. Nerd was pretty good at shaking the trees and scaring up a service dodger.

The Internet was our biggest resource for finding people.

Once in a while, we would scam them right into the office with some creative ruse and lay the paper on them. Linda would phone the mark and say he or she had just won a hundred-dollar gift card—just come in and pick it up. Clancy's favorite was the use of a borrowed UPS uniform. He'd deliver the subpoena in a box with some broken glass. The mark would sign for it, and Clancy would shake the box to rattle the broken glass and tell him or her to open it so they both could verify the damage for the insurance. He'd whip out his cell and photo the mark holding the subpoena. We tried to photo all the serves to avoid the denials.

Sometimes, it would take weeks to corner the slick ones, but the clients paid well because we got the desired results when their in-house people couldn't. One time, Scott Mathew told me he'd give a newly hired attorney some paper to serve just to see if they had anything on the ball. Sadly, he discovered most of them "couldn't find their asses in the dark with either hand." So Nerd was going out that night to run down six duckers for Scott. Success with two or three would probably keep the lights on at the office for another month.

A tap on the door preceded Ruth's entrance.

"I wanted to thank you for the job before Linda and I take off. We're getting me settled into her apartment," she said.

"You two are going to live together in her small apartment?"

"Temporarily, till I find a place."

"Welcome aboard. Maybe we can meet tomorrow, fill me in about yourself. And by the way, it was the coffee." I was messing with her.

"You're the boss."

Her confused look made me smile. "That's not how Linda sees it."

As I suspected, Art was asleep in his office. I shook him awake, to his displeasure. "Come on, buddy. We have a game to watch." That got him off the couch and headed down the hall to the men's room while I got ready to lock up. I checked on the coffeepot and was happy to see it had been washed and set up for the next day.

Art came back, his face splashed and his hair wet-combed.

"Who's playing?" was his way of saying he was in. Pizza delivery and a six-pack of cold ones would make it a good evening watching my Dodgers do their thing while babysitting my associate.

Chapter 9

Mrs. Scarsdale

"Jeez, Rollo, you look beat," was Linda's greeting. She seemed to relish critiquing my morning appearance. "By the way, your fly's open." She made me look and Ruth laugh. It wasn't.

I went to my office without responding to the frivolity. But just as I sat, Linda entered with a mug of coffee in one hand and two maple glazed balanced on a napkin in the other.

"You two are having a lot of fun at my expense. You think this offering will make up for it?" I asked, giving her my best *poor-me* smile.

"You stay out late last night?"

"Sadly, no. I had a hard time sleeping. Between Art's snoring and thinking about Bob Howser's plight, it was after three before I finally dozed off. Then Art woke me up at six to get back to his place so he could get ready for court at ten. He'd left his ride at Brennan's yesterday after a four-plus martini lunch. I drove him to his car. I told him to call Uber next time. So please keep me in coffee."

"You didn't stop downstairs for a double-shot espresso?"

"Why you hating on me? Enough already."

I feigned a wound and wondered who had ratted me out on the espresso. "Did Nerd have any luck last night?"

"You mean with all that paper he went out to serve or afterward?"

"The paper. Although we think you know everything that goes on around here, I just don't want to believe you'd know about that."

"Yes, he scored big time. Five out of six. He had one of the Local 433 guys get him up to the crane office, and he nailed all of them as they showed up for work this morning. I notified Scott's paralegal and sent the proofs of service to them via courier." She went back for more laughs with our new employee.

Alone with my thoughts and Nerd's computer workup on Bob Howser, I sorted through the chaff looking for the wheat, or at least a place to start. So far, all my conversations with Bob seemed to have helped him more than me. As I searched for a thread, my sorrow for Bob continued to grow. Not because he was dying but because he was dying alone. That's when I made my first decision in the case and extracted the page that had the sister's info. I picked up the phone and punched in her number.

"Hello?" a woman answered on the fifth ring.

"Mrs. Scarsdale?"

"Who's calling?" A cautious tone in her voice.

"My name is Roland Michaels, a friend of Robert Howser. I'm trying to reach his sister."

"This is she."

"Do you have a few minutes to talk about a situation that has come up in Bob's life?"

The words *friend* and *situation* seemed better for that conversation.

"Well, yes. Is my brother all right?"

"That's why I'm calling. Bob has no idea I'm reaching out to you, but I feel I must. Bob's facing something I don't think he should be facing alone. He's going to be very angry with me for calling you, but I can handle the heat. You're his only relative I know of, and I don't think your brother has many friends, no close ones for sure."

"And how is it you know my brother, Mr. ... ah Michaels, is it?" she asked, voicing her skepticism.

"Yes. I work for Bob."

"And what is he facing that has you so concerned? Is he ill?"

"Yes, Mrs. Scarsdale, he has cancer," I said, wishing I hadn't been saying that over the phone.

"Oh my God! Poor Bobby, poor Bobby ... What hospital is he in?"

"It's not like that. He has some time before that. His doctors give him a few months. I'm trying to get his things in order, so to speak, and I could use some help. He told me you two weren't very close, and he's adamant about refusing to burden you with his problems at this stage of his life," I said. She was sobbing. "I think his pride is getting in his way, and all the treatments he's been through could be affecting his judgment."

"I haven't seen him since our brother, Paul, was killed in an accident in ninety-five, over twenty years ago. Being at the funeral was very awkward for him. I'm sure the only reason he came was because I'd begged him to. He tried to fit in. In fact, Paul's kids were happy to discover they had an uncle. My two children knew of him but had never met Bobby all their young lives. When he left to return to LA, he promised to keep in touch. I heard from him a couple of times that first year, but then nothing. My letters were never answered—no calls, nothing at all. Then about a year ago, he called me out of the blue. Said he was researching our family tree, tracing our roots. He had some Internet company send me a DNA test kit. I mailed them the swabs as he had asked, and they forwarded the results to Bobby. Then after a thank-you call, no contact again," she said, surprising me with how much she was willing to share.

"He's an introvert, expresses himself through his work, I guess, but he's still tracing the family roots," I said, injecting an excuse on Bob's behalf.

"Our brother used to tease him awfully telling Bobby he was adopted and should go back to where he came from. They never got along. Paul showed a strong dislike for Bobby for as long as I can remember. It was wrong, I knew, and I would get in between them when we were young, but—"

"Yes, Mrs. Scarsdale, Bob told me about their relationship and how you would stick up for him as best you could."

"Well, not to excuse our brother's conduct, but Bobby was always a little strange, you know, mysterious, secretive, withdrawn. Mother seemed to favor Paul over Bobby, in fact over both of us. The only times Bobby was genuinely happy was when he was with Father. They seemed to have their own private connection going on. They'd sneak off somewhere and come back never telling where they'd been, what they'd done, but Paul and I knew that whatever it was, we were not to be a part of it ... and ... well ... What is it you want from me, Mr. Michaels?"

"Would you give Bob a call? You can tell him I called, told you he was ill, and could use someone to talk to."

"And then what? I wouldn't know what to say to him. I did my part in trying to mend our relationship after our brother's funeral, but he chose to keep us all out of his life, living on the West Coast... I ... I ..."

"Do you love your brother, Mrs. Scarsdale?"

"I ..." She paused. "I'll call him."

Chapter 10

Families

I was feeling good about having tipped off the sister and getting her to commit to calling Bob. I wondered how he liked the Bobby nickname she used for him. I found it endearing, and once I heard her use it, I knew there was this big-sister thing between them I hoped I'd tapped into.

My cold coffee caused me to wonder why Linda was failing me, so I went to investigate with cup in hand. She and Ruth were deeply engrossed in the contents of Michaels & Associates files. I could only hope she was training Ruth about her filing system because Linda was the only one who knew where anything could be found around the office. For that reason, I went to the credenza in the conference room and poured my own, feeling it was the least I could do. However, upon passing back through, I asked, "When is the new desk coming in so the credenza and coffee setup can be put back where it rightfully belongs?"

"Friday," Linda growled. "You can move that stuff whenever you feel like it. Have at it."

That got me scurrying back to my desk before she took a bite out of me. I got back into the computer search that Nerd had prepared and was looking at what he had on the thirty-five-hundred-dollar uncle some PI had identified as Bob's father's brother. Ruth interrupted on the intercom.

"Clancy on line one for you."

I punched the lit button. "How's Vegas?" I asked.

"Hot for April," he said. "Listen, our client and his wife are heading back home discouraged. Local police haven't been as helpful as Mom and Dad thought they should be. I tried to explain to them that a missing sixteen-year-old from LA is not the highest priority for these guys, especially a runaway. Well, the mother goes off on me and wants hubby to give me the boot and hire somebody who'll do something. He calms her down a bit and agrees to keep us out here through the weekend before he explores other options. We have over a hundred and thirty hours in this. We know she's being turned out, but I think the truck-stop thing got too hot for them. Tremaine probably got word of us showing the pictures and throwing cash around. Maybe he's got her in a crib somewhere, so Sylvia and I will try downtown tonight, check out some of the street people. That's what this guy did in LA, a real hustler. I'm meeting with metro vice at six. I'll pitch them for some help. Parents said they would pay a big bonus for some help. I'd like to send our man Nerd out on the street in Hollywood, see if he can scare up a phone for the pimp. What do you think?"

"Sure, do it. You have his number, right?"

"Yes. But wait, there's more. You should have told Linda to give me the thousand like I'd asked. Sylvia and I are close to tap city here."

"You sending me two for the price of one? All I pay is separate shipping and handling? Which debit card do you have?"

"The Visa Dodger Blue one."

"I'll have her put another five hundred on it. Lay off the steak and lobster."

That was my parting shot. I went back to the outer office and told Linda to load Clancy's debit card with the extra five hundred we should've given him to begin with. But I had to agree with Linda. "Rules are rules. If you're not going to follow them, why have them?"

The ladies were up to their elbows with case files, over four years' worth. Big ones, small ones, some dead ends, some happy endings. During the years, we'd built a rep for finding people. We started with skip tracing, collecting debts, finding hidden cars for repo. Somebody's kid runs away, stuff like that. The case that put us on the map didn't pay much, but the resulting four-column spread in the *Los Angeles Times* started the good times rolling for Michaels & Associates.

In May 2013, a construction worker named Roberto Hernandez walked into our office and told us his story of being young and dumb more than a quarter century prior and fathering a child in a common-law relationship. Five months after giving birth, the eighteen-year-old mother packed up with the baby and disappeared. The father had a copy of the son's LA County birth certificate but no other documentation. The mother's name was listed as Consuela Rivera, the father's Roberto Hernandez. She had run away from her parents, illegals living in East LA, to move in with Roberto shortly after they'd met. She was soon pregnant with his child, but he felt marriage would be the same trap his father had stepped into. Their relationship deteriorated, and to his relief, she was gone. But doubt and guilt ultimately drove him to search for his son, albeit twenty-seven years later.

Three months later, Clancy and I found the son in an El Paso, Texas, cemetery. Killed at the age of sixteen in a motorcycle accident. Roberto Hernandez Robles. Born June 26, 1985. Died September 11, 2001. You can't make this stuff up. Sure, the work that we put into the search was remarkable, but the date of Roberto's death made the case newsworthy. We had a lead on the mother and had given it to the client for him to pursue.

Three weeks prior to the anniversary of 9/11, our phones started to ring. El Paso's Spanish-speaking TV station got wind of the Hernandez story and called us to verify our client's account prior to airing on 9/11. Our in-house Spanish-speaking partner puffed it up and leaked it to two Los Angeles stations. Soon, we were busy handling a dozen custody disputes in which spouses had absconded with children. There are hundreds of these cases reported in Los Angeles every year, but few victims have the wherewithal to hire people to track down a stolen child.

But Bob Howser's case was different. He refused to believe he was who he had been told he was. Could he have been right, or was he just uncomfortable with the answers he'd been given? Our country is populated with lots of people who can trace their family trees back to the *Mayflower*. Bob Howser had never met a grandparent, didn't believe the woman listed on his birth certificate was really his mother, and secretly hoped he wasn't related in any way to his deceased older brother. I wondered if he felt different when growing up because he looked different from his brother and sister.

It wasn't until he had the DNA profiles of himself and his sister that he really knew that although they shared the same father, they had different mothers. Was a mistake made in the DNA sampling? Then why would the male DNA match, which would also rule out a mix-up in the maternity ward? What about the birth certificate? And what about his dream?

The uncle's name stared at me from the page. Meyer Howser. An immigration document from

February 17, 1933, showed Meyer's DOB as 12/01/1930, and Bob's father, Silvan Howser's DOB as 07/30/1922. No other Howsers were listed on the sheet. An eleven-year-old and a two-year-old crossing the Atlantic without their parents? Doubtful. But up near the top of the page was listed an Ayelet Heuer with a DOB of 05/04/1903. Country of origin listed as France on each. Could have been. It fit with what Bob had told me. I planned to follow up with him on his grandparents' info. Maybe the sister might know a name. All three names were Jewish. That fit in with what Bob had said about the Nazis.

"Your ex on line two. Are you here?" Ruth asked. I picked up without answering Ruth's question.

"Hello, Marie. What's up?" I asked, trying for cheerful.

"You didn't forget your daughter's school play tomorrow night, did you?"

"Of course not." I lied. I turned my desk calendar page to Friday. There it was in red. "Meet you there, okay?"

"I guess I don't have to remind you it's your weekend with the kids. Did you want to take them after the play? If so, I'll pack their bags."

"You think they want to spend two nights at my place?"

"Probably. Your son loves getting away with murder, and your daughter loves that beast you call a cat."

"El Gato is a great cat. Don't bad-mouth him. See you at the auditorium about a quarter to curtain."

"Mom and Dad will be with us ... You okay with that?"

"Why wouldn't I be? The real question is are they good with me being there?"

"They hate your guts," she said, laughing.

"Hey, there's that, but you know I'm like a cheap steak, right?"

"Tough or all fat?" was a dig masquerading as a joking question.

"Good one. See you tomorrow night."

Chapter 11

Client Relations

I arrived at Michaels & Associates at ten fifteen on Friday morning to find Linda and Ruth deeply engaged on Ruth's computer. When neither acknowledged my "Good morning, ladies," I joined them to see what they were up to. My "What's up?" got Ruth to point at her computer screen, which showed me standing by the two girls looking at the computer.

"Manny hooked up a CCTV security system last night," Ruth said as she punched up a view of my office, and then the conference room, and then one of Art working at his desk, then a split-screen quad shot of all four rooms of our suite. "But wait." She moved the cursor and clicked the mouse, bringing up Art again.

"Hey, Art, Rollo's here," Linda said, getting in on the fun. He looked up into the camera and waved.

"I've been waiting over an hour to talk to you, Rollo. Come on in here," Art said from the computer speakers. So I did.

Armani silk looked good on Art, but it was probably a bad choice to be wearing when standing before a judge who was going to be taking your assets and giving them to your ex. Tough to plead poverty wearing a thousand-dollar suit and two-hundred-dollar loafers. I would have opted for some old jeans myself.

"Hey, Art, at least lose the tie," I said. "And the pocket hankie too."

"Yeah, I know. I'm leaving my jacket in the car. I didn't cleanup for court. I have a client meeting at four this afternoon, and Ernie Fischer wants a prenup. He says another marriage like his last could put him in the poorhouse." He laughed at the retelling of his client's joke and waved me to a chair.

"Does he know his lawyer wasn't smart enough to have one for himself?" I asked, earning me his favorite form of exclamation lately, the middle-finger salute. *Left-handed? Wow. Ambidextrous, partner.*

Before we could take our conversation to the next level, we were interrupted by loud voices in the outer office. It sounded like a highly pissed-off Robert Howser. No surprise. I walked out to greet him with an engaging smile.

"Hi, Bob."

"Don't give me that 'Hi Bob' crap. You had no business telling Sis about my being ill. I told you that in the strictest of confidence," he said, starting loud but fading to a whisper at the end.

"I'm sorry, Bob. Let's go into my office and I'll fill you in on the why." I led him through the door. "Ruth, will you bring us some coffee, please?" We took our seats and waited for the coffee without speaking. Bob stared out the window while I took out Nerd's workup.

"Here you are, gentlemen," Ruth said, placing the tray on my desk. "If I remember, Mr. Howser takes his black also. Would either of you like a pastry?"

"None for me, thank you," Bob said in a much calmer manner. I shook my head, and she left.

"So she called you like I'd asked. Did you talk to her, tell her what's going on?"

"What was there to tell? You'd already told her I was a dead man walking. Why would you do that knowing I didn't want sympathy from anyone? I hired you to find out who I am, not create a guest list for my funeral."

He was unloading on me. "Did you tell her I was working for you?"

"She said you told her you were my friend and also worked for me. That was presumptuous on your part, don't you think?"

He was getting worked up again.

"Maybe. I'd like it if we were friends. Makes my job easier. Listen, Bob, all I was trying to do was get your sister on our side. She's already told me stuff about your childhood that you haven't."

"Yeah? Like what?"

"I'll get to that, but first, I want to be sure you understand that how I conduct this investigation is how it's going to be. You want answers, and I'll do my best to get them, but sometimes, toes might get stepped on. Feelings might get hurt. But damn it, we're on a deadline here. We can't pussyfoot around. Either you want answers or you don't. Which is it?"

Telling a client how it was like that had cost me a few cases, but I felt pretty safe with Bob. I was sure that unlike many clients, Bob really had nothing to hide.

"I get it, but it was tough talking with her. We were blubbering, telling each other 'I'm sorry,' wishing for do-overs. Now she wants to come out here. I don't know if I can handle that."

There was a knock on the door, and Linda stuck her head in. "The new desk has arrived. We want to move the credenza back in here while you and Art are still here to help."

"You're getting your coffeepot back?" Bob asked with a grin.

I gave him a wink and told Linda, "Let's do it."

Twenty minutes later, my office was filled with the aroma of freshly brewed coffee with notes of vanilla, maple, and cinnamon from the pastry box. Bob had a smear of raspberry jelly on the front of his shirt. The powdered sugar made his lips even paler. I gave him a napkin and finished my maple-glazed French in four bites. There was no denying I was a doughnut junkie as I went to the credenza for another one. Bob hesitated before declining my offer of a second jelly-filled.

"So tell me what Sis told you that I hadn't."

"She said your asshole brother used to tell you that you were adopted and should go back to where you came from, hateful shit like that. She said he wouldn't let up, and she would get into it with him, and your father gave him the business for it a few times, but bro never quit in spite of the punishments."

"I'm sure he hated me. I just never understood it." He shook his head. He looked out the window, maybe looking for a memory, maybe not. "She called Paul an asshole?"

"No. That was me editorializing. What can you tell me about your father's brother, Uncle Meyer?" I asked, bringing him back in from wherever he was wandering outside the window.

"It was strange, really. Uncle Meyer made a big fuss at Father's service, said a Jew's funeral should be in the Jewish tradition, and objected to a Presbyterian minister officiating at the burial. My uncle was also the executor of Father's will. But I never heard anything about him after that."

"Did your family go to a church or synagogue when you were a kid?"

"No. Mother was Catholic, Father agnostic, but we always had a Christmas tree and exchanged gifts. Mother and Father would go to parties around the holidays. They'd take us to the Macy's parade. I remember Mother taking me to sit on Santa's lap at Macy's once, maybe when I was four or five ... events like that."

"Does the name Heuer or Hauer ring any bells?"

"No, I don't recall anyone with either surname. Should I?"

"How about Ayelet?"

"Yes, there was a portrait in our house of my grandmother, Father's mother. Her name was written on the back of the canvas."

Bingo! I had to share. "How close did you examine those immigration documents the genealogist sent you?"

"All I got from them was the day Father and Uncle arrived at Ellis Island. Why?"

"Your grandmother was listed right on top of the page as Ayelet Heuer. For some reason, the boys were listed as Howser."

Chapter 12

Developments

As if on cue, Nerd walked into my office carrying his coffee mug. Our biggest, strongest crewmember had a knack of avoiding Linda's furniture-rearranging mania. I introduced him to Bob.

Bob, being a college graduate and all, took the opportunity to say his goodbyes probably hoping I'd get back to working his case.

"Now you show up after Art and I moved all the furniture," I said, pointing to the coffee setup. "Grab a cup."

"I was in the shop downstairs enjoying lunch when the delivery truck showed up. My soup would a got cold. Listen, you okay with me helping out Clancy and Sylvia on their runaway?" he asked while pouring coffee and three packs of sugar into his mug. I made a face. He warmed mine with a splash. "Never heard of black and sweet?"

"Never considered it in the context of coffee. Listen, the runaway's parents are thinking to dump us for lack of progress. They think we should be able to get Vegas PD to jump all over it. Clancy could use a lead on the kid's pimp-slash-boyfriend. Maybe you could put the fear of God in some of the street people, get the word out," I said, setting parameters.

"I'll need a fifty for a friend to cover my back. You good on that?"

"Who?"

"Lucien. He scary enough for ya?"

"Might be overkill you two together. Remember, you scare 'em to death, they can't tell you anything. Get the cash from the bail fund. But before you go, I need some more on the Howser case."

I gave him a rundown of what I'd found and what I needed.

"I'm on it, boss."

"When you get done, maybe you could help me rearrange my office so I don't have to get up from my desk to get a refill."

Fridays were customarily a four o'clock getaway day at Michaels & Associates. The local bars would start filling up around five, and the action was good for the single set and those who lied about being members of the single set. But that night, I'd be a father, something I truly sucked at. Ruth and Linda said their goodbyes and left me to lock up. I called Mrs. Johnson, my apartment manager, who kept my place presentable and my laundry laundered. I'd told her my kids would be coming a day early for our weekend visit. I asked her to lay in some milk, cookies, ice cream, and a bag of kitty treats my daughter used to teach El Gato tricks. In typical cat fashion, he would perform his tricks only for her, and even then only begrudgingly. Mrs. Johnson said everything would be done as per my request.

It was one thirty on the East Coast, so I gave Bob's Sis a call.

"Is that you, Mr. Michaels?" She'd no doubt been alerted by her caller ID.

"Yes, it's me, Rollo, Mrs. Scarsdale. Bob told me you called. I want to thank you for that. How do you feel it went?"

"A bit awkward at first, but he didn't hang up. He seemed angry at you for spilling the beans so to speak. He said you exaggerated the friend thing. I told him I believed you were being his friend by calling me, and I got him to admit it. We talked about half an hour—a lot of tears and 'do you remembers.' I told him I intend on going out there. He hemmed and hawed a bit but finally agreed. It's just a matter of getting a few things arranged here before I can leave, maybe a week or two. How did he seem to you?"

"He was a bit hot under the collar when he showed up here this morning, but a couple of doughnuts and some really good coffee turned him around. Your pending trip out here has him nervous. It's like he doesn't know how to act in that situation. I told him he'd be fine. Overall, I could sense his relief that the cat was out of the bag."

"That's a good thing, I believe. I'm so glad you notified me, Mr. Michaels, and thank you for following up. Can I impose on you to keep me informed, in the loop, so to speak, you know?"

Is she mocking my overuse of clichés? "It's a small loop, Mrs. Scarsdale—you, me, and Bob. No problem. Speaking of which, when's the last time you heard from Uncle Meyer?" I was getting to the nitty-gritty.

"Oh yes, the family tree business. Our uncle kind of went away shortly after Father died. He handled the disposition of Father's estate and returned to Connecticut. He was a strange one, made a fuss at Father's funeral, something about the family forsaking our Jewish heritage. That reminds me, the last I heard of him was that he went to Israel during the Yom Kippur War. I think that was in 1973. I doubt he's alive. He'd be in his late eighties by now. I guess he could be."

"Did you ever meet any of your grandparents?"

"No. My parents said they had all passed before any of us were born. Mother had a wedding photograph of her parents, but I have no idea what may have happened to it after Mother passed. Father sent us all off to boarding school in Connecticut. In fact, Uncle Meyer used to check up on the three of us there from time to time. I remember him taking us to a Jewish restaurant for breakfast. He'd insist we eat potato latkes with scrambled eggs and lox, onion bagels with cream cheese, and we loved it. I'm sure he's dead by now after eating all that cholesterol. How could anything get through those arteries?"

"You're making me hungry," I said, eliciting a laugh from her. "Another quick question if you have time. Do you know what happened to the portrait of your father's mother, Ayelet?"

"The last time I saw that painting of my grandmother, it was hanging in Father's dining room. Paul inherited the house and all that was in it. Bobby and I received all the cash. In 1971, two hundred and fifty thousand was a lot of money ..."

Her voice trailed off.

"You and Bob split it?"

"No. We each received that amount. Uncle Meyer also was given a large sum for being the executor."

"Can you ask your sister-in-law if she has the painting?"

"Yes, but why?"

"To see if anything else is written on it besides Ayelet."

I got to my apartment a little after five, just enough time for a quick shower and shave, a splash of Polo, and clean clothes for my daughter's acting debut. The seven o'clock curtain meant I would be taking the canyon roads and surface streets to Taft High in Woodland Hills.

It was five after six, and I was northbound on Highland just crossing Hollywood when my cell rang. It was Nerd. I punched up speaker.

"Yes?"

"Guess who I got in the backseat with Lucien?"

"I'm up to my ass in rush-hour traffic, Emanuel. Tell me."

"Clancy's favorite pimp, Alphonse Tremaine."

"You shittin' me?"

"What would you like us to do with him?"

"Make him give up the girl. Is he cooperating?"

"Oh you can count on it. But the boy is in pretty bad shape. Arm in a cast, stitches over his eye, teeth missing. He'd had the shit stomped out of him. Says it happened three days ago in Vegas, a trick upset with the service Alfie had provided. When he got out of emergency, his honey had split, and he came back to Hollywood."

"You sure he's not holding out?"

"Listen," he said.

And I did. I heard Alphonse Tremaine screaming loud enough to make the hair on the back of my neck stand up.

"Do you think he's holding out?" he asked me.

"Okay, I get it. Call Clancy. He'll have a few questions for him. Then take Tremaine to Hollywood Station. Clancy will tell you which vice cop to turn him over to," I said as I started up Laurel Canyon. The cars in front of me said I was probably going to miss the curtain going up.

Chapter 13

Showbiz

The play was titled “The Bright Blue Mailbox Suicide Note,” and the theater program said my daughter, Melissa Michaels, was playing Melissa. All the characters in the play were named after the actors playing them. I could see where that would help the director, Zoey Simms, Taft High’s drama teacher.

The play was about a high school boy who finds a suicide note in his mailbox and what happens next. A heavy topic I thought until I took my seat and watched. Wow. The kids put on a show with performances that could have come only from a real understanding of the topic.

I felt pride in my daughter’s delivery and self-confidence moving about the stage in front of an almost-full house. Her boyfriend, Jake, who played the kid who finds the suicide note, absolutely killed it. His stage presence demanded the audience's attention. After the cast took their bows, Miss Simms gave a brief overview of why that particular play had been chosen by her drama class.

"Arial Fowler would have been nineteen tomorrow if she had not taken her own life three years ago. Suicide is the third-leading cause of death of teenagers. More teens die from suicide than cancer, heart disease, AIDS, birth defects, lung disease, flu, and pneumonia *combined.* We all know that traffic fatalities are the leading cause, but many experts believe a lot of those are actually suicides too.

"Suicide prevention begins with awareness. Thus, our effort here tonight. We hope you leave us tonight with a better understanding of this problem facing our youth. We have printed the phone number for the Los Angeles Suicide Prevention Hotline on the back of tonight's program. I hope you'll never have to use it.

"The very purpose of theater is to inform. Its secondary purpose is to entertain. We hope we have done both. Thank you for being here."

The audience was moved to stand and applaud. I flashed back to my time in uniform rolling on a suicide call, a thirteen-year-old who had swallowed a bunch of his mom's sleeping pills because of acne.

Another bow and the cast beat feet to line up outside the auditorium for kudos, hugs, and handshakes. As I made my way toward my daughter, the very distinct voice of my ex nailed me. "Late again, Rollo?"

I turned to plead for mercy but stopped right after my "Hello, Marie" came out. That she looked great was nothing new, but the studly guy she had in an arm lock was. My ex-in-laws stood behind their daughter and her date obviously pained by my presence.

"Rollo, this is my friend, Rex," she said. He tried to free his arm probably to shake hands, but she wouldn't let go.

"Rex," I said with a nod. My "Hi Mom and Dad" doubled down on the awkwardness I felt and their discomfort. "Everybody like the show?"

That had the four of them talking at once. My son, Brandon, came running up to lay a hug on me, saving us all from further forced smiles.

"Hey Dad, shoot anybody lately?"

That turned heads and drew wary glances from those closest in the crowd.

"No champ, been a slow week. Let's grab your sister and head over the hill. Nice seeing you all," was the best I could do for a goodbye.

"Don't bring the kids home too late Sunday night."

Marie was obsessed with getting in the last word.

Melissa broke ranks and rushed Brandon and me for a group hug ignoring her mother and grandparents. "Thanks for coming, Dad! Did you like our play?"

"Awesome," I said, using the most overused word in the millennial lexicon. *Not cool, Dad.*

"You nailed it, Mel," Brandon added.

Melissa went over and graciously accepted praise from the rest of the family. That freed up Rex to amble over to me.

"Marie's raised a couple of great kids there, Rollo," he said, offering his hand, which I shook.

"Her role as mother was never a problem with us. I was the problem plain and simple," I said while watching my son take his grandfather's car keys and run toward the parking area. "What do you do for a living?"

"I'm an investment adviser," he said, handing me his card, which I put in my suit jacket pocket. "I understand you're a PI. That must be interesting."

"At times." I saw my son struggling to get two suitcases and a garment bag to balance at the edge of the curb. *How long are they planning to stay with me?* I seized the opportunity to get away from Rex while my feelings about him remained neutral. I was sure my kids would give me an earful over the weekend.

"Hey, champ, I'll keep an eye on this stuff while you get your sister. I'm dying for a Tommy's Burger. How about you?"

"Awesome!"

Chapter 14

Weekend Dad

Tommy's double cheeseburger with chili packed enough carb-loaded calories to keep a guy going for a whole day. They'd clogged more LA arteries than General Motors. Adding a large fries and a soda to it and you exceed your RDAs for sugar, salt, and fat for two days. They're also addictive.

When we hit Tommy's on Hollyweird Boulevard, it was ten thirty on a Friday night and the joint was packed. Ordering to go was the only sensible option. The people-watching my kids did during our half-hour wait was better for them than any three-unit sociology course at UCLA. I'd made enough stops there to earn a doctorate.

By the time we got to my apartment and parked, the car smelled just like Tommy's. I left my windows opened an inch all the way around, but I knew it would take more than one night to get the *eau de Tommy's* out of my car.

I had shut my cell down for the play and as usual had forgotten to turn it back on until we settled in my little kitchen. Three missed calls—Nerd, Clancy, and Nerd a second time. Voice mail nothing. After we ate and the kids unpacked, I punched up the last call first.

"Where you been, boss?" Nerd asked.

"At a play. What's up?"

"The vice detail wouldn't take Tremaine off our hands. Said until a victim signs a complaint, we got nothing. I had Clancy talk to them, but they wouldn't budge. The watch commander asked Tremaine if he wanted to press charges against Lucien and me for crissakes! I dropped your name, and *el jefe* got real huffy. He said they didn't need any of Michaels's humbug bullshit in Hollywood Division."

"What's his name?" I bristled.

"Lieutenant Harris. You know him?"

"Books have been written about him, *The Peter Principle* for one. What did you do with Tremaine?"

"Took him home."

"Where's he live?"

"That's *home* as in *my house*. Protective custody kind of thing at least till Clancy finishes up in Vegas."

"O M G, Big Man. Your kindness and generosity know no bounds," was all I could come up with. "Lucien helping with the babysitting?"

"Yeah, he's with it. Guy loves this shit. Listen, Tremaine says he'll help all he can if we don't kill him. Clancy told him we'd take him up on that. Then Tremaine wants to know if there's a reward out, and Clancy promised him 10 percent. Crazy."

"All of us are. Did you have time to dig a little more into Uncle Meyer?"

"You're kiddin' me, right?" he asked as if I'd just groin-shot him.

"Maybe tomorrow then. I'm going to call Clancy, see what the plan is. Did he follow up with the client?"

"No clue, boss."

I checked on the kids. Brandon had taken out the PlayStation loaded up with Black Ops and was fully engrossed. Melissa was on her Android, probably with Jake. I went back to the kitchen, where El Gato had his head stuck in a Tommy's bag greasing his whiskers. It was Clancy's turn to give his definition of the word *developments*.

"You never answer when I call," he whined.

"You never leave me a voice mail."

"Can't be too careful. Someone might get hold of your phone. Have you talked to Nerd?"

"Yes. Said he's having some statutory rapist pimp houseguest in for a sleepover. What did he give you? Anything on the girl?"

"As you've probably heard, the pimp got his ass kicked by a couple of rednecks and wound up in the ER. Police were called, but Tremaine wasn't in the system and refused to make a beat-down report. The responding officers took down his name and left. They went back to the station and handed in their log. Their supervisor sees the name and sends the officers back out to the hospital, but our boy had already limped off into the dark side of Vegas. Evidently, his attackers had put the fear of God into him.

"He told me he was back in Hollywood the next day. He has no idea where his star attraction had gone. He gave me their crash pad. It checked out. Neighbors say neither one of them has been around since Tuesday. They identified them both off my photos. I got hold of the Child Exploitation Unit and gave them all the info, but they won't do anything until Monday. So me and Syl are walking the streets and will head home tomorrow evening."

"Did you call Mommy and Daddy?"

"Yes, right after that prick at Hollywood Station busted everybody's balls. Daddy says he's calling Mayor Garcetti to make a personnel complaint on Harris. Good luck with that," he said, his frustration coming through.

"Hey, pard, you never know, it being an election year. Call me if a miracle happens. See you Monday."

The clock on the kitchen wall said midnight as I let the cat out of the Tommy's bag and wiped him down with a wet paper towel, which pissed him off. He hissed and ran to my daughter for some love and protection. She of course obliged.

"All right you two, time for bed. I have a big day planned for us tomorrow," I said, knowing full well I hadn't a clue what we'd be doing. Brandon wanted just two more minutes to kill those who had tormented him on the fifty-five-inch TV screen. Melissa yawned and claimed first dibs on the bathroom. I used the remote to power down the TV and pulled out the sofa bed for them. My housekeeper had made it up without me telling her. A bigger tip was in order. We were all racked out by one.

My usual Saturday-morning sleep-in was interrupted by gaming sounds I recognized as Grand Theft Auto. The bedside clock said 8:42, one hand chasing the other as long as I remembered to change the battery every six months. I staggered into the living room, where my two pajama-clad children had assumed their usual positions. Brandon was focused on PlayStation 3, and Mel was giving her thumbs a workout on her phone. Neither looked up or said anything as I slipped into the bathroom before the sight of me could scare them.

Thirty minutes later, I announced, "Next."

"Good morning, Dad," my daughter responded. "What's on today's schedule?"

"How about the pier in Santa Monica and a walk on the beach?" I asked, probing.

"Been there done that. You forget?"

"How about an early supper in Chinatown and then a play at the LA Center?" was my countermove.

"Two plays in one weekend, Dad?" was Brandon voicing his dissent.

"You two think you might like to visit the Los Angeles Police Museum, see why your old man's the way he is? We could catch dinner in Chinatown and do a Hulu movie back here afterward."

Thankfully, they bit, taking the pressure off this weekend-dad fool.

The kids showered and dressed. We downed half a box of cornflakes with a couple of bananas and a quart of milk before hitting the road. York Boulevard is a main drag in the Highland Park district of Los Angeles. The old Highland Park Police Station had been rescued from the wrecking ball and had been turned into a museum. It had opened its doors in the nineties. I was proud of my time with LAPD and proud of the men and women dedicated to being and preserving its history. That my kids were showing an interest was a surprising bonus.

We were getting a guided tour instead of the self-guided audio when my cell vibrated. A quick glance showed it was an LAPD call. I made the customary gestures and ducked out.

“Michaels.”

“Commander Grahek here, Rollo,” he said, letting me know it was business. “What can you tell me about two of your employees bringing in a beat-up suspect to Hollywood Station last night?”

Whoa. Clancy’s client does have juice.

“If that’s how the department wants to play it, not much, Commander,” I answered in case they were circling the wagons.

"Are not Emanuel Hemmings and Lucien Clark in your employ?"

"They work for me."

"And was not Tremaine's arm in a cast and his eyes stitched up?"

"That's what I was told."

"And didn't your business partner call the Hollywood watch commander on the phone and call him an asshole?"

It seemed he was reading off a checklist.

"I prize Clancy for his insight and candor, traits he developed during his twenty years of service with the very department in which you've achieved success."

"Well, Mr. Glib, we now have the chief chewing on my boss's ass, and you know how things roll downhill around here, so I'd appreciate a little help with this. We're not trying to cover up some stupid decision that might have been made last night."

"When my guys told the lieutenant that Tremaine was a suspect in a Hollywood juvie case

I had an interest in, he blew them off. He wasn't interested in the facts. He told them, and let me quote, 'Hollywood doesn't need any of Michaels's humbug bullshit.' Now that makes it personal. Surely your office knows this guy Harris wouldn't make a pimple on a real cop's ass."

"I'm not going to engage in demeaning a member of this department. Can you help me out here, Rollo, or not?"

"I'll call Clancy, have him call you from Vegas and fill you in. Put that in your owe-Rollo-one column. How's the wife and kids?"

"Debbie's great. The boys are both at USC spring ballin'. Can you believe we open against Western Michigan September two?"

"Beats the hell outta the ass-whippin' Alabama started them off with last year," I said, trying to move the conversation along. "Let me get hold of Clancy. Call me if you need more."

"I appreciate it, partner," he said. He was referring to our time in a radio car more than a decade earlier. "And how are Marie and your young ones?"

"Rod, we've been divorced over five years. This is my weekend with Melissa and Brandon, and you're cutting into it. Gotta go."

I did.

Sylvia answered Clancy's cell. He was on the buffet line for his second go-around. "I don't know where he puts it, Rollo."

"You look at his butt lately?" I said, unable not to.

"That's just mean, Rollo. I won't tell him you said that. Listen, this case is killing my feet. I was thinking about letting Clancy pimp me out just so I could get off them. And *here's Clancy!*"

"What's up?" he asked.

"I just got off the phone with Commander Grahek from West Bureau. Told him you'd give him a call, a rundown on the case. Evidently, our client does have some juice."

"Didn't you work patrol with Grahek back in the day?"

"Yeah. Be up front with him. Rod's one of the good guys." I looked up and saw Melissa giving me her best *What?* pose. "I got to go. Keep me posted."

She and I caught up with Brandon and our docent. Another couple had joined our group. The docent smiled at me and asked if everything was okay. I nodded, and he got back into his spiel about the vintage paddy wagon from way before my time. My son wounded me with, "Did you ever drive one of those, Dad?"

Our tour was running out of steam after another hour, and we had some time to kill, so we went by the old police academy on our way to Chinatown. No Dodger home game so no traffic. A few men and women were running on the track, and many families were picnicking all over Elysian Park. I pulled into the upper lot. We all got out. The Revolver & Athletic Club Café had reopened just a few months before after having been closed for two years for a much-needed makeover. Keeping with tradition, they still weren't opening on weekends.

The view of downtown LA had changed quite a bit since my days in the academy. No doubt I had too. I'd joined LAPD a year before Mel was born, and I made sergeant just before Brandon became an actuality. My theory of how time accelerated as we passed through it, seemed more a reality than an illusion. The view of an empty Dodger stadium reminded me that the more time marched on, the more the Bums went backward. Maybe the season would be different.

I watched my kids looking at the same panorama I was seeing and wondered what they were thinking as feelings of guilt and inadequacy washed over me.

"Let's go," I said, hoping to shake it off. "I'm thinking egg rolls."

LA's Chinatown covers about four square blocks of downtown Los Angeles, a small area when compared to the one in San Francisco and miniscule compared to New York's. But a lot of LA legend, lore, and history can be traced to that section of North Broadway, most of it between Bernard and College. The LAPD had written a lot of it. My first assignment out of the academy seventeen years earlier was to the Central Area when they worked out of Parker Center.

Built in the fifties to house the brass and specialized detective, traffic, and patrol functions, the building had been put on the wrecking-ball waiting list the past year. Los Angeles continued to grow and change, its institutions struggling to keep pace but seemingly always a decade behind.

I self-parked in a four-story structure on Hill Street not wishing to entrust my Escalade to a valet. We walked across Ballard and entered Chinatown through an alley dotted with shops built into doorways and vestibules. My daughter came upon a small shrine and took a photo of Buddha with her phone. She got one of me and her brother looking at junk hanging in the doorway of another shop. Having spotted no suitable souvenirs, we moved on to the restaurant of my choosing. I always suspected most of the restaurants here shared kitchens or at least recipes.

We had no problem getting seated that Saturday afternoon. Egg rolls, won-ton soup, a variety of dim sum, and pork fried rice made the kids happy. I had the beef lo mein all to myself. I passed on a cocktail and had hot tea while the kids slurped Cokes. My daughter took another call from Jake; she excused herself from the table to bounce an "I love you" back and forth with her persistent pursuer. *Or is Jake a stalker?* The reality of my daughter's age and physical development snuck up on me as if I hadn't been paying attention or had been too busy to. She'd soon be a young woman, while her brother would still be wrestling with puberty.

Melissa came back to the table as our waiter delivered the bill and customary fortune cookies. I told them they could choose their own fortune, I'd stick with the fortune they left. Rock, paper, scissors had Mel pick first. We read our fortunes aloud to each other and laughed. Mel collected the little strips of paper saying she'd save them to see if they came true. The waiter boxed our leftovers and put three almond cookies in the bag with them, enhancing his tip by another three bucks.

Eating out of the way, we did the courtyard walk and headed to the memorial sign commemorating the death of LAPD Officer Duane C. Johnson, who had been killed in the line of duty in a Chinatown jewelry store robbery in December 1984. I explained the details of the incident to the kids as they'd been explained to me by my training officer so many years earlier. I walked them to Bamboo Lane to where the shootout had occurred. It was a sobering experience for the three of us.

"What's Jake up to?" I asked on the way to the car.

"He's going to a party at a friend's house in West Hills, said he'd send some pictures ... like he was rubbing it in that I couldn't go."

"You couldn't go?"

"Not without missing a weekend with my dad," she said, forcing a smile.

The silence on the drive back to my apartment had me regretting my performance as tour guide. I asked about my ex and Rex to change the mood without turning on the radio, knowing the kids would make fun of my oldies station.

"Mom said you'd ask about him," Mel said.

"He's okay," Brandon said. "But he doesn't like baseball. He's a football fan. He has season tickets for the Rams. He's taking us to the season opener at the Coliseum in September against Houston, I think. Guys on TV said the new stadium wouldn't be ready until 2020."

"Oh boy," Melissa said derisively. "I don't want to go to either place."

"You don't like football?" I asked.

"Rex is just sucking up to impress Mom."

Anger? "Why wouldn't you want him to do nice things for your mom? That's what a man's supposed to do."

"I think it's being a phony," she said as I parked on the street in front of my apartment.

"Doesn't Jake do things to impress you?"

"That's different."

Her emotions were fighting with her logic. I let it drop. I let the kids set up Hulu with my roomie El Gato, the TV being too smart for me. We chose the Tom Hanks movie *Bridge of Spies*, his latest, *Sully* not yet available on Hulu or Netflix. We took potty breaks, popped corn, melted butter, and poured sodas before hitting the play button at 8:35, only an hour since eating the fortune cookies.

I spotted my daughter periodically checking her phone for party shots of Jake and friends. The movie was about Francis Gary Powers, the U-2 pilot shot down over Russia in May 1960, fifteen years before I'd been born. What I knew about Powers I'd learned in high school as a footnote to Cold War history. Our teacher, Mr. Cassidy, a Vietnam-era marine, made a big deal out of the irony of Powers's death. Seventeen years after surviving his spy plane getting shot down over Russia by a SAM missile at an altitude of over seventy thousand feet, Powers died doing LA traffic reports when his helicopter ran out of fuel at less than one thousand feet.

I'd always admired Tom Hanks's work since seeing the movie *Big* back when I wanted to grow up to be a song-and-dance man. He was great again. Brandon's critique revolved around Powers's escape from the disintegrating spy plane after it was struck by the Soviet missile. Melissa was impressed by Hanks's understated performance while sustaining the suspense even though we knew how it would end. *Only one play and she gets it.*

The next day was a beach day. Out to the Valley for suits and belly boards, chancing the discomfort that Rex might have spent the night. We'd also make a stop at my favorite Italian deli for subs and libations before the drive through the canyon to the Pacific Coast Highway. Weather was supposed to be in the eighties in the Valley by noon, making beach temps about seventy-five.

Chapter 15

Quality Time

Not a cloud could be seen in the Valley, but as we came down out of the canyon to the coast, we saw a big cloud bank lying a mile or so out to sea. We'd be good as long as the offshore breeze kept the clouds at bay. I set out the blanket, anchored it with my cooler of goodies from Cavaretta's, and stretched out in the sun. The kids stuck a toe in the water and reported to me what I'd already figured out—the water was cold. There were quite a few people on the beach but not so many in the water. While Brandon slid across the wet sand on his skim board, Mel sat on our blanket scrolling through pictures on her phone, presumably from the previous night's party in West Hills.

"Any pics you want to share?" I asked.

"Sure," she said, scooting over.

"Is that a Bud or a Coors Jake's swigging?" I asked.

"Does it make a difference?"

"In case I might want to buy him a beer it does. Does he drink when you guys go out?"

"No, only when he's out with his friends," she said guardedly.

"You drinking beer?"

"On occasion. The most I ever had was at Crystal's house. I had a beer and a half ... made me giggly."

"What about pot? Any weed smokers in your circle?" I asked, making her more fidgety.

"Dad, are you interrogating me?"

"Yes. You know I don't want you screwing yourself up."

"I know, Dad, but I won't. I've been thinking ... you know, about what you said about guys doing things to impress girls ... You know, not the show-off-y stuff but the nice stuff. I guess the football game is just Rex trying to do something nice."

"Listen, Mel, your mother deserves to be happy. I couldn't do it. Maybe Rex can." I put my arm around her shoulder.

"Can't you and Mom patch things up, you come home?"

There were tears in her eyes. There was a pain in my heart.

"No, sweetness. That wouldn't be good for any of us." I choked back some tears myself.

A chill told me the temperature had dropped. I noticed a change in the direction of the breeze. Brandon had hit the water to wash the sand off and came running back to where Mel and I sat. He wrapped himself in a towel and plopped down with a shiver.

"You get sand in your eyes, Dad?" he asked.

"Yes, guess I did, son. How about we eat?" That was like a command.

We got out our spread, opened the sodas, and unwrapped the subs. Chips, a bag of pickles, and another of pepperoncini completed our repast.

"The clouds are getting closer," Mel announced.

"Yeah, but the sun's still warm. What do you think, Dad?" Brandon asked.

"I love Cavaretta's subs," I said, chowing down while enjoying the closeness of my children and wishing the day would last forever. But I knew it couldn't, and it didn't.

Twenty minutes later, the onshore breeze became wind. Although the sun still shone brightly, the temp had dropped ten degrees in the hour and a half since we'd set up camp. Brandon's trunks were still wet. He'd covered himself with two towels but was shivering again. By the time we finished our food and drinks, the sun had caught up with the clouds to hide and take the rest of the afternoon off.

"Okay, kids, time to fold up our tent and head back to the Valley."

It hurt me to say it. We got everything to the car in one trip. Surf was up, and a bunch of wetsuits were having at it. All they needed was the theme from *Hawaii Five-O* to inspire bigger waves.

I dropped the kids off at their grandparents' home, not going in for the obvious reasons. I gave them each some pocket money, and we all promised to talk on the phone during the coming two weeks before my court-ordered visitations would allow me another visit. But visitation was never really a problem unless my ex had a conflict. We always worked something out. Well, almost always.

When I got to my apartment around six thirty, I fired up a frozen Red Baron to enjoy with Sunday-night baseball and a few cold ones left over from the other night of babysitting Art. I was feeling good about my weekend parenting yet sad the time had passed so quickly. The score of the game was already 2–0, the Sox over the Yanks in the bottom of the third. I kicked off my shoes just as my phone rang. Caller ID told me it was Clancy. I muted the game.

"What's up, pard?"

"A miracle! We found her!" he yelled.

"Awesome!" I said, a weekend with my kids showing. "Good work."

"Good work my ass. Blind luck, Rollo, blind luck."

"I'm listening."

"We left Vegas early after leaving messages with their juvenile unit and their vice detail. We decided we'd hit the truck stops on the way back. We had a quick dinner at the second one, gassed up at the third, talking to a few working girls at the diesel pumps at each stop, showing pics like we've been doing for a week. Nothing. The fourth stop, all the coffee and iced tea had us in the restrooms. I'm quick and zip it up and wait outside the ladies' for Sylvia. And I wait, and I wait. 'Hey, Syl!' I shout through the door. 'Chastity and I will be out in a few more minutes. Get us a booth,' she says.

"I can't believe what I'm hearing, so I step into the john. Sylvia is at the sinks cleaning the kid up. 'Hi, Chastity,' is all I can say, and back out the door to get the booth, like I was told. Can you believe it?"

"Now what? Did you notify the parents? How about Nerd and Lucien? Where are you now?"

"Still sitting in the booth waiting on the girls. I'm going to let the kid talk to the parents on my phone if she wants. We should hit Hollywood sometime after midnight. Here come the girls. Call you later. You can tell Nerd what's up. Gotta go, bro."

Clancy didn't give himself the credit he deserved. His tenacity doing the legwork, chasing the leads, and not quitting even when the client lost faith was how that girl had been found. Luck had had very little to do with it. Luck was often the result of hard work. I heard the *ka-ching* of Linda's imaginary cash register as my mind quickly calculated everybody's hours on the Morrow case—over two hundred plus expenses. I phoned Manny the Nerd to give him the good news.

"How are you and Alphonse Tremaine getting along?" I asked.

"It's like him and Lucien are engaged in some kind of eating competition. Had to send Lucien for takeout four times today. We haven't found anything this pimp won't eat. What's new? Clancy back yet?"

"Don't say anything to Lucien or your new BFF, but Clancy's found the kid and is headed our way. Tomorrow morning, you can take Tremaine back to Hollywood and dump him on the juvenile unit. Your cover story is he was a voluntary participant in the search for Chastity Morrow. Clancy will meet you there along with the parents. I have no idea if Chastity will roll on Tremaine or if the parents will even cooperate, but we still get paid," I said.

"I bet the father would pay Lucien some big bucks to make that pimp's ass disappear," he said, maybe jokingly.

"You guys make your own deals. Leave Michaels & Associates out of it," I replied with a laugh. "I'm officially canceling Monday morning's associates' meeting."

"Linda won't like that, boss. By the way, I might have found something on Uncle Meyer for you. I'll be in after visiting the Wilcox police shop in the morning," he said, referring to the Hollywood police station.

"Don't let him sneak out the window while you're sleeping."

"Thanks for all your confidence, but Lucien and I are taking turns watching him. Have a good night's sleep while the rest of us are working."

He was gone to increase his paycheck and Michaels & Associates' total billable hours.

I unmuted my TV. The Yanks were up, top of the sixth, score tied 2–2, man on third, one out. It was raining boos as the bunter was called out on a close play at first. I smelled something burning. *Oh shit! My pizza!*

Chapter 16

Susan Cochran

Twenty minutes to nine on a Monday morning found me with a paper coffee cup containing two shots of espresso in one hand, the *Los Angeles Times* tucked under my arm, and my key to the offices poised to penetrate the deadbolt when a woman's voice spoiled my aim with a "Mr. Michaels?"

I turned to see a twenty-something looker with long, blonde hair that framed her perfectly made-up face. She clutched a bulging alligator attaché to her ample bosom; her exposed cleavage threatened to blind me. A soft "Yes?" was all I could muster at that hour of the morning. I refocused on the key-into-lock thing to keep from staring. The door opened just as Linda and Ruth stepped out of the elevator. I led the procession of women into the outer office feeling like a very fortunate Pied Piper.

Ruth took my newspaper and espresso into my office while Linda got between me and the young woman, who was obviously not there to hurt me.

"How may I help you?" Linda asked.

"Actually, I'm here to see Mr. Michaels," she responded. "Vincenzo Costello referred me."

"Yes, he called last week, Miss ...?" I said, trying to take control.

"Cochran, Susan Cochran," she said, extending her hand around my bodyguard to shake mine. *Nice grip. Very nice hand.*

Linda, probably unhappy I was holding on, broke us up by asking, "And what is this about, Miss Cochran?"

"My brother. Our mother is very sick, and I need to find him before ..."

"Please come into my office where we can sit and discuss this," I said while leading the way, Linda not following. "And how is it you're acquainted with Mr. Costello?"

"Actually, I'm not. He's a friend of Mama's," she said as Ruth finished her morning ritual of making me a pot of coffee and fidgeting around the credenza apparently reluctant to leave me alone with this prospective client, probably at Linda's direction.

"Thank you, Ruth. By the way, tell Linda I've canceled this morning's meeting." That got her to leave. I noticed she left without closing the door. I poured two cups. "Sugar or cream?" I asked the client.

"Both please."

We got back to business. "So you want us to find your brother. Tell me why you can't find him." I looked right into her eyes to avoid other distractions.

"Jack came out here about a year ago looking for a fresh start. He wanted to get into the movie business. Other than a few Christmas cards, we didn't hear much from him. The last time we got a call from him was shortly after he arrived in California. He wanted me to send him some money. I didn't have it, but I figured he'd hit up Mom. So I borrowed six hundred from Mr. Costello."

"You mailed him a check?" I asked, hoping to make this easy.

"No. Mr. Costello wired it and said he'd put it on Jack's account."

So Big Vinnie is carrying Jack on the books? "Then what?"

"That was the last we spoke. Our mother says she hasn't heard from him either. She might be telling the truth. Anyhow, Mr. Costello says you're the person who can find my brother," she said while opening her attaché and placing two thousand in cash and a high school yearbook photo of her brother on my desk along with a printout of his vitals, including a Social Security number.

I handed her a sign-up sheet and a receipt for the retainer. I finished my double-shot espresso even though it was cold and watched Miss Cochran fill out the forms. *Nice handwriting*. I felt caffeine surge through my veins and wake up all my body parts. At least I thought it was the caffeine.

"How much time do we have here?" I asked.

"I'm flying back to New York tomorrow. What did you have in mind?" she asked with a flirty smile.

"Your mother, how sick is she?"

That made her blink.

"She's not good, but she's still at home. We're thinking of a nursing facility. The doctors say her condition will worsen. We're hoping to get Jack back home to stay with her."

"We?"

"My mother and I ... I can't deal with this all by myself."

Her concern for her mom made me wonder why she hadn't just called from New York instead of coming all the way out to LA.

"Who's keeping an eye on your mother while you're here talking to me?"

"Uncle Vinnie. He said it would be best if I talked to you in person, so I flew out Friday. He said a couple of days in Los Angeles would do me some good."

Uncle Vinnie? What happened to Mr. Costello? But when I looked at the stack of cash sitting on my desk, I decided not to pry.

"I'll see what we can turn up and call you by next week," I said, handing her my card. "Call me if you hear anything or think of something that might help find your brother."

We both rose, and as she got to the door, I said, "Tell Mr. Costello I said hello."

"I don't know when I'll be seeing him again, but I'm supposed to call him before I leave Los Angeles to tell him how our meeting went."

"I hope you'll put in a good word for me."

"I'd like to tell him you took me to dinner tonight."

"Actually, Mr. Michaels is tied up tonight," Linda said, interceding on my behalf as they both vied for position in my doorway.

One case closes and another begins. I decided to put Nerd on it and have Clancy do any legwork while I worked on the Howser case. I'd have to deal with Big Vinnie if he got word I'd pieced out work he sent me. He demanded personal attention. I assumed he was giving Jack Cochran's sister his personal attention also. Her story didn't quite sit right in my head, but I certainly couldn't turn down Big Vinnie's request for a favor. And Miss Cochran was sure easy to look at.

I put the cash in the safe and went to the outer office to give Linda the sign-up sheet Susan Cochran had filled out along with photo and handwritten vitals on the missing brother.

"Where is everybody?" Linda asked as if her little dustup with our newest client had never occurred; that prompted me to ask myself, *Did I imagine it?*

I ran down my reason for canceling the associates' meeting. Art came out from his office to chastise me for not letting him know before he'd driven all the way in. I apologized and went back to my office. Linda followed.

"How was your weekend with Melissa and Brandon?" she asked, getting a cup of coffee and putting a splash in mine.

"I don't think I screwed it up. I wish you could have seen the play. A star was born."

"Melissa stole the show?"

"Oh she was terrific, that's for sure, but her boyfriend absolutely starred."

That afternoon, I remembered to call Dr. Sheldon, my shrink for the past two years. I caught her before she did battle with her evening commute.

"Roland, how may I help you?"

"I need a huge favor, Doc."

"You're not canceling again, are you?"

"Well, no, not really. Let me explain."

And I did. For the next ten minutes, I ran down the Howser case to her, answered her questions, and gave her some of my observations for whatever they were worth.

"Very well, Roland, time being a factor and all, but if Mr. Howser doesn't call me, you better show up for your appointment."

"Thanks, Doc. He'll call."

Chapter 17

Political Incorrectness

Turns out the canceled Monday-morning meeting was only postponed to nine o'clock Tuesday morning. The conference table had everyone sitting around it but Nerd, who looked on from the comfort of his own desk where the credenza and coffee setup had been kept from me for almost a year. Ruth gave a brief bio and told of her excitement to be onboard the Michaels's express. Clancy gave a rundown of the Morrow case, the arrest of Tremaine for stat rape, prostitution, and four other felonies the deputy DA planned on filing. He topped off his report with props to Nerd. The $9,800 in additional billing would cover a couple of paydays. We all applauded.

I then brought up the Cochran case and assigned Nerd and Clancy to do the digging. Where we stood on the Howser case was left up in the air as I awaited further info on Uncle Meyer's status of being among the living.

Linda gave a rundown of the financials, indicating things would be tight until the Morrows paid up. Art was currently without an assignment.

He said he planned on meeting with a personal injury law firm in Westwood to pitch our services. Their firm did mostly wrongful deaths and serious bodily injury cases excepting traffics unless commercial vehicles were involved. Sticking it to businesses seemed to be that firm's trademark. I reminded him to cite our work for Scott Mathew and the Ironworkers Local and not forget to mention our exceptional success rate in subpoena service and our unmatched ability in locating reluctant witnesses. He countered by suggesting I might come along with him to close the deal. *Sorry, Art, I didn't mean to insult your intelligence, but time for you to score one for the team.*

Around noon, Clancy came into my office. He had just gotten off the phone with the commanding officer of Hollywood Division, Captain Joe Mariani, who wanted to know if we could make the Harris complaint go away.

"Doesn't he know the mayor was the one our client lit the fire under? What did you tell him?"

"Told him I'd talk to our client and get back to him," he answered.

"Mariani is a good man. He can't help which lieutenant gets sent to his division. Why does he care about Harris?"

"Harris is married to the daughter of Assistant Chief Connie Williams, who made the inquiry. The cap said he'd never even spoken to Williams during his entire career. Mariani thinks if he can quash the beef, he can get her to move her son-in-law out of his division and make everybody happy."

"Yeah, everybody except the next command that gets stuck with Harris. But maybe we could put one in the bank. Let me call his boss at West Bureau and see what he thinks. Have a seat. I'll put it on speaker." And I did after first getting some coffee and one of my French maple glazed. I punched up Commander Grahek. His adjutant put me on hold.

The political maneuverings that go on in large police organizations are truly Machiavellian and would make any Italian prince proud.

"Rollo, I heard your missing juvenile is home with her parents and her boyfriend is stashed away in county facing some serious jail time," he said, skipping the hellos.

"I didn't know Harris married up so high. You didn't mention that when we had our little talk."

"What difference does it make?"

"His mother-in-law phoned Captain Mariani, who in turn called Clancy wanting to know if the complaint could go away. Do you think Williams knows the chief of police is involved at the behest of our mayor?"

"Did Mariani say Assistant Chief Williams asked him to do that?" Grahek pressed, causing Clancy to shake his head no.

"No. Mariani is too smart to say that even if she did. Should I tell Clancy to make a call to our client?" I asked.

"Damn you, Rollo, you really put me in a tight spot here. This is a political football we just can't punt. If I don't tell my boss we had this conversation, I'm toast. It's your call to make or not. I like Mariani, but he should have called his boss before he called you guys."

"Tell you what, partner, I'll call Mariani and have him call you, then maybe you can tell your boss my friend Joe Mariani laid this on you. You guys decide if Clancy calls our client to suggest he ask the mayor to stop this ball of crap from rolling all over everyone involved. Clancy will gladly do what your boss thinks appropriate. And remember, Mariani is a friend, so don't chew on him, fair enough?"

"Geez, I have to say something. I just can't let it slide."

"Sure you can. I'll tell him how much he owes his boss."

"Thanks, bud. I'll owe you one," he said, sounding relieved.

"One my ass. That's at least two," I said and hung up before he could hit back.

Mariani had made a mistake by not contacting his boss before calling Clancy. Crap rolling downhill gathers more than just momentum. The chief expected decisive action. I was betting Assistant Chief Williams might have stepped in the crap. At least Grahek would make an effort to extricate Mariani from the mire. I told Clancy to sit on it until the next day. Hoping to save Mariani from trying to serve two masters, I called him.

“Rollo Michaels, why are you still causing people grief?” he asked.

“One of the many personality defects I’m still working on. I think you should call Commander Grahek at West Bureau and tell him about the call you got from Assistant Chief Williams.”

“Why?”

“So he can forget he heard it from me and remember he heard it from you,” I said. There was a long silence before he replied.

“Thanks, Rollo.”

Around three o’clock, Clancy reported he’d received another call from Captain Mariani requesting him not to notify our client about withdrawing his complaint. I suspected that would be a good ending for everyone except for Lieutenant Harris, upon whose shoulders the ball of downhill-rolling crap would come to rest. Unfortunately, Michaels & Associates had made another enemy in the ranks of the police. That list was getting longer.

Linda had gotten a call from Bob Howser inviting her, Ruth, and me to dinner on the west side at Gladstone's, Malibu's iconic seafood restaurant for the past forty-something years. Word had it the place could be closing come October. We were to meet there at the bar prior to the seven-thirty reservations Bob had made. The new Bob had evidently decided we were to be his friends. I felt I'd better get a boot in Manny the Nerd's butt so I could give Bob something.

Of course, Nerd had already anticipated my needs and delivered. He found a Meyer Heuer who was indeed alive and residing in a Jewish home for the aged just outside Bridgeport, Connecticut. The printout said the facility was an assisted-living setup with a nursing staff, pool, rec room, and rehab services. Nerd had called to verify the uncle's residency and was told to call back later as Mr. Heuer was at dinner. I called Bob's sister with the news.

"Mr. Michaels, is everything all right?"

"Yes, Mrs. Scarsdale. In fact, I'm calling to share some great news. We've located Uncle Meyer alive and well. He's in an assisted-living facility just outside Bridgeport. From what I found out, the place is not the usual nursing home. Its website makes it out as resort-like—swimming pool, rec room, walking trails, even a theater."

"Oh how wonderful! Bob must be pleased."

"I haven't told him yet. We'll be meeting tonight. Did you get hold of your sister-in-law?"

"No. I was told she was on a South American tour. My niece said she's due back next Tuesday, a week from today. I'll let you know what she has to say as soon as I talk with her."

"That'll be great, Mrs. Scarsdale. Maybe she'll be willing to talk with me, or Bob for that matter."

"I'll urge her to do so. Thanks for keeping me in the loop still."

"Yes, ma'am. I hope we can pull all the pieces together. Goodbye for now, Mrs. Scarsdale."

"Goodbye," she said and hung up.

I wasn't ready to tell her about the DNA results. I was pretty sure it wouldn't be a problem for her, but I thought I should probably have Bob sign off on it first. Linda came in to tell me she and

Ruth were going home to get ready for our dinner with Bob.

"You might want to clean up a bit yourself." She liked giving parting shots.

Chapter 18

Dinner with Friends

The Tuesday-evening run out Sunset Boulevard to the Pacific Coast Highway was not the dog-eat-dog trip it would have been on a Friday or Saturday evening. I was fifteen minutes early and chose to spend the time listening to some Queen on K-Earth 101 while I sat in Gladstone's parking lot doing some people watching. I hadn't had an alcoholic beverage since nursing a beer and a houseguest on Thursday. I wondered how a Jack on the rocks would go with the grilled swordfish steak I'd been thinking about since Linda told me of Bob Howser's invite. As I sang along with Freddie Mercury, "We are the champions of the …" Linda tapped on the passenger side window. She and Ruth were early too.

We found Bob waiting for us at the bar. Obviously, he'd been early too. Real early. I grabbed him by the arm as he slipped from his bar stool rising to greet us.

"Oops," he said, using the back of the stool to steady himself. Hoisting his cocktail, he said, "To my friends" and drained it. Hugs were exchanged all around, especially the one for Ruth. The restaurant hostess saved Ruth by announcing our table was ready. Bob clung to Ruth's arm while she helped him navigate the crowd as we were led to our window table. A sunset was in our near future. The girls had the window seats, and the boys had the outer seats to protect the girls. Menus were passed. Bob insisted on a bottle of Dom, so bubbly it was. My planned Jack Daniels left to wait yet another night.

The sommelier popped the cork and poured with flair. Bob started with a toast. "Here's to living life to its fullest." That was followed by a chorus of "Cheers!"

Our perky young server was all over us with smiles and a recap of the evening's specials and suggested appetizers. Bob led off with a half-dozen oysters to be followed by the baked cod. Ruth passed on an appetizer; she ordered a dinner salad and the shrimp scampi with a pasta side. Linda and I split a shrimp cocktail, and she went as usual with the salmon. I stuck to my plan—swordfish with rice pilaf and a grilled asparagus side.

Both food and service were great. Bob slowed down on the booze, ate the extra roll, and was pretty much sober by dessert time. He had tried to give Ruth one of his oysters, implying he couldn't be responsible for his conduct if he ate them all. Small talk laced with double entendres got us through a dinner flavored with merriment. So when Bob asked Ruth if she would split a crème brûlée with him, I wasn't surprised by her yes. Linda and I did the same. And as we all enjoyed coffee, it seemed the appropriate time to bring up his case.

"You up to talking a little about the case?" I asked him.

"I'm in the mood only for good news tonight. But wait. Now, if you don't tell me anything, I'll think you held back because you had bad news. That'll keep me awake all night worrying about what you didn't tell me."

"Guess that puts you on the hot seat, Rollo," Ruth said.

"Tell us something good" was Linda's contribution.

"We've found Uncle Meyer alive and well in Bridgeport, Connecticut. He's in an assisted-living facility and supposedly in good shape. Good news, no?"

"Yes, it's good he's alive, but how does that help us? Last time I talked to him was at a funeral. I asked him about my mother, and he walked away. He wouldn't say anything, just shook his head. I didn't want to make a scene, so I let him walk," Bob said as his demeanor changed. "How is it you could find him but those other PIs couldn't? You sure?"

"I'm sure, Bob. I'd like to go see him."

"What for? He won't tell you anything."

"Rollo has his ways, Bob," Linda chimed in.

"I guess if he can talk you out of quitting three times, my uncle doesn't stand a chance." His smile returned. "But I want to be there when you talk with him, Rollo."

"That's not how this works. I go see him, conduct the interview, then verify what he says with you and your sister. Then we can all pay him a visit, a family reunion kind of thing. Okay?" I asked.

His question "When?" signified it was a go.

"Linda will make the arrangements," I said and licked the last of the crème brûlée from my spoon. If I'd been at home, I'd have licked the ramekin clean too.

Chapter 19

All in a Day's Work

Wednesday at Michaels & Associates had me conferencing with Linda, Nerd, or Art for most of the morning unless interrupted by calls from Bob Howser, LAPD brass, or Sylvia, Clancy's wife. She wanted to tell me Clancy needed the rest of the week off, with no explanation. That put finding Susan Cochran's brother back on me. *Why wouldn't Clancy tell me he needed time off himself?*

Art said his contact at Meridian & Sons, the Westwood law firm, took his pitch under advisement. However, they were also interested in some personal security for a client and wanted to know if we could supply around-the-clock security for a client pursuing a personal injury lawsuit against a business front for some Russian wannabe gangsters. We were often asked to provide security in the form of off-duty police personnel but would pass on that one. A friend of mine, a retired law enforcement guy from the sheriff's office, would be a good referral, so I advised Art to make the call. Networking is always a good practice in our line of work.

Art had more. "They also laid four subpoenas on me just nine days to go before trial. They think opposing counsel may have stashed the witnesses. This may be a test of some kind or just something to make me go away and leave them alone."

"Hook up with Nerd. No more than an hour of computer time on each. Sounds like if we find one, they'll all fall into place."

Manny the Nerd walked in as Art gathered up his notes and coffee mug.

"Heard you two talking about me. Thought I'd barge in and stick up for myself," he said while papering my desk with background stuff on John Cochran, a.k.a. Smiling Jack, his sister Susan, and his mother, Madalyn.

"Do me a favor and spend some time with Ruth as you go over the stuff Art needs on some subpoenas. Show her the ropes, and let me know your take on her computer skills," I said. When the intercom announced I had a call from my BFF, Bob Howser, they left. “Close the door please.”

“Hey, Bob, what’s up?”

“I have a two o’clock with our shrink. Anything you want me to tell her?”

“Tell her I miss her and will call sometime soon to reschedule. How do you like the doctor?”

“She sounds like a very nice lady over the phone. She has me down for two more visits next week, then she says, ‘We shall see.’ By the way, she thinks highly of you. You two have something going on?”

“No way, Jose.”

“How about we go for a beer after work?” he asked, putting me on the spot and causing me to grope for an answer.

“I’ll buy if that’ll help your decision making.”

“Deal. Free beer is one of my favorite things. We can talk over a few more things on the case. How about the Golden State Café on North Fairfax?”

“Does this mean I have to pay for burgers too?”

"Well, of course. Five thirtyish okay?"

"You think the girls would like to join us?"

"No chicks will hit on us if we're with the girls."

"Well, there's always that. See you there."

I had time to catch up on my reading of the materials Nerd had dug up on John Joseph Cochran. Seems our boy, called Jack by his sister, has been a bad boy most of his life. He'd had multiple arrests in New York and had done hard time for felonious assault. His last arrest, some four years back, was for homicide. Nerd couldn't find a disposition on that case. The only other thing he could find was a New York driver's license renewal two years ago but then nothing. Nothing came up on him in California. Nerd said the guy was hiding, or had left the country, or was dead. I called Susan Cochran with the news.

Her voice mail said my call was important, so I left my cell number and told her we should talk. I gave her cell number to Nerd and told him to run it. Ten minutes later, he told me it was a burner phone with a New York area code in Queens. His printouts showed over a dozen Susan Cochran listings in the greater metro area and another hundred S. Cochrans. Nerd wanted to know if he should run them all down. I told him no, that I'd wait for her call and press her for more info. There was something about her I couldn't quite figure. The trouble with juggling all these cases is you sometimes drop the ball, miss the clues. You get too busy to pay attention.

Linda set me up with a flight to New York's Kennedy on Thursday with a return set for Tuesday night. A car from Enterprise had me one rental away from a free seven-day rental with another upgrade. We were also sitting on over twenty-five thousand frequent-flier miles I'd promised Linda she could use to visit her parents in Indiana over maybe a couple of weeks in June. Hopefully, Ruth would have learned enough to hold Michaels & Associates together while Linda vacationed. I hadn't made the call to Bob's sister, so I didn't know if she could see me sometime that Monday. After brewing a fresh pot of coffee to get me through the afternoon, I made the call.

"Good evening, Mr. Michaels," she said, keeping it formal in spite of my efforts to get past that. You try to take down the barriers they use to protect their secrets.

"It's two thirty here on the West Coast. Is this a convenient time for you, Mrs. Scarsdale?"

"Why yes it is. I usually have a light supper around seven. You have an update for me?"

"I was hoping to see you this coming Monday after I meet with your uncle."

"Well, I guess, as long as it's not too late in the day ... Can you give me a time?"

"Around noon. Maybe we could do lunch on Bob's dime since this is about his case."

"That won't be necessary, Mr. Michaels," she said.

I sensed a little coolness in her tone. "Is something wrong, Mrs. Scarsdale?"

"I don't wish to discuss it right now."

That told me something was wrong.

"Monday at noon it is then. Goodbye, Mr. Michaels," she said abruptly and hung up, leaving me to speculate on what might have been the matter.

I would be taking the ferry from Long Island's Port Jefferson to Bridgeport on Sunday. My plan was to cold-call Meyer Heuer, not give him a chance to refuse, but before that, I wanted to know what was going on with Mrs. Scarsdale.

While in New York, I was also hoping to get a little more info on Smiling Jack Cochran, maybe talk to the mother, spend a little more time with the sister to find out what it was about her that had me uneasy, beside her cleavage. I knew I was attracted to her sexually, but there had to be a reason she presented herself like that. I could also use my contacts at NYPD, maybe see why we couldn't find a dispo on the murder case. Could I get it all done in four days? That wouldn't allow much time to check in with Big Vinnie Costello and ask about his connection to the Cochrans.

"Susan Cochran on two. She says she's returning your call," Ruth announced on the intercom.

I pressed the button feeling a spurt of excited energy like some damn high schooler. "Miss Cochran, I was just thinking about you. Thanks for getting back to me."

"You found my brother?" she asked, her tone of disbelief coming through loud and clear.

"No we haven't. In fact, there's no record of your brother ever being here or anywhere else in California. I think we might have to take the search nationwide. I was also wondering why you failed to tell me your brother was a criminal, Miss Cochran."

"Please call me Susan, Rollo, and what difference does that make?"

"It might be the reason he's either hiding out, maybe left the country, or he could even be dead," I said, laying it on to get her reaction.

"Oh Jesus! Why would that be?"

"Judging by his rap sheet, Jack could have gotten himself killed. I think I should be coming to New York, see if any of his old friends might know something. I'll need more money for expenses, or you could hire someone there to see if any leads are to be found."

"How much more money will it take?"

"Another thousand, maybe fifteen hundred."

"Geez, Rollo, I don't know if we can do that. I'll get back to you tomorrow, okay?"

She seemed to be pleading.

"Maybe we can get by with five hundred if I can have another week or so, maybe travel on some other client's dime. Call me when you decide, Susan."

That finished our call. I buzzed Ruth back on the intercom. "What was the caller ID on the Cochran call?"

"Blocked," Ruth said.

"That's strange. Why hide the number on a burner?"

"You asking me?"

"No, just thinking out loud. Sorry."

"Can I sneak in for a cup of coffee?"

"Of course. Feel free anytime."

"Well, the door was closed."

"Knock if I'm alone. If I'm with someone, flash the hotline."

"The what?"

"Ask Linda. You want coffee or what? My ear is starting to hurt."

Ruth double-tapped the door and made a beeline to the coffee credenza while I punched up Susan Cochran's burner cell number. It rang four times and went to voice mail again. "I had something else to ask you. You have my cell number" was my message. Ruth was hovering. I put down the phone. "Yes, Ruth?"

"I could use an advance," she said, holding her cup up to cover her blushing.

"How much?"

"A thousand?"

"That's not an advance. That's a loan. What's Linda paying you?"

"Six," she said. Her coffee was looking to escape a nervous cup.

"A month?" I smiled, trying to put her at ease. "Why come to me, not Linda?"

"She said there was a rule and the associates wouldn't go for it," she said. Her discomfort was showing. "I wouldn't ask this except that a family emergency has come up with my mother in Phoenix."

"I see." I lied. I spun the dial on my gun safe and took out ten big ones. "Tell no one," I commanded and slid the bills to her. "Pay me back when you can. How did it work out with Manny today?"

"I learned a lot. Manny is simply incredible. Thank you, boss."

"Remember, Linda's the boss. I'm outta here. Can't keep Bob waiting." I closed the safe and spun the dial.

Chapter 20

Mental Health

"How did you and the doc hit it off?" I asked Bob as our server delivered two drafts of the current craft beer they were pushing at Golden State.

He wiped a beer-foam mustache from his lip. "Good ... I think. You know, I spent an hour filling out forms, medical history, et cetera. So I thought we were going to talk about my cancer, the prognosis, the impending doom, stuff like that. But she asks, 'Why are you here?' So I tell her, 'Rollo sent me.' You know, keep it light, make her smile. Well, she doesn't buy that, no, and the smile is gone. And the next question is, get this, 'Are you gay?' Can you believe it?"

"So what did you say?" I said, throwing him off stride.

"What the hell do you think I said?" he asked, raising his voice. "I said, 'Hell no! Why do you ask?' And she points out I'm a lifelong bachelor, living alone, and had put your name down to be notified in case of emergency."

"Hey, Bob, I'm flattered, but why me, not Sis?"

"I figured you'd get the ball rolling in the right direction. If Sis is coming out for a visit, maybe I'll talk to her about it, but for now, you're it. Okay?"

"I guess."

But it really wasn't. I'd have to tell him why later.

Our waitress saved me. "You fellas ready to order?" Bob went mainstream with the classic burger and fries. The memory of Friday night's Tommy's burgers still lingered in my head and maybe my car, so I opted for Golden State Café's lamb burger and a side of sweet potato wedges with a garlic aioli dip.

"Bring us another round of beer with it please," Bob said. He looked at me. "And put it all on one check."

"Well, thank you, Bob. Listen—I'll be flying to New York tomorrow to talk to Uncle Meyer, Sis, and hopefully your sister-in-law."

"Geez. Tomorrow? I thought you were going this weekend. Wait a minute ... My sister-in-law?" His voice rose toward the end of his delivery.

"We talk to everybody we can," I said as he turned in his chair to lean on the brick wall as if to admire what the restaurant had done to utilize every bit of its small space.

"When do I go?" he asked.

"Let's see what shakes out. You're only a five-hour flight away. I promise to keep you posted. I'll need you to drop some more money on Linda tomorrow or Friday. Airfare, car rental, hotel, a couple of meals. I wanted to take Sis to lunch, but she squelched that idea. Anything said in your latest phone conversation with her to tick her off?"

"Yeah. I told her the DNA test showed that I was only her half-brother, that we had different mothers. She was really upset I'd held back on sharing the results."

"She'll get over it," I hoped aloud.

"I explained to her that I was coming clean, that I couldn't expect others to be forthcoming if I wasn't up front with them. Well, I told our shrink about the conversation this afternoon, and she said I needed to consider other peoples' feelings. Seems I can't win."

"Do me the favor of getting back with Sis, and tell her I suspected something was up when she gave me the cold shoulder today. She probably thinks I was complicit in the decision to keep info from her. Make sure she knows I had nothing to do with it. Got it?" I asked. He nodded.

Our burgers and trimmings arrived with the beers to wash them down just in case we bit off more than we could chew. Bob told me about stopping off at his old company to say hello to a few of his former employees. When he saw he was making everyone uncomfortable because of his walking-dead status, he got the hell out of there and cried like a baby when he got to his car.

Bob didn't seem as enthused about his choices as I was with mine. He pushed his plate away leaving half his fries and the last two bites of his burger. I assumed the telling of his visit to his old business had dulled his appetite. *Or something else?*

“You okay, Bob?”

“I’m good. Just a lot of food. Want another beer?” he asked.

“No thanks, buddy. I should get it in gear. Have to pack for the trip, go over my notes. Anything you want me to say to your uncle Meyer?”

“Tell him I hope to be seeing him soon.”

“Bob, I hope to make that happen. I’ll keep you posted.”

Chapter 21

Much Maligned

It fell on Linda to drive me to LAX to catch my nonstop to Kennedy leaving shortly after noon. But before we left the office, a courier delivered another five hundred from Big Vinnie with a note that simply said, C/ME! *Succinctly put, big fella.* I stuck the cash in my wallet, and we left giving us two hours for traffic, baggage check-in, and TSA.

We took Wilshire Boulevard all the way to Sepulveda, avoiding any chance of getting snared in any freeway jams. Linda asked for my itinerary. I told her my plans emphasizing the "subject to change" aspect of what it was we did.

"Thanks for fronting Ruth the thousand," she said.

"I told her not to tell anybody," I said, feigning annoyance.

"God's sake, Rollo, I'm her best friend. Why do you think I sent her to you? Like I thought you wouldn't give it to her?" she said, pulling up to United's curbside check-in.

"Presumptuous, no?" I asked, getting out of her car. "If she stiffs me, it's on you."

"Oh K M A," using code as if the baggage guy might have been listening.

I fetched my suitcase from the backseat. "Linda, I'd love to, but I gotta plane to catch. Rain check?"

I closed the door, and she left without answering, leaving me to watch as she pulled from the curb and drove away. *Seriously? I was only joking.*

Inside, I showed my ticket and driver's license and gave them my suitcase in exchange for a claim check, which rarely ever got scrutinized, and my boarding pass. I went with the herd and again showed my ID and freshly printed boarding pass to enter the maze that was TSA screening.

Thanks to the 24-7 insatiable news cycle, we're all familiar with the complaints of air travelers put out by some TSA agent trying to do his or her job. Bombarded with tales of intolerable delays, intrusive searches, rudeness, and insensitivity, we approach the screening process with great angst and trepidation. But if we consider the hundreds of millions going through TSA screening compared to the relatively few whose noses get bent out of shape, we should take solace in knowing TSA is doing a great job. Most of the tests they fail were designed as training exercises to keep screeners on their toes. All the negative press, the testing of patience and skills, and the very nature of the mission have created stress and frustration few workers are willing to put up with. Cops understand, and first responders, ER personnel, all have empathy. But most travelers don't have a clue.

Fifteen minutes had passed from the time I'd entered the line to the time I slipped back into my loafers and put all my junk back in my pockets. I enjoyed a full-body scan, a chest pat, and visual of my Saint Christopher medal while some clown one screening line over complained because his supposed carry-on was too big. How the agent remained cool I know not, but I would have gladly slapped the snot out of the clown challenging her if asked.

I was forty minutes early, so I made the obligatory stop at the Starbucks for a double-shot espresso and a couple of scones with butter. I snagged an abandoned *USA Today* in hopes of new insight into the Dodgers' prospects. The front page shouted that Trump had offended someone else. I wondered how a billionaire got so in touch with the working class.

"United Flight 831 nonstop to New York's Kennedy is now boarding at gate 70A."

That was my cue to finish my scone and wash it down with a few sips from the two-dollar bottle of water I'd bought with the long-gone espresso. Heading down to the gate and the horde gathering to get onboard, I hoped the seating gods would be kind to me.

Chapter 22

Friendly Skies

Unlike most of my other fellow passengers, I was in no hurry to get onboard the previously known Friendly Skies, so I lagged behind, outwaiting all but a couple of my fellow travelers. The flight attendant greeted me with a smile as I crossed the threshold with my water and reading materials. I made my way past the forward galley, closets, and bathroom to the promise of first-class comfort only to find my seat occupied. And of course it was occupied by the jerk who'd given the TSA screeners a hard time.

"Excuse me, but you're in my seat" was as nice as I cared to be.

"I don't think so, buddy. Better check your ticket again."

That made my Mr. Nice Guy go far away.

"First off, I'm not your buddy, and aren't you the jerk who was giving the TSA gal a hard time? Get out of my seat."

"Is there a problem?" Miss Welcoming Smile interjected.

"This rude man thinks I'm in his seat. Perhaps you can straighten him out," Mr. Jerk responded.

She examined the seat number on my boarding pass, a seat Linda had forked out a little over eight hundred for, and said to Mr. Jerk, "I'm sorry, sir, but may I see your seat assignment so I can assist you to your proper seat?" Her smile had to be hurting her face by that point. Unfortunately, she didn't call airport security to drag him kicking and screaming off the plane.

After Mr. Jerk was repositioned thirty-two inches to my left and I was about to take my seat, a whiff of jasmine and lemon blossoms tantalized my nose. Enter Miss OMG Gorgeous.

Her "May I squeeze past?" made me mistakenly move from the aisle to the space in front of my seat. "Oh I'm sorry, I mean to get *there*," pointing to the window seat next to mine. As I moved again to let her pass, I vowed to burn incense to honor the seating gods every chance I got from then on and forever.

During the flight, she read *Variety* while I tried concentrating on the sports pages and thinking the *Wall Street Journal* might have been more impressive. The contrast between her Chablis and my Maker's Mark started a conversation. She was an actress. I was a PI. She was going to New York for a publicity film shoot. I was going on a case. It was her first trip to New York. I'd been raised there. Her name was Monique. Mine was Rollo. Monique was not her real name, nor was Rollo mine. By the time we landed, I had her life story, she had my card with my cell on the back, and I had her number.

"Is someone meeting you?" I asked, hoping for a negative.

"There's supposed to be a limo to pick me up, take me to my hotel, the Crowne Plaza in Times Square. Can you believe it?" she asked excitedly.

"You'll love it I'm sure," I said, knowing a week's pay could probably get me the room next to her for one night. "Who will be staying with you?"

"The producer said he'd be right next door to look out for me, take care of incidentals until I return to LA next Friday."

Darkness had descended over New York a good hour before our scheduled landing. Stacking had caused a fifteen-minute delay, but that allowed for some aerial sightseeing by my seatmate. I pointed out some landmarks to her between her oohs and ahhs. She was excited to see the Freedom Tower because her agent and filmmaker had promised a trip to the observation deck for some publicity shots.

Once we landed, we walked together to baggage claim. Sure enough, there was the uniformed driver standing among a dozen like-clad men and two women holding up name placards. One of the lady driver's sign read, "Monique Duvall."

"Hope to talk again, Mr. Michaels," Monique said, and off she went cell phone in hand, making what surely had to be a very important call. *Mr. Michaels? Really?*

My "Good luck!" hit her right between the shoulder blades as she handed the driver her claim checks and small carry-on.

When my bag finally came down the chute, I noticed it was tagged. One of those terrible TSA people had probably had to fondle my underwear to keep us travelers safe in the sky.

Suitcase in tow, I ventured forth in search of the shuttle to take me to my car rental. Getting onto the vehicle turned out to be a contact sport—too many players for the number of available positions. Once on and my suitcase stowed, I sat as the doors closed on the jerk with the oversized carry-on and the wrong seat. I flipped him off and smiled. It pays to court favor with the seating gods.

Chapter 23

New York

My rental-car experience was not without tribulation either. My reserved SUV had morphed into a clown car, or I could upgrade to a Cadillac sedan for a few dollars more. The hard guy in me demanded someone in charge to explain why I should pay for their screwup. Apologies were accepted. The Caddy was mine for a reduced rate, and I had a voucher for a future upgrade; that was deemed an appropriate remedy for such a loyal customer's inconvenience. I would have preferred the SUV, but ...

More than an hour had passed from touchdown to getting on the road that promised a way out of the airport. I negotiated a few wrong turns and with the aid of poor signage managed to get on the Van Wyck. Not the way I wanted to go, but it wasn't too far before I found my way to Long Island's much-maligned expressway, the LIE.

Fortunately, at that late hour, it was not the world's longest parking lot.

In less than an hour of driving, my room at the Hyatt Regency on the Jericho Turnpike in Hauppauge was but a few minutes away. The thought of food took hold of my sleepy brain and led me to an all-night diner a half mile after exiting the LIE. Although I'd grown up about ten miles from there, I remembered very little about the lay of the land other than that I was traveling north.

The San Remo Diner was a long way from the San Remo neighborhood I remembered as a kid, but the lights were on, and there were cars out front, and people in the booths, and a couple of guys at one end of the counter. I went in and took a stool at the end of the counter away from the entrance.

"What'll it be?" the counterman asked, his salt-and-pepper hair secured by a red, white, and blue bandanna.

"Coffee," I said, examining the laminated five-by-eight menu while he poured me a mug.

"How 'bout some eats?" He was prompting me.

"What do you suggest?"

"I'm not a mind reader." He added a smile to his New Yorker directness.

"Two over easy, wheat toast, crisp me up some hash browns too," I said to my tired-looking host.

"Wasn't that easier?" he asked with a bigger smile. "Where you from?"

"CI." That was what people from Central Islip called the place.

"Yeah? Don't think I've seen you here before."

"True, I'm lost," I said, giving him the business as I watched him throw a handful of potato shreds onto a few drops of the oil dancing on his hot griddle.

"How 'bout some bacon or ham?"

He was upselling me like he owned the place.

"You got a piece of steak back there?"

"Sure do. Thin or thick?"

"Thick. Medium rare would be great," I said, keeping up with the cadence to our rap.

"I think I can do that," he said, enjoying his work.

"Maybe some grilled onion with the meat?"

"Hey, CI, you're pushing your luck here."

"Hey San Remo Diner Man, I'm a good tipper," I said, ending it to head toward the sign that read "Restrooms."

After washing up, I called the Fort Salonga Hideaway. The bartender answered on the third ring. "The Hideaway," he shouted over the jukebox blare.

"I want to leave a message for my uncle. Tell him I just got in town and will see him in the morning, got it?"

"Who is this, and who the hell's your uncle?"

"Hey, whatsamaddayou?" I asked, not quite getting the Vinnie vernacular right.

The FBI wiretap logged the call on 04/14/17 2351hrs.

My plate was resting on the cooler side of the griddle. The counterman/cook placed it before me as I retook my stool. A small mound of grilled onions adorned the top of my steak, the hash browns were browned like I'd asked, and two slices of wheat toast sat on a bread plate sided by a ramekin of whipped butter.

"So what's your name, CI?"

"Rollo. And yours?" I asked, spreading some butter and testing my over-easies with a toast point. The yolk oozed out perfectly.

"Ed, but people on this side of the expressway call me Irish. How'd you get lost?"

"Joined the army twenty-something years ago and never looked back. Should I call you Ed or Irish?"

I could have cut into my steak with a butter knife. *Impressive.* I put a couple of ringlets of sautéed onion on a bite of the meat and closed my eyes to savor the flavor. *If this is a dream, the steak would be bigger.* I opened my eyes.

"Irish works best. Fewer people turn around when someone shouts it out. So what brings you back?"

"Visiting my uncle Vinnie in Fort Salonga. Where'd this steak come from? It's unbelievable."

"That's aged top sirloin at its best, not our usual breakfast steak. We don't tell where we get them from," he said with a wink. "What's your uncle's last name? Maybe I know him."

"Costello, Vincenzo Costello. You know him? By the way, Irish, you're a great cook."

I was enjoying my steak-and-eggs midnight repast. I purposely refused to spoil the potatoes with ketchup from the counter squeeze bottle. I wanted to show my appreciation for his considerable skills.

"Big Vinnie's your uncle?" Irish asked, wide-eyed.

"So you know him?" I asked rather than answering his question. *Maybe just a little squeeze of ketchup? No, don't do it, Rollo, no! ... God, I hope it's Heinz.*

"Well, I don't *know him* know him," he said, making air quotes. "But I know who he is. Owns the Hideaway." He poured me a warm-up before tending to the couple in the booth and the two drunks at the other end of the counter.

A few more of the late-night crowd took up seats, so Irish hustled to take their orders, cook their food and serve it, all that while keeping my coffee mug topped too.

"Your boss too tight to get you some help in here?" I asked while paying the bill.

"Shit, CI, I *am* the boss." He laughed. "My waitress went home sick a couple of hours ago. You want to run tables for me?"

"There was a time."

Chapter 24

Sweet Dreams

It was going on one in the morning when I checked in at the Hyatt Regency just up the turnpike from the San Remo Diner and the magic of Irish. I laughed when the desk clerk told me breakfast would be served from six to nine in the morning. His perplexed look caused me to explain, "I hope to be sleeping at least until ten."

I schlepped my suitcase to my second-floor room, hung the Do Not Disturb sign on the door knob, and unpacked. I thought about retrieving ice from down the hall but decided I was too tired. I felt grubby, so I hit the shower. Ten minutes of hot and one minute of cold and I was done. I turned on Fox News and was catching the 2:00 a.m. replay of O'Reilly substitute when my phone chimed to let me know I had a text message. It also was a reminder to plug in the charger so my cell would be ready for some heavy usage the next day. I checked the text. It was Monique. Her "Thanks for being such a good seatmate" made me wonder. "Thanks for being you" was the best I could do.

My brain was still on LA time, but my body wasn't buying it. Cross-country flying always kicked my ass, and the hotel's king-sized bed and six pillows demanded I shut off the talking heads and turn out the lights. I soon fell fast asleep. My last conscious thoughts were of Monique's text, then a peculiar dream.

I want to leave but am drawn into the room captured by the presence of evil. The smell of booze and stale smoke catches in my throat, my heart pounds, my skin twitches. I gasp for breath not comprehending what I'm seeing.

"What you lookin' at?" the beast growls.

"Nothing," I whisper, averting my eyes as it rises from a whimpering girl.

"Nothin' is right. You ain't saw nothin' here. Now get the fuck out," it says. It sneers, its eyes glowing with menace.

I turn from the beast, bile in my throat, tears welling up in my eleven-year-old eyes. I flee wetting myself as I run to my father's office to get the revolver from its hiding place in his desk. I've been there many times to play with it, spinning the cylinder, touching the bullets, cocking the hammer, sighting down the barrel, pulling the trigger.

I wipe the tears from my eyes and the sweat from my hands. I am empowered by the heft of the cold metal in my hands. I walk back to the room I had fled but a moment ago and enter again. The beast rises from the girl and stares in disbelief as I raise the pistol and shoot Evil in its face. The explosion of the bullet recoils up my boy arms, shocking my senses. Evil slides from the bed and lies dead on the floor. And the girl screams and screams and screams.

I hear shouts and heavy footsteps behind me. Powerful hands grab me and take the pistol from my grasp. Father puts his jacket over my head and ushers me down the hallway ordering his men to "Clean this up."

We enter my bedroom, and I can hear myself moan and more tears flow and not just from me. "Shush. It's just a bad dream," Father says, rocking me to sleep in his arms, the reassuring smells of Aqua Velva and Marlboros telling me I am safe from Evil protected by the sheer force of my father's being.

I was startled awake by my phone. It took a few more rings for me to get my bearings. The bedside clock said 8:38 as I reached for the still-ringing phone. Too late. It went to voice mail. I sat on the edge of the bed, yawned, stretched, yawned again, then staggered toward the bathroom in the semidarkness of drawn curtains. Naturally, once I started to go, the phone rang a second time. I closed the door with my elbow. The phone stopped about the time I flushed. I went to the window and opened the drapes. It was raining, perfect sleep-in weather for a body still on LA time.

I checked the phone. Both calls from the same number, a local area code. I hit the call option. Two rings got me my faux uncle.

"Hey nephew, where the hell are you?"

His voice was as big as he was.

"In bed, Uncle, trying to sleep a little—"

"You're sleeping your life away. What time you gonna get here?"

"Give me a couple hours, wash up, dress, grab a bite—"

"Bullshit. You eat here. Cookie can fix you anything you want. Where'd you say you're at?"

"Hyatt Regency."

"In Hauppauge?"

"Yeah, Uncle—"

"You hurt me. Why ain't you staying with me and Angie? Geez—"

"Got in too late, big guy. Let me get movin'. I can be at the fort in less than an hour, okay?"

"See you there. Don't keep me waiting."

The FBI wiretap logged the call on 04/15/17 0857hrs.

Chapter 25

The Fort

The Fort Salonga Hideaway was headquarters for Big Vinnie Enterprises, those that were legal and those not so much. I hadn't been there since my father's funeral services over six years earlier. Not much had changed. Maybe the blacktop had been redone on the parking lot, the weathered wood siding may have been sprayed a few more times, and the signage appeared freshly repainted. The rollup shades in the second-floor windows were still at half-mast.

Vinnie's pride and joy, a fire-engine-red '32 Ford Roadster with a white ragtop, was parked in its usual spot. Wood barrier horses stood guard on either side just in case some fool wanted to park too close. The sun bouncing off its three coats of wax made the car sparkle like a jewel. All appeared right with the world and the fort.

Three other cars and a pickup were lined up along the front of the joint, and a big beer delivery truck was doing its business around back. I parked between two of the cars and went in. Ceiling fans whirled as they hung from exposed beams. The jukebox was silent as one of five giant screens played CNN for my uncle Vinnie, still a die-hard liberal.

All eyes were on me as I stepped in. Vinnie was leaning against the bar, Alejandro Reynolds, his bartender/bouncer, was on the other side of the mahogany. Ozzie Arturino gave me the nod and a smile from his seat at the table just inside the door, his back to the wall, the *Daily Racing Form* before him. I walked up to the bar. "Hope I haven't kept you waiting too long" was my funny.

"Nipote mio, so good to see you," Vinnie said, wrapping his huge arms around me. "Ali, you remember Charlie Michaels's kid, Roland, don't you?"

"Sure do, boss," Ali said, reaching across the bar to shake hands. "How ya doin', kid? Long time no see."

"I'm great, Ali, livin' the life. I see not much has changed around here. How's the family?"

That made Uncle Vinnie scowl and shake his head.

"Kathy's moved on, but Rocco's in college, Suffolk County CC, doin' good. You and that little Sicilian girl have a couple of kids too, right?"

"Yeah, Ali. Melissa is seventeen, and Brandon is fourteen. They live with Marie. Get to see 'em like every other weekend."

That put a further drag on the conversation, so Vinnie jumped in.

"Come on, nephew, let's get Cookie to fix us up with something."

He led me away from a bummed-out bartender to Cookie's kitchen. "I should have warned you about mentioning family to Alejandro. His old lady is marrying some schmuck from Mineola tomorrow. He's really depressed. I'm afraid he might do something stupid, ya know?"

"Roland!" Cookie shouted. "Look at you! Is that a gray hair I see in those curls? Get over here, give this old gal a hug."

And I did. Loretta had gotten her start as a sous chef with my father's hotel more than thirty years back. She was a kitchen constant as a parade of chefs passed through the doors. She even found time to show me a few kitchen tricks. When the feds shut Pop down, Vinnie took her in.

"How 'bout fixin' us up some breakfast grub, Cookie?" Big Man asked as we sat at a small table in the kitchen office.

"So you find anything out for the Cochran girl?"

That got us right down to business.

"Her brother's a bum, and don't tell me you didn't know that when you sent her to me. Anyway, I couldn't find a trace of him in California. Zilch, like in zero. I'm guessing he's changed his name, left the country, or is dead. Anyhow, I'm scheduled to check in with a friend who's a New York detective, see if he can get me some names of known associates and the like. There's also no disposition on his last known arrest that needs to be looked at, which was for a murder and in the city by the way."

"I told her if anyone can find her brother, it'd be you. But did you notice how beautiful that girl is? You should probably be splittin' your fee with me puttin' that girl in your life," he said, grinning ear to ear.

"Hey, I gave her a thousand-dollar discount bein' you're payin' an' all," I said, letting him know I was wise to his ways.

Cookie placed plates of toasted bagels with cream cheese smears and lox-and-onion omelets before us. OJ and steaming cups of coffee helped to completely cover the table.

"This was your father's favorite breakfast, Roland, you remember?" Cookie was beaming.

"You bet, Loretta, and thanks bunches for making it."

If I keep eating like this, I'll need new clothes ... probably be comfortable having sex only in the dark.

Our small talk between bites, sips, and gulps consisted of "How's business?" I asked. "Good," he said. "I make a buck here and there." "How's the family?" "Angie's fine, a happy grandmamma." "Marie's dating. The kids are fine."

I agreed to check in with him over the weekend, keep him up to date on the search for John Cochran. Maybe a Sunday dinner at his home in Northport.

"Angie will make us some of her lasagna. It's the best, remember?"

"Who could forget?"

I remembered Angie had given the recipe to my ex.

Chapter 26

Brooklyn's Eighty-Third Precinct

Dick Stines was a high school classmate of mine who'd gone to City College on his daddy's dime instead of joining the military with the rest of his hooligan friends. His daddy was a sergeant with the NYPD and certainly knew who my father was, and more important, he knew what my father and his associates did for a living. But he could never prove it. His daddy got Dick into the police academy when Dick graduated from junior college just before he turned twenty-one. I was still in the army, an E-5 with a year to go on active duty. I had plans for a wedding and a career at the NSA upon discharge.

My wedding happened a little sooner than planned. That caused many to think a shotgun had been involved. The truth was that on returning from overseas, I was sent to Ft. Meade to finish my enlistment while training for my civilian job as one of NSA's thousands of analysts. My fiancée wanted to get a jump on marriage and our future by setting up our home off base. But her parents wouldn't pay the freight unless we were married; thus, my first marriage took place during a quiet gathering in a New Jersey courthouse six months before the long-planned, big, Italian church wedding on Long Island.

Two years before that, while I was mastering the Korean alphabet at the Defense Language Institute, Marie, my intended, surprised me with a visit chaperoned by her aunt and uncle from Los Angeles. I took them around and showed them the sights; Marie was smitten. So when it came time to commit to my planned career with the NSA, she wanted California instead. After six months of sitting at a desk reading transcripts of Korean messages so they could be properly sorted and routed, I found it easy to have second guesses about my career choice. Soon, I was California Dreamin' all the way to LA a week after my separation from the army.

I ran into Dick Stines at our ten-year high school reunion. He was then a seven-year NYPD veteran patrolman working Manhattan South and would soon promote to detective. He registered surprise that I was a two-year member of LAPD. His first question was, “What did your father say?” I told him my father had never pictured me in that line of work but had no problem with me wearing a badge, but my move to LA hadn’t been forgiven.

The night of the reunion, Dick and I hit all the bars where a classmate might buy us a drink and we could reciprocate. We wound up at my father’s place. From then on, bonded by tying one on together and the fraternalism of the brotherhood of the badge, we became the best of friends. Marie and I hosted Dick and his wife, Claire, in Los Angeles, and we next hooked up at his father’s funeral in late September 2001. Sergeant Albert Stines died in the rubble of the World Trade Center’s North Tower on 9/11.

I had called him Wednesday to tell him I’d be in New York Friday and ask if he could help me out on the Cochran case; I gave him some of the particulars. Strangely enough, Cochran’s homicide arrest had been made in the very precinct his father had been assigned to on 9/11. We agreed to meet there at three. I made the run to Knickerbocker Avenue in a little over an hour from my hotel after making a few calls—one to him, one to Linda, and one to the assisted-living facility where Meyer Heuer resided.

Everything was a go. Dick was already at the Eighty-Third and wanted to know what I was driving so he could arrange for parking. Linda said that Bob had dropped off another $2,000 that morning and that the bill on the Morrow case, totaling $11,600 and change minus the $4,500 in deposits already paid, was going out in the afternoon mail. I was told Rabbi Heuer was still in residence and just fine.

Rabbi?

Sunday visiting hours were 9:00 a.m. to 5:00 p.m.

Dick met me outside the stationhouse and directed me to a yellow zone down the block after putting a Pass placard on my dash. Handshakes and hugs and in we went. A few civilians were doing business at the desk while others sat on a bench awaiting their turns. Dick took me over to a row of pictures on the lobby wall honoring fallen officers of the Eighty-Third, eleven in all. Albert Stines smiled at me. I noted the 9/11/01 designation on two of the other pictures too. I was moved.

Dick tagged me with a visitor's badge before we were buzzed through a door and climbed the stairs to the detective squad. I was introduced as "Sergeant Michaels, LAPD." That was Dick's lie, not mine. It wasn't Dick's house, but we were made to feel at home because Dick was Albert's son. I shook hands with the lieutenant and exchanged nods with three of his detectives, a man and two women.

We went to a desk Dick borrowed from a choice of a half-dozen empty ones. He handed me a folder marked "Houston, Raymond C."

"Have a seat. That's all we have on the homicide. The murder book was signed out by Major Crimes in 2014."

I examined the inner flap. A notation said "FEDS" in large, handwritten letters. Another entry listed Cochran, John Joseph, a booking number 12053, and a charge of 187. His aliases were Jack, J. J., and Smiling Jack. His rap sheet, starting out as a thirteen-year-old, included theft, auto theft, petty theft, grand theft person, assault, assault and battery, and felonious assault for which he pulled a three-to-five in Attica, New York's infamous prison for bad boys.

Cochran's jacket and related reports including the arrest report would be at Majors. When Dick called there, he was told the case had been taken over by the feds–i.e., the US attorney, New York, Southern District. "Good luck with that," they advised.

"However," Dick said, "one of the detectives who originally caught this case retired two years ago lives on the island and will be meeting us for dinner at six."

"He got anything?" I asked.

"Says he does, but the guy's old school. He sounded sharp to me, knew who I was, says he remembers working a squad car with my father over thirty years ago. So we'll meet him at his favorite restaurant in East Islip. His son owns it. You remember East Islip, Rollo?"

"I do, Dick, I do. Listen, being this has turned into dinner, how about Claire joining us. I'm buying."

Chapter 27

Expense Accounts

The Irish Coffee Pub on Carleton Avenue was a white-tablecloth restaurant with uptown pricing, a full-service bar, and a well-thought-out wine list. For the second time that day, Dick Stines was waiting for me at a door. He was accompanied by the lovely Claire. A hug and a smooch was the price I happily paid for admission.

At six on a Friday, the place was already near capacity. The hostess led us straight to the best table in the house where a bear of a man stood to greet us. Claire almost disappeared in his arms. He shook Dick's hand and turned to me.

"Teddy McBride, this is Rollo Michaels. We went to CI High back in the nineties," Dick said as Teddy's big paw wrapped around my right hand.

"LAPD, eh? Never much liked Jack Webb telling the country you guys were tops. You think we're chopped liver?"

A big grin crossed his face.

"Thanks for seeing me, Ted. Jack Webb was a little before my time. I guess we should thank you guys for sending Bratton to the coast to straighten us out instead of Crazy Eddie" was my retort.

"You're welcome. As long as we kept Kelly from you poachers." He laughed.

We ordered cocktails and appetizers before entrée decisions. Of course I ordered the corned beef and cabbage, based on Ted's recommendation. Conversation was light, mostly Dick reminiscing about high school hijinks. I learned that Ted was called Bear during his forty-year tenure on the job, the last twelve as a homicide detective and squad boss. He was a 'Nam vet who had joined the department after eight years in the army. He had planned to be a lifer, but budget cuts squelched those plans, so the PD it was. He did stay in the army reserves, became a major, and got called up with his unit during the first Gulf War. Theodore "Bear" McBride was quite a guy.

Five years earlier, he'd loaned his son a chunk of money to buy the Irish Coffee Pub because he liked the corned beef. It was his daughter-in-law who seated us. Desserts and Irish coffees and we were two hours into the evening. Dick and Claire said they had to get home before nine because of Claire's mother being under the weather. I doubted that. Dick was giving me a chance to talk with Bear in private. We rose to say our goodbyes. While hugs and kisses were exchanged, Bear huddled with Dick probably to discuss me.

Bear and I sat back down. I waved our waiter over. I ordered another coffee sans whiskey. Bear was a real Irishman and ordered a double Bushmills 16 on the rocks. Once served, we got down to business.

"Here's to the Irish in you, Michaels. Your grandmother was from the old sod, wasn't she?" he asked, raising his glass and an eyebrow, a smile telling me he was letting me know he had checked me out.

"And my grandfather Michael Cassidy too."

I clinked his glass with my cup. *Linda's going to hammer me on this expense report.*

"Let me tell ya', Rollo, your guy is a real douchebag. His uncle, married to the mother's sister, gets caught dumping the body of an out-of-towner tourist over by Bay Ridge. We get the case because the vic's wife had reported him missing from their hotel the day before. It was a pretty easy matchup. The vic had a prosthetic foot. So the uncle is facing murder one, and we sweat him. He cracks, says he was only doing a favor for his nephew, Smiling Jack Cochran. We go out and pop Cochran for the murder and rebook the uncle for aiding and abetting. DA's happy, we got two jamokes off the streets, the bosses are happy. Sad things can happen in the Tombs, and sure enough, our aiding-and-abetting witness kills himself. We had to kick Cochran thirty-six hours later.

"Well, six months go by, and Major Crimes comes sniffing around for our case files. Seems a snitch tells the FBI he saw Cochran stab our victim right in the heart over an argument in a card game. So they scoop him up for the feds. Two weeks later, I spot Smiling Jack going into that mob hangout on Delancey. I call Majors, and they tell me, 'Fageddaboudit!'"

Teddy Bear McBride took a hit on his drink and wiped his lips, his eyes telling me he was enjoying the telling.

"I'm sure the feds had put him on the payroll. Five or so months later, Slats Salerno falls for racketeering, and his number two falls a short time after that. Well, pretty soon, some mobster genius figures Jack for a rat and Jack disappears. Dead? On the run? Witness protection? Your guess is as good as mine. I'm betting he's part of a Jersey landfill."

"Anybody ever check on the family? Mother, sister?" I asked.

"The mother filed a missing on him just before I retired. It's probably still open. Maybe Stines can check on it," he said, not knowing Dick had already faxed me a copy of that report after I'd called on Wednesday.

"And the sister?"

"Never met her."

Chapter 28

Mom

Saturday morning found me in Queens knocking on the door of Madalyn Cochran's third-floor apartment. I stood back and smiled for the peep.

"Yes?" came a woman's voice through the hollow-core door that should have only been on a closet.

"I'm here following up on the missing person's report you made on your son John, Mrs. Cochran," I said while holding up my ID. It could have been a credit card, which had actually worked for me in the past. The door opened, and a healthy, well-groomed woman stood before me. I handed her my credentials in case she was skeptical. She examined the photo on my PI license and my retired LAPD ID. When she handed them back, I noted her manicured and brightly polished nails.

"Those say you're from Los Angeles, not the NYPD, Mr. Michaels. I'm a little confused. You're not bringing me bad news, are you?"

"No, Mrs. Cochran, I'm not. I'm a private investigator. Your daughter hired me. She believes the police have given up on the case, and she wanted me to see if your son was in LA, but I couldn't find a trace of him. I was hoping you might be able to shed a little light on the circumstances of your son's disappearance."

"My daughter? Please come in."

She led me into the small bachelorette apartment. Well-coiffed and smartly dressed, she sure didn't seem to be suffering from any terminal illnesses.

I sat on the couch and spotted an ornately framed eight-by-ten glossy of Mrs. Cochran flanked by Jack on her one side and a younger version of Mrs. Cochran on the other. The three of them were standing in front of a Christmas tree, their broad smiles speaking of happier times.

"That was taken three Christmases ago," she said.

"Any other children?" I asked, already knowing the answer.

"No, just Jack and Suz," she said, nodding to the photo.

"When's the last time you spoke with your daughter, Mrs. Cochran?"

"Sadly, we're estranged. That beautiful girl you see in that photograph got mixed up in drugs over two years ago. The last time she was here, my jewelry disappeared. We had an awful fight, and she left, and ..." She stared at her hands. Almost a minute went by.

"Mrs. Cochran?"

"I'm sorry. What was your name?" She was looking at me as if seeing me for the first time.

"Roland Michaels, from Los Angeles." I handed her a business card. *Uh-oh.*

"Yes, Suz. She called from jail in Jersey City a few months later, wanted me to bail her out on a prostitution charge. I refused, hoping a jail sentence would get her off the drugs. Never heard from her again." Her eyes welled up with tears. "How did it all go so wrong?"

That was a question I hadn't anticipated or had an answer for.

"Susan showed me a couple of Christmas cards postmarked from Los Angeles. Do you recall getting them from Jack in 2015?"

"Last year?"

"Not this past Christmas—the one before," I said. She looked befuddled.

"Let me think ... No, we didn't receive any cards from Jack or anything else since he walked out that door, left all his stuff behind. I thought he'd been arrested again. After a week, I made a police report. You can't believe a word that girl tells you, Mr. ... what did you say your name was again?"

She retrieved a tissue from the box on the coffee table and blotted the corner of her eye.

"Michaels, Roland Michaels. It's on the card you're holding. I'm sorry to have upset you like this, Mrs. Cochran."

Her sudden change in demeanor and apparent confusion was a shock.

"I believe what the other detectives believe, that my son's dead. It's the nagging doubt that's so painful, and when my daughter left, I was devastated. You said Susan hired you? When you talk to her, please ask her to call me ... I have her number somewhere, but can't seem to find it ... And if you find ..."

"I will, Mrs. Cochran. I promise."

I called Susan Cochran when I got back to my car. Same pattern—no answer, leave a message. I did. "Susan, this is Rollo. I'm in town. It's imperative that I see you today."

I drove back to the San Remo Diner with visions of steak and eggs dancing in my head. Thankfully, Irish was working.

"What will it be, CI?" he shouted out, turning heads.

"The usual, San Remo Diner Man," I shouted even though he was no more than six feet away and bringing me a cup. Another patron wearing a sports coat and a white shirt opened at the collar walked up. When he sat on the stool to my right, I saw his badge.

"You from Central Islip?"

"Used to be. And you'd be ... who?" I asked so Irish could hear. He was facing the business on his griddle; he was hiding his embarrassment from when he saw the law approach me.

"Beau Wolfe, that's with an *e*, Suffolk County PD," he said, pulling his jacket open to display the badge I'd already seen. "Do I know you?"

"No, and I don't think I'd forget. Hey, Irish, cancel that order."

"You lose your appetite?" Wolfe asked, going for obnoxious and overshooting his mark.

As I stood and took out my wallet, Wolfe jumped back and reached for his shit. My "Little jumpy, Officer?" made it worse.

"Put your hands on the counter. Assume the position," he ordered, hand on gun.

"A good citizen gives you information and you burn him like this? Let that be a lesson to you, Irish," I said, placing a couple of bucks on the counter to cover the coffee before grabbing some counter. Wolfe gave me a pat-down and turned me around. I wasn't carrying.

"Let's see some ID, wise guy."

I gave him my California driver's license. "Why are you embarrassing the both of us like this, Officer Wolfe?" I asked loudly on behalf of the dozen or so other patrons enjoying the drama. His cheeks reddened.

"That's Detective Wolfe to you, pal. Vinnie Costello's your uncle?"

"Really, Detective, you're jacking me up to ask about my family tree? Give me my license back so I can leave. I'll let him know of your interest."

He handed my license back, and I left as Wolfe made a notation in his smartphone. Probably had my picture in there too. *WTF?*

He came out of the diner as I was pulling away and snapped a few more pictures. I flipped him the bird as he was phoning it in. My stomach said I was still hungry.

The FBI wiretap logged the call on 04/16/17 1123hrs.

I drove on over to the McDonald's on Commack Road. The two Egg McMuffins were a big step down from San Remo's fare, but I always found Mickey D's coffee more than just palatable. As I contemplated the rest of my day, my cell rang. Caller ID was blocked. I made an educated guess.

"Hello, Susan. Where are you?"

"Out and about. You said you had to see me. Can't we do this over the phone?"

"No, Susan. Hey, I thought you'd be more anxious to see me."

"Well, where then?"

"How about your mom's place in Brooklyn?" I said, setting a trap.

"No. I don't want to get her all stirred up again."

"Okay, how about the lobby of my hotel?"

She didn't respond. I waited. "Hello?"

"How about the Fort Salonga Hideaway? By the way, my mother doesn't live in Brooklyn, and don't you be bothering her," she said, avoiding a gaff.

"I can be there in a half hour." I was lying. I headed to my car.

"Me too," she said, probably lying too. I was guessing she was already there, having been told what to say to me by Big Vinnie himself.

Chapter 29

More Lies

It took fifteen minutes to get to the fort. The Mets pregame was on the screen over the bar, soccer was on a second screen, and golf was being talked about on another. Actually, the closed-captioning was telling the viewer what was being said about a missed putt, expletives deleted. Four people stood around the pool table watching a hotshot prancing around the table with the cue. Vinnie was at a small table conversing with my client. The loyal Ali occupied Vinnie's usual spot on this side of the bar while Sox Devine tended to customers taking up various stools. Joe Montebello was on door-watch duty and gave me the nod. Ozzie might have been running errands for Vinnie. I walked past a four-top who were digging into some of Cookie's fried chicken, the smell of which made me wish I hadn't done the McDonald's thing.

"Nipote mio! Viene qui. Susan says you just had to see her. You found her brother?" asked Vinnie.

"Not yet, Big Man, but I'm working on it. Mind if I steal her from you? I need to ask her a few things about her mother."

"Don't keep her too long. That guy with the pool stick is her boyfriend and might get pissed if you try to leave with her," he said, getting up and offering me his chair.

"You're early, Rollo. Anxious to see me?" she asked.

Does she always flirt?

"Absence makes the heart grow fonder," I shot back while taking the seat Vinnie had warmed up for me.

"Seemed like forever. So what's up?" she asked.

"Your mother says you're crazy and believes your brother is dead. She also told me you two had a big blowup a couple years back and haven't been in touch since."

"Okay, I lied. She's not terminal. She has mental issues, thinks I'm someone else, sometimes ... She kind of short-circuits, you know?"

"Alzheimer's?"

"Yes. Her doctor says it will only get worse. I can't deal with it anymore. The housekeeper walked out yesterday after finding a stash of meds my mother was supposed to be taking every day. She was spitting them out and hiding them, God knows for what."

"She all right alone? No one was there when I visited."

"The neighbor's popping in and out. I have a meeting at five with a new caregiver along with social services. Your uncle Vinnie made a few calls, got the ball rolling ... says the state will pick up most of the cost."

"What about the picture in the living room?"

Playing my trump card seemed to have knocked her off guard.

"The Christmas picture?" she asked, shaking her head. "That's Jack on one side and Aunt Suz, my mother's younger sister, on the other. I'm named after her. She died of an overdose after my uncle committed suicide, and Mom's never gotten over it."

That made me fold my hand.

"Was your uncle in jail when he killed himself?"

"Yes. How'd you know? You get that from your NYPD friends?"

"Maybe. Your boyfriend keeps looking over here. Does he have any reason to be insecure?"

"That's not my boyfriend. He's just a friend. I was talking to your uncle, and he said if the social services people dropped the ball, I should let him know and he'd get a housekeeper over there. You think that's a good idea?"

"Why not? He knows a lot of people, my uncle Vinnie. In fact, I have to tell him about somebody I had a little run-in with at lunch. Which reminds me, why don't you answer your phone when I call?"

"I never answer the phone. I just screen the voice mails and call back the ones I want to talk to. I always call you back, Rollo," she said and walked away to join the fun at the pool table. I watched—maybe to make sure she got there all right, maybe for another reason.

I joined Vinnie at the bar.

"What can I get you?" Ali asked, dropping a coaster on the bar as I sat on a stool.

"Something cold after watching her walk away."

That got them laughing.

"How 'bout a Heineken, no glass?"

"What did you have to see Susan about besides her ass?" Vinnie the comedian asked. Ali laughed probably out of a sense of duty. But I held back to show my serious side, Susan's derrière not being a thing jokes should be made of.

"I went to see her mother. What her mother told me didn't add up to Susan's story, so I needed some clarification. Seems her mom's not all there. Wish I would have known that before I went to see her. Susan tells me you're lining up some help for her?"

"I made some calls, called in a favor or two."

"Listen, Big Man—I know you knew Smiling Jack and who and what he was. Why did you keep me in the dark?"

"What's to tell? You seem to find out everything anyway," Vinnie said, his ears reddening a bit. "I didn't want to get involved with this and was hoping you'd put it to rest, give them closure. Not a month goes by I don't hear from Suz or her mother, so finally, I sent her to you, even fronted some of your fee. I know the guy's a piece of crap and the family would be better off if he's dead."

"I talked to my NYPD friends, and they tell me he's buried somewhere in New Jersey."

"They say everybody's buried there. If that was the case, you couldn't dig a hole there without digging somebody up. Don't you think I'd know about that if it had happened?"

"I guess you wouldn't waste my time and your money looking for a dead man. By the way, I had a run-in with a local PD this morning at the San Remo Diner, some guy named Beau Wolfe. He wanted to know if you were really my uncle."

"So I heard. You have to be more careful when name dropping."

"I hear ya, Uncle. He call you when I left the diner?"

That got me a nod.

"By the way, I have to pass on dinner tomorrow. I'll be in Connecticut on another case. How about Monday?"

"Monday night it is. Six o'clock good?"

"I'll be there. Looking forward to seeing my favorite aunt."

Back at the hotel, I decided to make some calls on behalf of my other client, Bob Howser. I started with calling for Sunday's ferry schedule. The 8:00 a.m. departure seemed a bit early, but I decided to give it a shot. If not, I could catch the 9:00 or the 10:00. Returns from Bridgeport were scheduled every hour on the half hour.

I turned the TV on to the Cooking Channel. A competitive challenge was down to two cooks competing against Bobby Flay making something out of stuff most people didn't eat. Luckily, my phone rang as they tried to make smoked eel and sweet potatoes go together. Caller ID said it was my son.

"Brando, how's my favorite son?"

"You have another one?"

"If I did, you'd still be my favorite. What's up?"

"You in New York?"

"Yes, out on Long Island, not in the city."

"When are you coming home?"

"Tuesday or Wednesday. Why?"

"I need to talk to you. I got a dog, but mom says I can't keep him because she doesn't want any animals in the house. She says Rex is allergic. Can you believe it? She wants me to give the dog away."

I could hear the emotional strain in his voice.

"I can't give the dog away. I can't. I won't."

"It's her house. She makes the rules, son."

"Before he came along, I could have a dog. It's not right."

"Talk Grandpa into letting your dog stay at their house until something changes at home. I'll see if there's anything I can do when I get back," I said, my stomach knotting up. "What's your dog's name?"

"Rex!" he shouted. He and his sister laughed hysterically. "Belated April Fools', Dad," they shouted in unison. "We love you."

"Clowns! You wait till I get home," I said, but I immediately realized that *home* meant something different to my children. "Thanks for the call and the joke. Be good and mind your mother. See you next weekend."

"Bye, Dad."

That left me wanting to cry. *Aarrgh!*

Next up, I checked in with Bob's sister, Mrs. Scarsdale, to let her know I was in town and would be going to visit Uncle Meyer in the morning.

"Mr. Michaels, I'm sorry I was curt with you the other day, but I was so shocked with what my brother had told me. I hope you can forgive me."

"There's nothing to forgive, ma'am. Being told something that overturns long-held beliefs is never easy. I'm glad Bob finally confided in you, and I hope it brings the two of you closer."

"Thank you, Rollo."

I considered that a breakthrough.

"And please call me Phyllis. My friends call me Phyllis."

"Well then, I look forward to seeing you Monday at noon, Phyllis. You sure you won't reconsider lunch on Bob?" I asked.

"Maybe. Let's see how things are Monday."

Chapter 30

Rabbi Heuer

It was an overcast morning on the North Shore—it was in the mid-fifties, the sun waiting for the clouds to get out of its way. Standing by the railing and letting an occasional spray of salt water invigorate my face, I looked down into the cold, clear waters of the Long Island Sound that were as clear as I remembered. I reviewed what I knew about Bob's case and what I didn't know. I hoped to learn everything that Meyer Heuer knew about his brother's family, the circumstances of Bob's birth, and the accuracy of Bob's remembrances.

I had my props—Bob's birth certificate, which I knew to be bogus; the results of two DNA tests; and the immigration logs of Meyer, his brother, and their mother, Ayelet. Would he help me identify Bob's mother? The answer to that question would depend on my ability to engage him. I hoped I was ready. We were docking in Bridgeport. I returned to my rental car. Meyer Heuer was just a fifteen-minute drive away.

Just outside of Bridgeport, the Edelweiss Manor stood upon seven acres of rolling manicured lawns and ornamental trees. A few early daffodils stood proudly in red-mulched flowerbeds bordered with rock. The blacktop circular drive that appeared freshly swept curved around a small pond aerated by a fountain spraying water over a Zen-like arrangement of boulders. A discreet sign in the parking area directed all visitors to sign in at the reception desk. I followed its arrow to the entry.

The clock on the wall behind the welcome counter said it was 10:10. Holding a potted tea rose I'd bought at a Port Jefferson market, I smiled my friendly smile at the woman who looked up from her electronic workstation. *Work related? Video game? Porn?* Her equally friendly smile brought me back from further speculation.

"May I help you, sir?"

"I'm a friend of the Heuer family here to see Meyer Heuer."

She put me through the drill, checked with the resident, checked my ID, had me sign in, issued a visitor's pass, and paged me an escort. *Impressive precautions.*

"This is James. He will take you back to Rabbi Heuer's apartment. Please remember to return the visitor's badge and sign out when you leave, Mr. Michaels."

James led me out the front door to a golf cart and drove me around the building to a courtyard faced by a semicircle of attached, single-story apartments. The area also resembled a park with another fountain spraying more boulders and green space punctuated with patches of yellow, blue, and white crocus. Meyer Heuer must have done well for himself to afford such accommodations.

Silent James stopped the cart and pointed to the unit that had a little sign on a post that read, "Rabbi Heuer." A tall, thin man dressed in black except for a crisp, white shirt stood on the small porch in front of the door. A black yarmulke partially covered a head of white hair. Two wooden rocking chairs with a small table between were arranged to his left.

"Rabbi Heuer, my name is Roland Michaels, a friend of your niece Phyllis and your nephew Robert. How are you this morning, sir?"

"And what is it they want from me?"

"To know that you're well and will see them. They had no idea you were still alive until I found out you were here, not in Israel," I replied, sensing his skepticism. "May we talk, sir? I've come from California to do so, Rabbi. Please?" I placed the rose plant on the little table and offered my hand. He hesitated before shaking it without enthusiasm. He gestured to the farther of the two rocking chairs.

"Have a seat, Mr. Michaels," he said.

He waited for me to sit before he did. My opening move was to hand him my business card and tone down the formality with "Please, Rabbi, call me Rollo."

"Is that what Robert and Phyllis call you?"

"At least to my face," I said, going for humor.

"Get on with it then, Rollo."

"Fair enough, Rabbi. I'll start out with the bad news first. Robert is terminally ill. He maybe has three months left."

He stared at me and blinked a few times as he processed the information.

"He has brain cancer."

I told the rabbi all that Bob had shared with me about his illness.

"Oh the ... poor boy ... poor ... poor boy ..." he said in cadence with his slowly rocking chair.

"Bob came to me a couple of weeks ago and asked for my help to find out who he is, why he has vivid memories from his childhood, why he believes he was treated differently than his siblings were. Your nephew wants to know who he really is before his death, Rabbi."

His eyes were closed. He slowly rocked and whispered in Hebrew what I guessed to be a prayer. I told him about reaching out to Bob's sister, their recollections of the deaths of their father and mother, of Uncle Meyer's visits to their boarding school in Connecticut, their father's funeral, and the handling of the estate. He acknowledged each point I related with an affirmative nod. He turned his chair more toward me, opened his eyes, and spoke.

"My brother, Sylvan, was a very successful man in spite of his faults. He was the big brother and was obligated to watch out for us. Our mother worked ten to twelve hours a day to provide for us with the help of neighbors and our synagogue. Mother insisted we keep that French bastardization of our name, Howser. It was not a friendly world for Jews back then, not much better today."

He made eye contact with me for emphasis. *Good sign?*

"When Sylvan was eighteen, he attempted to join the army to fight the Nazis but was turned down because of a perforated eardrum. Mother was ecstatic with the news and took him to work to meet her boss. And so he became involved in the garment industry. By the time he was twenty, he was getting contracts to make clothing for dozens of retailers and farming the work out to subcontractors. At twenty-two, he branched out and factored receivables, made deals with the teamsters, the Italians, and most of all, he kept the peace in the garment district." The rabbi smiled and stared off at something I couldn't see accessing another memory. "He married an Irish girl, Colleen, a Catholic who thought Jews weren't Christ killers. Her parents didn't so much approve of Sylvan as they did his money. And soon Colleen bore him a son, Paul, and a year later, Phyllis was born. Life was good. And then ..." He slapped his knees and stood. "How about a soda or something, Rollo? My mouth is dry."

"Sure, whatever you're having," I said, sorry he'd stopped. I got up to follow him into the apartment. I needed to keep him engaged, keep the information flowing. "Let me help."

"No, I can do it without help. In case you haven't noticed, I'm in pretty good shape for a man in his eighties." He filled two glasses with ice and Sprite and handed me one. "Got most of my marbles too. Not like a lot of them around here."

"Your longevity the result of clean living?" I asked as we went to a combination sitting room and dining area. He put two coasters on the table and indicated that we sit.

"Ha ha. Where were we?"

I took the use of the collective pronoun as a good indicator of how I was doing. I looked around the sparsely furnished room and there hanging on the wall above a loveseat ... *Could it be?*

"Excuse me, Rabbi, is that the portrait of your mother, Ayelet Heuer?"

"No, Rollo, that's another Mrs. Heuer, my late wife, Esther. You know of my mother's portrait that hung in Sylvan's house in Manhattan?"

"Her name was written on the back. The best I could find out is that it went with the house to Paul."

"Why is this important to you?"

"Maybe something else is written on the portrait," I explained.

"I doubt it, but let's go see."

What?

As he went to the closet, I felt a tinge of excitement. He pulled out a blanket-wrapped bundle, untied the string, and removed a framed painting. "This is the portrait you speak of."

"Your mother was very beautiful," I said, not exaggerating. As her captivating eyes drew me in, the rabbi turned it around to show me the "Ayelet" written there but nothing else. "Have you ever examined the sides, Rabbi?"

"For what purpose?" he asked, starting to rewrap the portrait.

"Clues? Maybe a date or another name. I notice some of the paint is chaffing. I'm sure a professional restoration service could preserve it for future generations."

"Future generations? The Heuer name ends with me, the last Jew in the family," he said, his bitterness unmistakable.

Am I losing him? "Rabbi, the blood of your ancestors runs through the veins of all your brother's children and their children too."

"I know, Mr. Michaels, but if we forsake our heritage, the Nazis and their ilk win."

Mr. Michaels? Not good. "True, Rabbi, so don't let it happen. Make sure the families of Phyllis and Paul are aware of their history."

"You mean I must put my anger behind me and take a positive approach? Is that what you're telling me?"

A tightlipped smile made a brief appearance.

"I don't know your pain, Rabbi, but I think your niece would love to have the portrait of her grandmother."

"You may be right, Mr. Michaels."

"You were going to call me Rollo, remember?" I tapped his forearm, giving him the smile.

"And Rollo it is. Will you be seeing my niece soon?"

"Yes, tomorrow, and maybe Bob too."

"Then you must take the painting with you. Now where were we when you interrupted about the painting on the wall?" His natural smile was returning.

"You were telling me everything was going good for your brother, but then—"

"Then? Oh yes, then ..." He paused, gathering his thoughts. "Then my brother introduced me to the Gypsy." He became quiet and closed his eyes, his smile getting bigger.

"Gypsy?"

"Anna, the most beautiful girl I ever met. Dark, mysterious. My brother told me she and her family got to the United States from Brazil because they couldn't go back to Europe. The Nazis were rounding up Gypsies just like they were the Jews. One day out of the blue in 1949, my brother takes me to the old Madison Square Garden on Forty-Ninth Street and Eighth Avenue. I look up at the marquee and I see Ringling Brothers Circus. In we go, seats right down front. Naturally, I'm excited. I'd never been to a circus before. We watched the show, all of it, so much going on. Then during an equestrian act, this beautiful bareback rider goes racing by and shouts out my brother's name, 'Sylvan!'

"After the show, we waited outside for Anna, and after most of the crowd had gone, out she comes. She walks over to Sylvan, and they hug each other, then he introduces us. I can hardly speak. And then it hits me—Anna and my brother are involved."

His voice was losing steam. He stared out the window across the courtyard to another time encased in the mist of the fountain's spray. We sat in silence, the sky clouding over as if on cue. I drained the last of my Sprite and crunched an ice cube. After another minute that seemed like five, he continued.

"My God, I thought, what about my niece and nephew, their mother, everything? What will Mother do? I wanted to weep. But the girl is a charmer, and I can tell she's smitten. We go for a bite to eat, and she tells me of circus life on the road and how much she wants a regular life of her own. At eighteen, I wasn't smart enough to know she was saying this for my brother's edification, not mine.

"Later, we catch a cab and drop Anna off at her hotel. On the way to my brother's grand house where we all lived, he swears me to secrecy, makes me a part of his infidelity. He professes his love for Anna, for our mother, his children, and me, but he has no idea of what he's going to do. I ask him questions, but he has no answers."

Rabbi Heuer suddenly slapped the dining table. "How about we go to the dining hall and have some lunch? We can talk there. Most of the inmates leave on the weekends."

I followed him out, and we walked around the outside of the building. It was a bit cooler with a cloud layer bunching up as coastal Connecticut prepared for rain.

We entered an institutional-style cafeteria setting with trays and utensils and railings. The rabbi approved of my coffee and a bagel with a smear but chose a fruit cup and a raspberry iced tea for himself. I pop for the five and change telling him it was on Bob. His laugh, if an honest one, told me there was much more he wished to tell me.

He chose a table in front of double French doors far removed from the dozen or so people seated close to the serving line, some in wheelchairs, some with walkers parked next to their tables. From my seat, I saw a posting on the wall where we entered saying the occupancy limit was eighty. It started to rain.

"April showers, May flowers," he commented. "Our mother could hardly speak any English, but she sang along with that song whenever it played on the radio. That old Philco was one of the few luxuries she allowed in our apartment in the bowels of Manhattan before the war."

Such anecdotal, personal information was yet another indication that Bob's questions would soon have answers. Rabbi Heuer took a sip of tea and continued.

"A few days after Sylvan had taken me to the circus to meet Anna, our mother died. It was terrible. Sylvan and his wife had been at a dinner party, and Mother was left to watch the children. I'd been out with friends. When I came home, Paul was crying in his crib, Phyllis and Mother where cuddled together on the divan. I thought it curious that Paul's occasional wails hadn't woken them. I went to Mother to nudge her awake. My niece responded, but Mother didn't. I picked up the baby and put her in the crib with her brother and went back to the divan. Mother wouldn't wake up. She was dead.

"The police and an ambulance showed up, but I don't remember making the call. I do remember changing Paul's dirty diaper and getting him and Phyllis to sleep before Sylvan and Colleen got home. That was my first encounter with death."

"Awful. What was the cause of death?" I asked, lightly touching his arm again to show empathy.

"Heart. She had been seeing a specialist for some time, but up until that awful night, I never knew for what. My brother had never told me."

"Maybe because your mother didn't want him to."

"He never said, and I never asked. Perhaps you're right, but I resented it. Mother's death was difficult for all of us, particularly Sylvan. It really changed him. In fact, we were all changed, and the atmosphere around the house changed too. After the funeral, Sylvan hired a live-in housekeeper, a young Polish girl who lasted a week. Colleen objected to the way my brother looked at the girl, so she was gone. The fights were frequent. He let Colleen hire the next, an elderly Irish lady named Maggie, who could cook and be the nanny for the babies. Colleen then hired a housekeeper too. Sylvan said his money didn't grow on trees, so the housekeeper came in only two days a week.

"About that time, my brother got me a job making pickups and deliveries for three of his operations. I became a card-carrying member of the Teamsters Union Local 814. Some of what I picked up was bags of cash, lots of cash. What it was for I never knew, but I was sure it had to be illegal. I would deliver it to my brother, and he would put it in his safe. He said it was payment on loans he'd made. He tried to explain factoring to me, but I didn't want to know."

"You're not eating your fruit, Rabbi," I said after noting he had yet to taste it. He followed a couple of mouthfuls with more of his tea and continued.

"But that's not why you're here, is it, Rollo? You want to know about Robert and his mother, Anna Barbosa," he said, giving me the name and confirming my suspicions.

Yes!

"And how did Bob wind up being raised by your brother and Colleen?"

"We snatched him from his birth mother when he was a little over two," he said, shaking his head. "Ringling Brothers was back in town, so Sylvan arranged to meet Anna in Central Park. I had no idea his liaison had produced a child, nor did I know we were going there to take the child from his mother." He rubbed his temples as tears ran down his face. "I never would have gone with him, Rollo, believe me. I just didn't know."

I handed him a clean napkin from the dispenser. With a final shudder, he wiped his tears and blew his nose. I'd seen that scene play out many times—the guilt was released and the secret was no more.

"What about the authorities?"

"My brother gave Anna money, paid her off. And she took it. Every time the circus came to town, he gave her a stack of cash, always bringing their son with him. But the hardest thing for my brother was dealing with his wife, Colleen. I don't know how, but they did it. Sylvan probably threw himself at her feet, played on her Catholic forgiveness, and she went along with it."

We returned to the rabbi's apartment via an inner corridor that ran through the entire complex. We walked past the pool area, workout and physical therapy room, and the entertainment center before turning into a corridor marked "Town House Way." The place was definitely not a run-of-the-mill nursing home where many of the elderly were simply warehoused.

Two and a half hours with Meyer Heuer had him revealing bits and pieces of his life story—the changing of his name from Howser to Heuer; going to Israel and joining the Israeli army; marrying Esther, "a nice Jewish girl Mother would have loved," and his wife's death at the hands of a grenade-throwing Palestinian. Grief over her death resulted in his immersion in Judaism and his ultimate disaffection with Israeli politics. The pain of loss and the inability to put it behind him led to his return to America. Meyer Heuer was a most interesting man.

Before leaving, I asked if he was willing to meet with his niece and nephew. He assured me he would. I told him I'd arrange it. He handed me the blanket-wrapped portrait of his mother and said he hoped I was right about the children of his niece and nephew. We shook hands again, that time with feeling.

"Le hitra' ot, Rollo." A Hebrew goodbye.

"Toda, Rabbi. Shalom." That exhausted my Hebrew.

Chapter 31

Revelation

The rain accompanied me back to Bridgeport. I lined up with a bunch of other cars for the ferry ride back to Long Island and turned my phone back on to check for missed calls, voice mail, and texts. There was some of each. I tackled the text messages first. Brandon's text shouted, "YANKEES GAME?" I replied, "no all business darn it." The other was from Linda—"call bob" in lowercase. I sent her a "yes" from my library before the line of cars I was in started to move.

Once onboard, parked, and my engine turned off, I popped the Cadillac's trunk to check on my passenger. Ayelet Heuer rested comfortably in her blanket. I refocused on my phone and checked the two missed calls and the one voice mail. All were from Bob Howser. I called him fearing that once we pulled from the dock, I'd soon lose cell service.

"Finally, did you meet with him?"

Excited or impatient? "Who?"

"Very funny, wiseass. What did you find out?"

"What? No hello, Rollo, how you doing, how's my new best friend? Just 'What did you find out?' Well, Bob, your uncle Meyer came through, told me everything."

"Everything? What's everything?"

"Catch a plane. Meet me at your sister's house for lunch tomorrow. Pack for a family reunion. As we suspected, Uncle Meyer knew your mother and gave me her name. You knew her too ... Anna Barbosa, the circus performer."

"Oh my God Rollo! Anna! The circus! The lady on the horse! Oh my God! Anna. Oh my God. Where is she? Have you met her? ... Where is ... When can I ...?"

"Slow down, Bob, I just found out her name. If she's alive, she'd be three maybe four years older than Meyer, going on ninety or more. I wouldn't get my hopes up too high, my friend. Meet me at Phyllis's house and we'll take it from there. Talk to you then."

"Okay, okay, I get it. Listen, Rollo, thank you doesn't seem enough, but thank you. I'll see you tomorrow. My God. Anna."

He ended the call.

The ferry whistle blew, and we pulled from the ramp to cross the sound.

I hoped to put this case in the solved column the next day. I knew I could go to Florida, take Linda as my research assistant ... maybe spend some time in the sun at Bob's expense checking out what I hoped would be extensive archives at Ringling Brothers in Sarasota. But the Cochran case was going nowhere, and without a break, it might remain on the other side of the dead end confronting me.

By the time my wheels left the Port Jefferson dock, it was four thirty, the rain had stopped, and the sun was trying to burn through the clouds. I'd been going all day on a bagel with cream cheese, coffee, and soda. My stomach protested, so on my way back to the hotel for a snooze, I pulled into the parking lot of my favorite Long Island eatery, the now-familiar San Remo Diner. Hunger was interfering with good judgment and the chance of another encounter with Detective Wolfe.

Sunday was not a happening afternoon at the San Remo Diner. Two customers sat on opposite ends of the counter, a father with two young children took up a booth, probably his weekend with the kids. Irish wasn't working the griddle; a twenty-something in whites with a lot of ink work on his large arms was slinging the hash. I took a booth as far away from everyone as I could get.

A middle-aged waitress shuffled over to my table as if she had sore feet. She wore a forced smile on a nice-looking face lined with character. She slid me a menu. "Coffee?"

"How'd you know?"

"Been doin' this a while. Black, right?"

"You're good, Sandy," I said, reading her name tag. "I see Irish isn't working. What do you recommend I have for supper?"

"Real hungry?"

"Yes. Does it show?"

"Young man back there does a mean southern fried chicken, mashed potatoes, gravy, buttered corn, and buttermilk biscuits. Ought to fill a man up."

"Sounds good. How about a dinner salad to start, side of ranch," I said, handing her back the menu. The picture of what I'd just ordered was clipped to it. "Sunday Special $11.95, add a salad $1.95." I headed to the men's room to wash up for dinner. I was all soaped up when my cell rang. I dried off and removed the phone from my pocket. Caller ID was blocked. I let it go to voice mail. Whoever called had hung up without listening to my "You know how this works" message.

I returned to my booth to find an empty mug and a silverware roll-up on the table. As soon as I sat, Sandy came shuffling over with a metal coffeepot in one hand and my salad in the other.

"I made you fresh, you looking like a big tipper an' all."

"Well, thank you, Sandy. Ya know, I was hoping to catch Irish working today. I wanted to thank him for looking out for my uncle."

That got me a double take and a jaw drop.

"CI?"

"Rollo, Rollo Michaels. News travels fast around here I see." I flashed my smile and dimple. "Tell him I'm sorry I had to leave, but I didn't want a scene with his detective friend. No hard feelings."

She went back to the kitchen without saying a word but returned five minutes later with my steaming dinner and the ubiquitous coffeepot.

"Looks good, smells great," I said as she placed it before me and added a warm-up to my cup.

"I'll let Ed know you stopped by. Enjoy your dinner."

I was gnawing on a chicken leg, honey and butter on my fingers and biscuit crumbs on the table and my lap. Sandy was spot-on about the boy's southern fried.

Irish walked in the front door and made a beeline toward me. I washed down the chicken with a swallow of coffee.

"Hey Rollo, mind if I sit?"

He did without waiting for my answer. *Kinda ballsy.*

"I wanted to explain about—"

"Hey Irish," I said, raising my hands palms out to cut him off. "We're good here, buddy. You teach Popeye back there how to make this chicken?"

"Actually, he taught me," he answered, his concern replaced by a smile. "He's from South Carolina, Dixie through and through. His secret is buttermilk and sage, a little cayenne to boot. Listen, you sure you're not pissed? I was telling a friend from Central Islip about you coming in. Asked him if he knew you, told him your name ... that you were in town to see your uncle Vinnie. Well, a lot of the local cops eat here, so I guess Detective Wolfe overheard ... I'm really sorry, Rollo, I don't want you or your uncle to peg me for a snitch."

"It's not a problem, Irish. Fageddaboudit."

"But what about your uncle Vincenzo?"

"Who?" I asked, making a shush sign punctuated with furtive glances left and right. "Join me for a cup. Hey Sandy, bring Irish a cup of coffee."

"It'll be a minute. I'll have to brew the decaf," she shouted back.

"I'll have the real stuff, sweetheart," he yelled.

"Don't be bothering me if you're awake all night."

"You two married I take it," I said.

"Going on twenty years. Three kids, two in high school, one in college," he said as a family of four was just sitting down at a booth to help Sandy and Irish with college tuition.

Chapter 32

Reunion Day

I slept to almost ten Monday morning but still arrived at Phyllis Scarsdale's condo complex a few minutes early. The guard at the gate had my name on his list and called her to let her know I'd arrived. He gave me the directions to Strawberry Lane, the gate went up, and I went in. A crew of Latino gardeners were snipping and mowing on both sides of the street, so I parked in her driveway. She stood on the front steps to greet me.

"Good morning, Rollo. Welcome," she shouted over the cacophony of mowers, weed-eaters, and leaf-blowers.

"I'm a bit early. I grew up on the island, but this is my first trip to Mount Sinai," I said, shaking her hand as her blue eyes gave me the once-over. "Your brother's not here yet?"

"No. He phoned from the Islip airport at eleven twenty and said he was just getting into his rental to make the drive out. Let's get inside away from all this noise."

"I have something in the trunk for you from Uncle Meyer." I retrieved it. She held the front door open as I carried it in. "It's the portrait of your grandmother. Uncle Meyer wanted you to have it."

"How wonderful! My sister-in-law called this morning from Belize. She said they never had the painting and speculated it could have gone with the sale of the house."

She took the bundled painting from me. Removing the blanket that had kept her grandmother warm for so many years, she propped the painting against the foyer wall. "Truly a beautiful woman. I think I was three when she passed."

"Your uncle Meyer married a woman in Israel who looked very much like her," I said.

"He told you that?"

"Actually, he has his wife's portrait hanging in his living room," I said as Ayelet gazed at the two of us. "Something smells good, Phyllis. I guess we're not lunching at some local bistro."

"We're eating out ... on the patio." She beamed and pointed to an umbrella table outside the sliding patio doors. Her small manicured backyard bordered a golf course fairway where a pair of carts were chasing balls.

"You play golf?" I asked.

"Not as much as I used to. My husband loved the game," she said, pointing to a number of trophies on the mantle of the large corner fireplace. "Can I get you a beverage while we wait for Bobby?"

"Did I catch a whiff of coffee coming from the kitchen?"

"You did. Do you take it with anything, Rollo?"

"Black, please," I said, following her to the source.

"My brother was so excited last evening when he called. He said Uncle Meyer told you everything about Bobby's mother and our family secrets," she said, stirring sugar and cream into hers.

"He shared only one family secret with me. If there are more, you and your brother will have to coax them out of your uncle Meyer. He's anxious to see you both."

"And how is he?"

"Unbelievably fit and sharp as a tack. He's led an unusual and most interesting life you and Bob ought to hear about."

The phone on the kitchen wall chirped two quick rings.

"It's the gate. Bobby's here." She picked up the phone. "Send him up, Kenneth."

I could see she was already tearing up as she headed to the door to welcome the brother she hadn't seen in over twenty years. I'd wait out on the patio to let them have their private moment knowing the last of Robert Howser's days would be some of the best of his life.

While getting cleaned up and dressed for dinner with the Costellos, I couldn't stop thinking of the emotional reunion I'd witnessed over a lunch that ended up hardly eaten. I had a tough time not tearing up with Phyllis and Bob. They had dozens of questions I couldn't answer especially when I told them their uncle was a rabbi. A trip was planned to Connecticut the next day and then another to Sarasota, Florida, in the near future to visit the headquarters of Ringling Brothers Barnum & Bailey Circus.

After lunch, Phyllis remembered the portrait of Ayelet standing against the wall in her living room. She led Bob to it and again, the tears flowed. When the topic of removing the painting from the frame it had sat in for over eight decades came up, I suggested it be done by professionals. I left them as they reminisced about the past and made plans for the future. Bob was effusive in praising me and promised "a little something" real soon in the mail.

My cell's ringing intruded on these pleasant thoughts. I didn't bother to look at the who. "Hello?"

"Hey, we miss you around here," Ruth said. "Linda wanted me to give you an update on the goings on at Michaels & Associates."

"Make it quick. I have to get to the bank for another roll of quarters for this vibrating bed."

"You're alone, I hope."

"Only if I run out of quarters. Don't tell the boss either."

"I'll need a raise." She laughed.

"Take ten dollars off the thousand I loaned you."

"Deal. Two things the boss thought you should know. First, everyone showed up for the weekly meeting except you. Second, we got a check for eleven thousand and a thank-you note from Clancy's favorite actor."

"Well, it just so happens I have some good news too. I solved—"

"We heard. Bob already told us. I announced it at the meeting this morning. We're on a roll."

"We certainly are. Gotta go. See you guys Wednesday."

"Thought you were coming back tomorrow."

"True, but Linda's picking me up after five. See ya."

The Costellos also lived in a gated community on the North Shore, theirs in the town of Northport. Though there were no markers commemorating it, it was the town of my father's birth. Big Vinnie liked to say that's why he lived there. But my father said the Costello family's loan-sharking business actually got them in on the ground floor of a land development company. That enterprise built the twenty-six-house complex then known as Northport Shores.

I was surprised to see that the security setup at the entrance was all electronic. CCTV was prominent every way I looked. Access was gained by a card reader or a call to a resident who could buzz you in or tell you to get lost. I pressed the button next to Costello and smiled. Big Vinnie's voice boomed out, "We gave at the office. Go away."

"Let me speak to the lady of the house see if she wants what I'm peddling, old man."

"I got your old man right here."

The gate opened. "Make a right and take the second left. We're three houses down on the sound side. Don't get lost."

The Cape Cod look was the theme of this posh neighborhood of blue-and-white, two-story homes on quarter-acre plots. Angie and Big Man were waiting on their front porch both pointing to the driveway for me to park. My aunt had put on a few pounds since the last time I saw her at her niece Barbara's wedding a few years back. Angie was still a real looker at a bit over forty. I got the bouquet of roses from the floorboard and stepped out of the car as she came forward to greet me.

"Oh Rollo! For me?" she exclaimed, taking the arrangement and kissing my cheek.

"No, Aunt Angie," I said, taking her in my arms for a hug. "They're for Uncle Vinnie. Hurry up and get them in water. You know how grumpy he can get when his things wilt."

"Hey, watch that talk, nipote mio," he said, punctuating his words with a light punch to my arm. "You've been here before, no?"

"No, I haven't. Last time I had Angie's lasagna was at Dad's wake."

We followed Angela inside. The smell of baking pasta was making my juices flow.

"Come on then, I'll show you around while your aunt gets my flowers a drink."

After a quick tour, we were on the patio, the Long Island Sound two hundred yards away. The air had cooled considerably from the time I'd left my hotel, making me glad I'd chosen to wear a suit sans tie. "You have some place here, mi arrendo. Aunt Angie must have had quite a dowry."

"Yeah, idiot, I married her for her money. Listen, I don't want to talk business in front of your aunt." I nodded. "So tell me what's going on with the thing you're looking into for the Cochrans?"

He clearly hadn't taken me outside to show me the view.

"I talked to the retired detective who caught the homicide case Cochran had been arrested for. Like I told you, he thinks Jack's long dead. But there are a lot of inconsistencies in what people are telling me. Right now, I have my computer guy searching for a hit on Jack's Social Security number. There's no employment history, but a lot of people use the number for a password. Should hear back Wednesday on that."

"I want to get the mother and daughter off my back. The mother is a cousin of my mother-in-law, like a second cousin to Angie, so keep me up to date," he said.

Small world.

"Dinner's on the table, boys," Angie announced, and we went to the beautifully set table prepared for us in the dining room.

We clasped hands, and Big Vinnie Costello said grace, requesting a blessing of our meal and those about to enjoy life's bounty. An antipasti of tomato slices topped with capers, anchovy fillets, and a sprinkle of Romano cheese served on a bed of butter lettuce and drizzled with a garlic-infused olive oil and drops of balsamic vinegar preceded the lasagna. The basket of hot toasted garlic bread topped with fresh rosemary attested to Angela's culinary talents. Of course, the lasagna was her signature dish; the recipe traced back to her great-great-grandmother, who probably got it from her mother. My ex used the same lasagna recipe, but there had to be something Angie held back on her.

Dinner conversation revolved around me, my children, and how my failed marriage to a Sicilian girl who happened to be another of Angela's second cousins had saddened them. Another bottle of wine helped keep the conversation flowing. I told them of the case that had brought me to New York and Connecticut. Aunt Angie thought it would make a wonderful movie. A dessert of tiramisu and cups of espresso with shots of Strega ended a perfect meal.

Angela gave us the boot with her "Why don't you two get some fresh air, enjoy a cigar while I clean up a bit. Rollo, do you indulge?"

"In most everything but drugs, Aunt Angela," I confessed as I followed Vinnie to the patio, where he opened a box of Don Carlos Belicosos.

"These were a gift from a Dominican friend. You ever smoke a twelve-dollar cigar?" Vinnie asked.

"No, Uncle, how could I afford to?"

"Well, you're gonna now." He beamed. He was happy to splurge on the son of a lost friend.

We bit, spit, and lit all in accordance with a centuries-old ritual. I blew a smoke ring of pleasantly scented, flavorful smoke. I watched it rise and take its time to dissipate in the still night air. Vinnie lived the good life and was proud to show it.

Angie soon joined us, carrying a tray of more coffee and the bottle of Strega. She took a couple of hits on her husband's cigar and said something in Italian that made them laugh. I think I knew. Another shot of the liqueur had me a bit buzzed, but it was a wonderful evening with time to sober up. I told a few jokes that got more laughs than they deserved, and the night, like the smoke, dissipated in a cool breeze now coming in off the sound. It was time for goodbyes and last hugs and promises that might or might not be kept.

I was soon in my bed at the Hyatt Regency when there was a knock on my door. I looked through the peep. It was Susan Cochran. *What could she possibly want?*

Chapter 33

Familiar Ground

The seating gods were angry with me. I'd forgotten to burn the promised incense, so they had abandoned me on my return flight to LA. The belching window seater next to me also had bladder issues, making a nap impossible. A game app on my phone kept me going for about an hour before my seatmate started to kibitz.

"You probably should've put up a wall to keep them out," he said, causing a device shutdown.

"I don't want to run down my battery." I lied. I put my phone away. The *Wall Street Journal*, bought to impress, told me why the Trump presidency was moving the market ever higher. The sports pages told me Kershaw was the best Dodger pitcher ever, ignoring a guy named Koufax. My seatmate told me he needed the bathroom yet again. Another two hours and two cocktails had me watching the line for the first-class lavatory.

Seeing an opportunity, I made the break for the lavatory door just as air turbulence became an issue. That coupled with the captain's authoritative voice ordering all passengers to their seats did nothing for my aim. My janitorial skills allowed me to make the bathroom functional again.

Soon we were descending and I could see the Santa Monica mountains meet the Pacific on our final approach to LAX. A smooth landing and a long stop-and-go taxi ride had us to our gate.

"Welcome to Los Angeles" was punctuated by the clicking sounds of a hundred seatbelts unfastening. The longest five and a half hours of my life were behind me and I felt a rush of excitement to be getting off this plane. I retrieved my jacket from the overhead and checked the pocket for the little trinket I'd bought Linda at the Kennedy terminal while waiting to board. *Got it.*

"Thanks for flying with us. Watch your step." Up and out the gangway into the hubbub of LAX. I spotted the Starbucks kiosk and stopped for a fix. A double-shot espresso would surely provide the juice to get me to baggage claim. As I gave the barista my two-shot order, my phone rang. It was Linda.

"Hey, baby." I had my Barry White on.

"Meet you at the baggage carousel," she said, ignoring my sweet tones.

As I came down the escalator following the signs to baggage claim, there stood Linda. She was wearing a smile and a chauffeur's cap and holding a handmade sign that read "Mr. Michaels." *Why does seeing her make me feel so good?*

I went along with the gag, handing her my claim check. "It's pretty big, miss. Do you think you can handle it?"

"Now you're just bragging, hot shot," she said, taking a swipe at me with her sign. People scurried around us just in case. We went to United's carousel to await my suitcase. She filled me in on Ruth's quick trip to Phoenix and her mom's financial problems at that point being handled by the Phoenix PD and her mom's bank. Mom had been hacked, and her credit card, linked to her checking account, had caused a nightmare Mom couldn't handle. Four hours after Ruth took charge, the bank did the right thing. Should be another week to get it all straightened out.

Linda's Manny, my Nerd, scored on the four subpoena services Art's Westwood lawyer pals had given us as a test. So next, they wanted us to find unknown witnesses to an industrial gas leak that had blown the roof off a warehouse in Bell, California, killing two. Putting a twenty-billable-hour limit on us sounded like another assignment to placate Art and make us go away. Travel time alone could eat that up.

The buzzer signaled action at the carousel. My suitcase was the third bag out. *Really? My flying experience is ending on a happy note?*

As I sat next to Linda on the drive home, I was overcome by feelings of guilt about last night's tryst at the Hyatt Regency as if I owed Linda my fidelity. *Where is that coming from?* Linda and I had gone at it for a while, a serious effort on both our parts. But we broke it off when she shot down my marriage proposal. My reaction to her rejection had probably scared her and had given me another thing to talk to my shrink about. Linda could always press my buttons knowingly and unknowingly. That time, it was the one marked "Replay."

It had been just past midnight when Susan had come to my door Monday night. She had been drinking but wasn't drunk. She was carrying a bottle of champagne. Said it was her birthday and wanted me as a birthday present. I sure as hell didn't want to disappoint her.

Five New York nights had my biorhythms adjusted to East Coast time, so I was wide awake at seven in spite of only four hours of sleep. The amazing woman sharing my bed was another story. I had showered, shaved, and dressed without waking her. My stealthy suitcase stuffing and slipping out the door would have made any ninja proud. I was most pleased with my self-discipline. Acting on the urge to kiss her butterfly tattoo yet again would have kept me in New York till who knows when.

I'd grabbed a coffee and a cheese Danish and left the Hyatt Regency to take the Southern State Parkway back to Kennedy. Once there, turning in the Cadillac was much easier than getting it. Unfortunately, chaos awaited at the terminal. The plane that was to take me to LA was delayed at another airport for unknown reasons. It would take United three hours to get us on another bird. I used the time to drink too much coffee and browse the duty-free shop.

So there I was in Linda's car traveling east on Wilshire through Beverly Hills and worrying about the ten-spot I'd left for housekeeping on the dresser of a New York hotel. *What if Susan thought the money was for something else?*

"You hungry?" Linda asked, saving me from further self-recriminations.

"You mean like dinner or maybe some tacos and margaritas?"

"I'm good with El Cholo's," she said, driving past our office and making a right on Western.

We waited at the crowded bar for a table, sipping Dos Equis from the bottle.

"Do you think I could be mistaken for the most interesting man in the world?"

"Not a chance."

That seemed like a rush to judgment on Linda's part.

"You guys miss me?"

"We survived. Ruth is driving to Phoenix tomorrow to check on her mom."

"She coming back?" I said.

"Why wouldn't she?" she asked.

"She owes me money."

"Ro-yo party of two," the hostess called.

"That would be us," I said, interpreting for Linda. We followed the young lady to a small booth away from the kitchen and bar. Chips and salsa were placed before us, two more beers and taco plates were ordered, for me the taco de carne and Linda the pollo. I handed her the little gift box.

"What's this?" she asked, blue eyes shining.

"A little something for holding down the fort while I was in New York." I lied. It was all about the guilt. I watched her smile as she opened the box.

"I don't wear pearls," she said, stepping on my heart.

"How many strands do you have?"

"None."

"Precisely. So now you can wear them."

The following morning, jet lag had caught up with me along with the previous night's refried beans. I finally arrived at the office in the early afternoon having survived over eighteen hours with only limited amounts of caffeine. I'd used my last K-cup when I got up around eleven, so I went right to the pot on my credenza. The nose told me the half pot had been sitting on the heat for hours. But like any coffee junkie, I didn't care. I downed a cup of the vile brew while cooking up a fresh batch. I knew I wasn't well when I passed on the maple-glazed French doughnuts in the tray by the coffee maker.

I eased into my desk chair. The thought of a nap seemed to be more important than my overflowing inbox. I closed my eyes.

"Susan Cochran on line two," Linda announced over the intercom.

I opened my eyes to find my inbox was still full. I sipped my coffee, which was cold. *How long was I out?* I picked up. "Hello, Susan."

"Rollo, you're not going to believe this, but I got a birthday card from my brother. I can't believe it! I just knew he was alive!"

"What's the postmark?"

"He's in South Dakota. Deadwood, South Dakota, 57732. He mailed it Saturday, the sixteenth. You remember my birthday, don't you?"

"Yes. Who could forget? What does he say?"

"Well, it's not really a birthday card. It's a postcard from the Holiday Inn Express. The other side, he wrote 'Happy B Day', and he signed it, 'Love, Jay Jay Smiley'."

"So you recognize the handwriting?" I asked, trying to tie it down.

"Not so much that. He went by his initials, but I always spelled them out, j-a-y j-a-y. The Smiley name is a play on another of his nicknames."

Her ID seemed pretty positive to me.

"I called the Holiday Inn and they said he wasn't a guest, and the manager told me he never worked there either. What do you think?"

"It's a lead we should check out. He could be there or might have just been passing through. I'll do some checking and get back to you."

The events that followed—courier cash delivery, Linda's chauffeur service, a repeat tempting of the seating gods—led me to a four-day jackpot not of my own making. *Or was it?*

Chapter 34

Deadwood Law

It was over four hours since Smiling Jack Cochran had died at my feet, and I'd worn handcuffs for most of that time. But the cuffs were off, and Sheriff Bullock was being nice, making his play as interrogator. He obviously wasn't taking me for Cochran's killer.

"So, Michaels, how do you know John Smiley?"

I decided to start with the truth and save the lies for when they'd be needed.

"Your victim's real name is John Joseph Cochran, not John Smiley. He's a career criminal from New York with a rap sheet you should probably know about. I think it got too hot for him back east, so he came here to hide out."

"They do background checks at the casinos. No way he's an ex-con." Bullock stared at me waiting for more.

I shook my head, finding that revelation puzzling.

"Cochran's only redeeming quality is or was to make a deck of cards do his bidding, a talent honed while doing a two-year stretch in the joint. When he got out he ran crooked card games for some New York wise guys. They'd bring in whales, and Smiling Jack would harpoon and the sharks would swoop in and skin 'em. The victims would be on the hook for a lifetime."

"Smiling Jack?"

"Mob guys love nicknames. Smiling Jack got his handle when a game went sour. He got caught dealing from the bottom to a chronic loser, causing a scene. Cochran just smiled at the guy then stuck a knife in his chest, thus the Smiling Jack moniker. A couple of New York's finest spotted the victim being dumped into the bay by Jack's uncle. Faced with serious hard time, the guy gave Jack up. So Jack was arrested for the homicide. Lucky for Jack, his uncle committed suicide while they were both in jail awaiting trial."

"Suicide?" Bullock asked, pouring more coffee.

"Nobody believes it, but they had to let Jack out of jail and back to his job with the boys. But then, a fed informant said he'd been an eyewitness, and they snatched Jack up again. My guess is they turned Jack because a week later he was back on the streets. A few months go by, and the people Jack works for are indicted on RICO charges. I guess the case brought too much heat, and soon, Jack was in the wind. That was over a year ago. About two weeks ago, his sister, Susan Cochran, hired me to find him, supposedly in Los Angeles."

"So how does a PI from Los Angeles wind up finding a New York wise guy hiding out in our fair Black Hills community?"

"Good detective work," I said, warming up for the lies with a half-truth as Bullock gave me the look. I took a sip of the surprisingly good brew and continued.

"Although the sister says she'd received cards from him and had wired money to him, there was no trace of Jack ever being in LA. So I hit Sis up for some more money and made the trip to New York. I verified the mother had filed a missing person report. My NYPD contact also told me Jack's murder arrest was dropped for lack of evidence, and Missing Persons assumed Jack to be part of a Jersey landfill.

"I visited good ol' mom in Queens. She looked really well for someone said to be terminally ill. She wasn't aware her daughter had hired me to find Jack. She believes her son to be dead. She said she always knew he would come to a bad end. I asked about the Christmas cards, but she didn't have a clue what I was talking about. Mom claimed to have never heard from her son since the day he walked out of her home almost two years ago. I asked for a more recent picture than the high school picture the sister had given me. Mom only had a picture from 2014, told me it was a family shot of her and her kids. The three of them stood in front of a Christmas tree beaming at the camera.

"I asked if she had another daughter, and she said, 'Only Susan' and that she hadn't heard from her in a couple of years. Claims the daughter got mixed up in drugs and stole from her, so she threw her out. About now, I conclude Mom is a few cards short of a full deck mixing up events, dates, and people. So I split, leaving her with promises of calls from both the son and daughter."

"Well, is she or isn't she?" Bullock asked.

"When I caught up with my client and asked what gives, she told me Mom's losing it. Yes, she knew about the picture in the living room, but the girl in the picture is actually her mom's sister, Aunt Suz."

I could see all this was making the sheriff's head hurt.

The detective from the crime scene stuck his head in the door. "FBI on line two," he said.

"I'm busy here. Tell them I'll call back," Bullock said.

"You'll want to take this one, Sheriff. It's about our boy here."

"Take Mr. Michaels to a holding cell while I talk to the FBI," Bullock told his detective.

I picked up my cup from the desk as I rose from the chair. "Can I get a little more for the road?"

"Get him out of here," Bullock barked, and I was led away by the detective after he took the cup from me and placed it on the sheriff's desk.

When I asked Bullock's man what time dinner was served, I was told I'd missed the evening meal but breakfast was at 0600. Then he let the cat out of the bag.

"You're in deep doo-doo with the feds, Michaels. They don't like it when one of their witness protection clients gets executed. I can only assume you're holding back on us. We just don't find your story credible. Maybe you don't appreciate how deep the shit you're in is. Responding deputies find you standing over a body with a gun in your hand. Our victim has two gunshot wounds, and we recover two shell casings on the floor. They match the ammo in your weapon. We find gunshot residue on your hand and the vic's blood on your other hand. And to top it all off, we have an eyeball wit to the shooting," he said, making it obvious he'd been listening in on my conversation with Bullock. But I was pretty sure they didn't make me as Smiling Jack's killer.

"This your first homicide, Detective?"

That didn't win him over, but Bullock came to my rescue.

"Feds request we hold you until the US marshals get here in the morning," Bullock said.

"What's the charge, Sheriff?" I knew he could tell me but also knew he didn't have to.

"Homicide."

"That's bullshit and you know it," I said.

"It'll work till the feds arrive. Take him down and book him. Sleep tight, Michaels. We're done here."

A uniformed deputy took me back to lockup. Prints and mug shots followed a cavity search, that indignation obviously payback for pissing off my captors. A metal cot topped with a thin mattress and a stainless steel commode with matching sink completed my cell's amenities. An old army blanket protected me from the steady sixty-eight degrees of the jail. The lights went out at ten sharp. As I lay on the cot, I saw snow falling outside my cell window, making me feel colder than it really was.

Thoughts of how I'd gotten there kept me from sleeping. Then there were the new developments—FBI, US marshals, witness protection. Had I been played by a pretty face and used to finger Jack Cochran for a mob hit? The question of why led me to the question of who. Only one name came to mind.

Chapter 35

Soldier Warm and Fuzzy

When Soldier Boy Mahan awoke in his hotel room, he felt the warmth of another human being snuggled beside him. The sound of her rhythmic breathing pleased his ear as he held her in his arm. He could feel each beat of her heart and marveled at the closeness he felt.

Her name was Dora. They met last night at the Number 10 Saloon. She was with a group of ladies a bunch of the local cowboys hovered around. She came over to the bar where he stood sipping his beer. She smiled at him as she ordered a draft.

"Be glad to buy that for you, Miss," was his move. A conversation ensued. Soon they had their own table, followed by dinner and dancing and a switch to bourbon and yet more dancing. Pretty well snockered, they made the walk to his hotel and a couple of failed attempts at drunken lovemaking. Now here he lay, fantasizing that he could lead a normal life, have someone special, raise a family ... She began to stir. He pulled her close not wanting those feelings to end.

She reached across his chest, touched his bandaged arm, and pulled her hand away. "You're bleeding."

Soldier looked down and saw he'd bled through his bandage and that some of the tape had pulled loose. "Good morning," he said. "I'll live."

"Let's clean you up and check this out." She led him to the bathroom. She removed his bandage and made a face. "Whoever sewed this up should have his license revoked. How'd you do this anyway?"

"Got hurt at the jobsite, sewed it myself."

She made a sour face and shook her head. "Men. Go figure. Get in the shower," she ordered. He did, and she followed. She washed him up, and after drying off, they redressed his wound.

"How 'bout some breakfast? I know a great spot over in Lead. What do you say?"

"Sure," he said.

Leaving the Do Not Disturb sign on the door, they walked from his hotel to the Deadwood City Parking Garage, got her car, and went to Lead. The great spot turned out to be a hillside cabin within shouting distance of a gold mine still cranking out ore.

"One of their tunnels runs about a quarter mile right under my house," she explained. She unlocked the door and led him into her home. Vaulted ceilings with exposed beams, rough-hewn furniture, and Native American rugs on plank flooring made the cabin seem larger than it was. They went to the kitchen, where he met Freckles, her cat, who seemed overly friendly to a stranger like him. While she cranked up the coffee, fried a couple of pork chops, and whipped up some eggs, Soldier walked about and came upon a curio cabinet filled with snow globes, maybe two dozen of them.

"What's with all these snow globes? You a collector?"

"My daughter was fascinated by them, so we bought her a few. Every now and then, I add one," she said, making him sorry for asking. As she put

Freckles out the door, she announced, "Breakfast is served."

They were about halfway through breakfast and the getting-to-know-you small talk when he asked about her husband and daughter.

"They were killed in a traffic accident. A big truck rolled on top of my husband's pickup. I really can't talk about—"

A knock on the door cut her off.

Soldier knew when authority knocked and immediately put the shock of what Dora had just told him into another part of his brain. Upon seeing the patrol car through the window, he wondered how the police could have been on him so soon. Dora went to the door and opened it. Two sheriff's deputies stood there hats in hand.

"Hi, Dora. Sorry to disturb you," said the taller man whose name tag read "Carpenter." "We're following up on the homicide that happened in the city lot last night. Sheriff Bullock wants us to interview anyone who was in the lot at the time of the shooting. Your car was there, and we want to know if you might have seen or heard anything."

"Come on in, Bill. Like some coffee?" she asked, stepping back from the door.

Both deputies entered causing Soldier's neck hairs to prickle. *Maybe you could fix 'em some eggs while you're at it*, he thought, but they declined her hospitality.

"We were all at the Number 10 when someone came in and said there'd been a shooting. I parked there about four thirty, didn't see anything," Dora said.

"You didn't pick up your car till after ten this morning?" Deputy Bill asked. Soldier saw that as an attempt at intimidation and rose to step in.

"We don't think drinking and driving's a good idea, Deputy," Soldier explained, wishing he'd had a gun.

"I don't either. And you'd be who?" he asked, turning his focus on Soldier.

"Why?" Soldier shot back, his hackles still raised.

"Like to know who it is I'm talking to. Let's see some ID." Deputy Bill bristled.

Soldier took out his wallet and handed the deputy a phony New Jersey driver's license that stated he was Jason Morton from Emerson.

"What brings you to the Black Hills, Mr. Morton?" Bill asked, not letting up and entering Soldier's personal space.

"Why are you hassling my friend, Bill?" Dora, defensive, raised her voice.

"It's okay, Dora. The deputy's just doing his job," Soldier said, still face to face with Bill. "I'm just visiting an old friend, deputy." He forced a smile playing their game and realizing he didn't really need a gun right at that point.

The deputy asked how long he'd been there and was he planning on staying and got answers of "A while" and "Maybe." The deputy handed back the ID, thanked Dora for her cooperation, not saying anything to Soldier. They left without realizing how close they had come but knowing they didn't like Dora's friend. Soldier decided he would get another gun as he was feeling a bit naked without one.

They picked at what was left of their breakfast, but Dora's revelation and the law's intrusion had dampened the atmosphere. Dora changed clothes and drove "Jason" back to his hotel. They agreed on dinner that evening, an awkward kiss sealing the deal. Soldier went to his car. He had some shopping to do. He purchased more stuff for his wound and another throwaway phone at a drugstore. He drove to a biker bar just outside of Sturgis, where he bought a beer for himself and a couple more for the two bikers at the pool table.

An hour later, he left with a pistol and a box of hollow points without having quibbled over price. He parked a block from his hotel and watched a sheriff's cruiser pull up to the entrance, let Rollo Michaels out, and drive away. Before getting out of his car, he used his new cell to call Dora. *Maybe this could work out.* He knew life was filled with maybes. As his call went unanswered, he also remembered how life could be filled with disappointment.

Chapter 36

Charges Dropped

At six in the morning, the lights came on in my cell. The breakfast passed through the bars was faux eggs and rubbery sausage. At least it was warm. The coffee was not from the sheriff's stash. Two slices of white bread made it all add up to seven hundred empty calories. I had just gotten past the gag reflex when the US marshals arrived.

Lying to the feds can be a big-time felony they like to hose you with akin to tax evasion and offshore numbered accounts. They put me through the drill and asked how I knew the victim and why I'd shot him. I responded with a request for an attorney. We were just getting warmed up when Bullock came in to tell the marshals that the FBI was on the phone, and they left.

"They won't be back," the sheriff said, unlocking the cell door. I followed him back to his office. "Sleep good?" That was more of a dig than a question.

"Like a baby." That wasn't to lie but to get one in for the home team.

"Guess your name set off a few alarms all over the federal data base. An FBI agent named Rene Monroe is flying in from DC. She wants me to release you when she gets here this afternoon. But I don't work for the FBI, so we'll get you un-arrested and take you back to your hotel."

"Why the change of heart?"

"FBI backs up your story, but Monroe wouldn't tell me more over the phone. So what's really going on here, Rollo?" he asked as he handed me my personal property minus my Walther. He poured me some of his great coffee as a peace offering.

"I haven't a clue." I lied, and he knew it. I traded in my prisoner garb for a pair of old jeans he'd dug up for me but kept the slippers. My clothing would be kept for evidence since it was already on its way to the state crime lab along with my Walther.

During the drive to my hotel, we engaged in cop talk, our preferred sidearm, and our mutual distrust of the feds. Bullock had been a big-city homicide dick in Denver and had come to Deadwood to retire. It was his ancestral home. I was starting to find it easy to like the guy.

"I'll see you when your FBI girlfriend hits town," he said. "Right now, I have a homicide to solve." As I got out, he added, "Don't leave town." He laughed. "Damn, I love saying that."

Once in my room, I dialed Susan Cochran in New York. Nothing different there. My "Call me, very important" on her voice mail got a response in five minutes.

"Hello, Susan."

"Where are you?"

"Deadwood."

"You found my brother?" she asked excitedly.

"I'm sorry, Susan, but Jack is dead. He was killed yesterday."

She wailed, and I listened, feeling like an ass for dropping it on her.

We talked for fifteen minutes, her sobbing, me trying to console. I told her Sheriff Bullock would contact her, funeral arrangements to be made, maybe grill her about me. But at least I knew she wasn't complicit in her brother's death, just used to finger him.

I took a long, hot shower and washed off most of the previous day. My toothbrush and razor had me feeling almost human again. The complimentary coffee maker did its thing, but the coffee it made didn't. I fell fast asleep on top of the covers. While I slept, my brain did replays of the shootout. In the dream, I noticed the shooter had turned toward me and fired without actually pointing his gun at me. And my return fire had hit the shooter knocking him down.

A pounding at the door woke me to a darkened room lit only by a sliver of fading daylight through the blackout curtains and the face of the bedside clock, which read 5:56.

"Come on, Michaels, open up," a female said, announcing FBI Agent Monroe had arrived. I fumbled for the nightstand light when a key opened the door allowing Bullock and Monroe to barge in.

"You okay, Rollo?" Bullock asked, hitting the wall switch, the light shocking my sleepy eyes. "Agent Monroe was worried you might go out the window on us." Monroe had obviously told him of our first meeting.

"This is the fourth floor, Sheriff." That got a big smile on Agent Monroe's face, which was even prettier than I remembered. My "How's the FBI's best-looking agent doing these days?" got a blush that the sheriff picked up on.

"Come on, Rollo. Get dressed. You got a whole lot of explaining to do," she said.

It wasn't a request.

"Turn around then."

"Why? You have some tattoos I don't know about?"

The implication had Bullock eye rolling.

We went back to Bullock's office, me in the caged backseat of his cruiser. Once there, I told my story, the version I'd given Bullock. Monroe was interested in who had hired me and how I'd found Smiling Jack. That was the part I'd held back from the sheriff, about the sister calling me to say she'd gotten a birthday postcard from her brother on Wednesday. The front of the card was the Deadwood Holiday Inn Express postmarked a week ago, April 16, Deadwood, SD. A computer search revealed a John Smiley was a resident of Deadwood and licensed by the state as a casino employee.

Agent Monroe wasn't impressed. She showed me a newspaper photo of a man in an army uniform with a Combat Infantry Badge and a bunch of service ribbons. She asked if that was the man I'd seen shoot Smiling Jack. I didn't think so, but maybe I'd seen him before.

"Do you know Vincenzo Costello?" she asked, her question confirming my suspicions that the shooter was somehow connected to Big Vinnie in her mind too.

"Big Vinnie? Yeah, we've met, but that's not him," I said, pointing to the picture.

Bullock rolled his eyes yet again.

I explained attending the wedding of Big Vinnie's niece almost two years earlier as a guest of the groom. Looking at the photo again, I realized Army Guy had been at that wedding too, but I held back that little tidbit.

We then watched a casino surveillance video. I pointed out the shooter to Bullock, but he was way ahead of me and showed us video of the same guy entering and exiting the parking garage before and after the shooting. He gave Monroe a DVD copy of all the relative video collected so far in exchange for a mugshot of Smiling Jack Cochran. Monroe left to check into her hotel. She was to meet Bullock for dinner later that evening. That told me Bullock was way, way ahead of me.

"I'm an old poker player, Rollo, and your tell was real easy to spot. Who's the guy in the newspaper clipping?"

"Not the guy I saw shoot Cochran," I replied, "unless ..."

"Unless what?"

"He was at the same wedding as Big Vinnie. Your department have a sketch artist?"

"I'm lucky to have a secretary, but the gal in our photo lab is a wiz on the computer," he replied. "But she went home hours ago."

"Let's get her back in here," I said. He was already dialing his phone, still way ahead of me.

Chapter 37

Soldier Moves

Earlier that afternoon, Soldier had watched Michaels shuffle in his paper slippers into the hotel as the cruiser drove off. He got out of his car and elected to use the hotel's side entrance. Looking through the window, he saw Michaels have a brief conversation with the desk clerk before getting on the elevator. Soldier went in and noticed the elevator went to the fourth floor. He took the stairs to his second-floor room.

He dumped his packages on the bed and loaded his new pistol and extra clips first, just in case. He stripped the bed, stuffing the sheets in a pillowcase along with the soiled towels. He changed clothes, packed, wiped the place down of his prints, and poured Drano down the sink and shower drains. He didn't want to leave any of his DNA. He took pride in leaving the place cleaner than it had been when he'd checked in.

He drove to Lead and sat on Dora's porch. He called her. He heard her cell ring inside the cabin. *Great. She doesn't have it with her.*

The afternoon sun, which had melted the previous night's snow, felt warm on his face. The chirping of birds drowned out the noise from the gold mine up the hill. *This is good.* He closed his eyes.

When Dora woke him, the sun was thinking about setting on the other side of the Black Hills.

"I kept calling your cell. Why didn't you answer?" she asked.

"It died, but I got a new one," he said, handing her his after pressing redial. "What we have here is a failure to communicate."

They laughed when her phone rang in the cabin.

"I left it on the table when I went to get my hair done. You like it?" she asked, doing a pirouette.

He did. "Where am I taking you for dinner?"

"The Elk Creek Steakhouse & Saloon. Might be the best steak in these here parts," she said, unlocking the door and leading him in. "Throw your bags in the bedroom."

That implied a lot to him. He wondered how she could be so accepting of him but quickly put that doubt out of his mind.

Two hours later, a jukebox was pumping country music out a door marked "Saloon," so Soldier led Dora through the one marked "Restaurant." They were greeted by a hearty hello and were quickly seated. When their waitress returned with their drinks, Dora ordered the petite prime rib after talking Soldier into trying the twelve-ounce New York–cut buffalo steak. He ordered a bottle of red from the wine list to go with their dinners. He noticed the dining room was filling up, the overflow being sent through the swinging door into the bar.

"Ain't never saw no buffalo cut in New York," he said with a feigned drawl, which got a good laugh from Dora. Soldier loved the way she lit up when she smiled. He liked how she ate, the way she tilted her head to listen to what he had to say. Her voice was like music, melodic and sweet. His previous encounters with candlelight, wine, and beautiful women had never felt this special.

Halfway through their meal, Soldier's stomach muscles tightened when he saw Rollo Michaels and a female companion walk in with Sheriff Bullock. Instantly on alert, he noticed the woman had a holstered automatic riding on her hip under her jacket. *Maybe Michaels won't recognize me.* He reached for the new gun in his waistband hoping he'd chambered a round.

Dora followed Soldier's gaze to the threesome being seated. Sheriff Bullock waved to her, and her "Hi, Sheriff" got the other two to turn around. Soldier wiped his brow with his napkin and held his wineglass to his nose until Michaels turned back around. Soldier cursed his luck. The old fight-or-flight thing was kicking in.

"What do you think of buffalo steak?" Dora asked.

"What?" Soldier asked, fingering the trigger of his gun.

"Your steak. How do you like buffalo?"

"Sure doesn't taste like chicken."

He released the safety as the sheriff stood and walked toward their table. Dora was clueless. He watched Bullock walk past them and toward the alcove marked with the restrooms sign. Soldier gestured their waitress to the table, put a hundred down, and asked her to box up their leftovers.

"I'm feeling a little queasy. Need some air. Meet you outside," he said, getting up to leave. He felt the lady cop staring a hole in the back of his head as he went through the connecting door to the bar. He waited inside the door to see if he was being followed. He went out the saloon door to the parking lot. He took up a position behind a pickup next to his rental and waited. Dora came out not followed. Soldier went around to the passenger door and held it open for her. She handed him the bag with their unfinished meals, which he put on the floorboard of the backseat.

"How you feelin,' baby?" she asked as he stole another look at the Elk Creek Steakhouse & Saloon to see if the sheriff of Deadwood was following with a posse.

"Evidently buffalo isn't my thing, or maybe I just needed some air. I'm sorry I ran out on you like that, but I thought I would lose it in there," he said, starting up the car.

They were silent during the first five minutes of the drive back to her cabin; he turned on the radio to fill the void. She reached over and turned the volume down.

"You expecting someone to be following us?" she asked between songs.

"Why you thinking like that?"

"You keep checking your mirrors," she said, turning the radio back up. She unbuckled her seat belt, slid on over, and snuggled up to him as Kenny Chesney and Grace Potter sang, "You and Tequila."

It felt good to him, contact with this woman. He inhaled the sweetness of her fragrance and was comforted by her closeness and warmth. But he continued to steal glances in the mirror, hoping nothing was catching up with them as he drove through the moonlit Black Hills.

Once back at the cabin, Dora put their dinner leftovers in her refrigerator and made coffee. Soldier slid his new pistol under the couch cushion and took off his shoes. He got a small fire going in the fireplace and was tending it when she brought in the fresh brew. He watched the light of the flames dance on her face and sparkle in her eyes and thought he'd melt when she smiled handing him his cup.

"Sorry you're not feeling good. Maybe you're coming down with something," she said as they moved to the couch.

He put his arm around her, nuzzling her cheek. *God, she smells good.* He pushed the concerns of an hour earlier to a different part of his brain. "Maybe I shouldn't eat buffalo," he said, identifying the smells as vanilla and orange blossoms as he kissed her cheek. "You make me better," he said. "What's on the agenda for tomorrow?"

"Church at nine o'clock. Do you want to go with me?"

"Aren't you afraid the roof will fall in?"

"I'm not if you're not," she said. They laughed.

Soldier was confused by his feelings. No one had ever made him feel so relaxed. He had never met a woman so at ease with herself, so unassuming, so real. He didn't know what was happening. *Let's see where this goes.*

They made love on the couch, fell asleep in each other's arms, and awoke shortly after the fire had died out. Dora led him to her bed, where their passion was rekindled. When their lovemaking was done, they lay contently entwined while their hearts stopped racing. Soldier could feel her heart beat as he held her and listened to the rhythm of her breathing as she fell asleep. A tear of happiness ran down his cheek. Soon, he too was asleep.

But his dreams were not those of a happy man. He dreamed of the dead. His mother, his father, his best friend. The dozen faces of those he'd killed morphed into images of Dora's husband and little girl reaching out to him from their graves. "Help us ... help us ... Help us!"

"Wake up, baby, wake up," Dora said while gently shaking him awake. "It's only a dream, Jason, only a dream."

He opened his eyes. Seeing only darkness, he pulled her close to him and whispered, "I'm so sorry, so sorry."

"Shush," she murmured.

They were soon asleep again.

Chapter 38

Elk Creek

Bullock took us to a steakhouse a fair drive from his office into the Black Hills. He told us of Sturgis and Spearfish, his love for the Black Hills, of hunting and fishing, and his dislike of clowns screwing up his personal time by getting murdered in his community.

The Elk Creek Steakhouse & Saloon's parking lot was filled with pickup trucks, country music, and the mouthwatering smells of roasting meats. Sheriff Bullock was warmly greeted, and we were whisked in ahead of two waiting couples. He smiled at a few of the patrons and waved at a couple two tables over.

Our waitress had water on the table and menus in our hands. She took our drink orders. I opted for a Jack Daniels with a splash of branch water, hoping to fit in. Agent Monroe was surprised they had Blue Moon on tap, and Designated Driver

Bullock requested coffee, black. He excused himself to wash up, stating he was having the usual. Our waitress pitched the Saturday night special—the prime rib, potato, and salad kind, not the .22-caliber throwaway Monroe and I envisioned. I bit, but Monroe opted for a trout filet, no spuds, just a small salad with vinegar and oil. *It figures.*

"Well, Rollo, why is it you keep popping up on my radar?" she asked.

"Just lucky I guess."

"Who, you or me?"

Her smile was a killer. Her parents had probably spent a fortune on it.

"I've been known to get lucky now and then. First time to South Dakota?" I was as charming as I could be as our drinks arrived. As she removed the orange slice from the rim of her beer glass, her gaze locked onto a male customer who passed our table on his way to the saloon's swinging doors.

"Yes," she answered. "I hope to check out Mount Rushmore before we leave."

"We, like you and me?"

My question went unanswered as Bullock returned.

Dinner was great. We avoided talking about the case at hand, cop talk, and the weather. We got Bullock to tell us of the sights to see and the things to do, as if we were tourists.

"You leave your suit and tie in Denver when you came to Deadwood to take this job?" Monroe asked the sheriff.

"The powers that be wanted the look, and playing the part got me reelected for another four years. Mustache just came natural. Tourists love it, and I'm real comfortable with it. But don't be fooled, Agent, I can do my job better than most, in case you're wondering" he said.

I really liked this guy.

"Honest, Seth, I didn't mean anything negative, but you don't look much like the senior detective lieutenant who retired six years ago. I truly like the new look."

Surprisingly, Agent Monroe grabbed the check, claiming her FBI expense account would take care of it. I doubted it, but I was without a client and on my own dime since John Cochran had stopped smiling. The conversation on the ride back to Deadwood was all business.

"Sheriff, who was the woman you waved at in the restaurant?" Monroe asked.

"Dora Cruz. Sad story there ... Husband and daughter killed in a wreck ... Run over by a logging truck," Bullock said.

"And the man she was with?"

"Don't know him. She's been dating a few locals ... Nothing serious that I know of. Why?"

"I thought I might know him or maybe seen him before. Strange they didn't leave together," she said.

Then it hit me. Take off the mustache and he'd look familiar to me too, and why wouldn't he? We were old acquaintances. We'd been to the same weddings. Maybe even exchanged gunfire like other people swapped Christmas cards. But I sat quietly. Was it because Bullock had had me locked up for a night, or was it because I was caged in the backseat of his cruiser, the one without door handles on the inside? Or maybe the only reason was because I was a jerk. But there was stuff I needed to know, and the best way for me to find out was to have a private conversation with Soldier Boy Mahan.

"Tell Agent Monroe about the photo my tech digitally enhanced," Bullock ordered, making me more comfortable with the decision I'd just made.

"You tell her. She's your tech."

And he did.

"Could be the shooter is this Mahan fella wearing fake facial hair. Probably long gone if it was him," Bullock said.

"Our wiretap got him telling Vinnie Costello he was going to stick around Deadwood for a few days to check out the sights. I'd bet he's still here," Monroe replied.

Wha—? Wiretaps? Really? Mistake? Or is she playing me? I had my own ideas about Mahan's whereabouts but didn't share.

"And the Bureau believes our killer is Mahan because—?"

"Because he's Big Vinnie's go-to guy," she said.

"Is there anything else I should be passing along to my detectives and deputies?" Bullock asked her, a little frustration seeping in.

Sheriff Bullock dropped us off at our hotel probably thinking we were or soon would be in the same room together. Inside, piano music drifted through the lobby from the bar.

"Buy me a nightcap?" Monroe asked.

"Sorry, but I'm totally worn out. Didn't sleep much in Bullock's jail cell, the amenities not being to my liking. Then you two interrupted the only sleep I've really gotten since arriving in Deadwood."

We said our good nights in the elevator, she off on three and me off on four. Thirty minutes later, I went down and moved my car to the side street to avoid the hotel's security cameras then returned to my room.

I had set the bedside alarm for three in the morning. At two o'clock, I was still waiting for it to go off. I fired up the little coffeepot and drank the two cups while putting on jeans, a black T, and my trusty Nikes. A navy windbreaker and my Yankee cap completed my impromptu black-ops uniform. The side doors were locked down after two in the morning, so I had to exit through the lobby. The desk clerk was nodding in front of a small-screen TV, so I left unnoticed except for the ever-present security cameras. I had my cap pulled down so they couldn't tell if it was me or Derek Jeter. I made my stealthy walk to my rental from the hotel. Armed and ready, I drove to Dora Cruz's home hoping to confront a stone killer. Maybe not one of my better ideas.

D. Cruz was listed in the phone book, and Garmin got me to her home by three thirty. I continued a full block past her place, turned around, and went past again. All was quiet, not even a dog barking. I parked in the parking lot of some kind of factory adjacent to Dora's cabin, put my car keys in the cup holder, and started walking across the lot to get to the rear of her house.

Bam! I was lit up by a spotlight from the factory roof and the headlights of a fast-approaching

Jeep. It skidded to a stop three feet in front of me. Two security guards jumped out holding shaking revolvers.

“Down on your knees, asshole,” one ordered.

“Get your hands up,” said the other, neither guard taking charge.

“I’m not kneeling down in the mud,” I said in a calm voice while raising my hands. “Let me explain, fellas.”

“Put your hands on the back of your head, and slowly turn around.”

I was handcuffed for the second time in two days. Not good. I was taken to the security shack and searched. All I had in my pocket was my driver’s license, a twenty-dollar bill, and an ebonite yawara stick. The inexperienced searcher missed my backup Glock 26 holstered in the small of my back where I easily hid it from him with my cuffed hands.

“Los Angeles? You lost or something?” the reader of my license questioned.

“Where am I?” went over their heads.

"And what the hell is this, a dildo?" one said, holding up my yawara stick.

"It's my girlfriend's."

That didn't improve the conversation. After they determined I wasn't a fountain of information, the sheriff's office was called. Shortly before dawn broke over the Black Hills of South Dakota, Deputy Bob showed up.

"Jeez, Michaels, what are you up to now?"

"About 220, Bob."

That didn't amuse the deputy, but my captors enjoyed the old gag.

"You know this guy, Deputy?" the older guard asked.

"Why you trespassing?" the deputy asked me, ignoring the other two.

"Prospecting? Actually, Deputy, I was looking for a place to piss." I fibbed while he was exchanging his handcuffs for theirs. "And get my Glock out of there. It might fall out and hurt someone."

"You boys best be gettin' your heads outta your asses 'fore somebody blows you away." He showed them my gun and watched them go pale then blazing red with embarrassment. He strapped me into the front passenger seat of his cruiser and took me to lockup. I sat in a holding cell. His shift was ending at eight, so he waited until then to notify his boss.

I sat for another hour before Bullock came in to spring me. I could tell he wasn't in the mood for frivolity. I followed him to his office.

"You must like my jail, Michaels. Let me hear why you're all dressed like some kind of ninja warrior and spare me the bullshit," he ordered while firing up his coffee maker.

"I was checking out Dora Cruz's abode, see if her boyfriend is the shooter," I said, deciding to come clean. "I think he might be Soldier Boy Mahan." That got me a stern lecture about cowboying in his jurisdiction and threats of more jail time no matter who my friends were. The coffee was ready. He poured two cups before he phoned Agent Monroe.

"Agent Monroe, Seth Bullock here ... We have your boyfriend in custody again ... Rollo

Michaels ... Yes, ma'am ... I'm sorry ... I apologize. He claims to have a lead on your hitman ... Yes, could be him ... Yes, ma'am ... We'll see you when you get here."

"How 'bout we get some breakfast, cowboy? Monroe says it'll take her an hour to get here. Hotel's five minutes away. Probably wants to pretty up for you," he said, a grin on his face even his big mustache couldn't hide.

"Not if it's jail food."

"You like waffles? If not, you can get anything you want. Coffee's not as good as mine but still better than most," he said, sliding my gun, holster, and ID across the desk. "It's not loaded. My deputy says you had that stuck in your ass. Probably wouldn't have found it without the heads-up. How many guns you bring with you?"

"Always a backup. And you know that's not really where it was. Where you taking me for breakfast?"

"The Lee Street Station Cafe, my cousin's place a few blocks from here. We can walk."

And we did. If he hadn't worked the pedestrians we passed as if it were an election year, a sleepy me would never have been able to keep up with him.

Chapter 39

Soldier Finds Jesus

Soldier Boy was amazed that Dora had him sitting in a church with a hundred or so redneck souls listening to a fire-and-brimstone preacher warn them of the "fires of hell." Looking directly at Soldier, he announced, "The end is near, sinner ... Repent!" Shouts of "Amen!" and "Hallelujah!" filled the small church, and they were all on their feet. The organist hit the keys and pumped out "Amazing Grace" as Dora and the rest of them belted out the gospel standard. Soldier couldn't believe he knew the words. "Amazing Grace ... sweet the sound ... saved a wretch like me ... I once was lost ... I'm found ... blind ... I see."

The music stopped, and they settled in the pews. A hundred pairs of eyes looked up at the young preacher in the pulpit.

"None of us knows for sure when our days on earth will end, but He does. So we should realize the end could be near for some of us sitting here today. Look at those sitting all around you. If not one of them, it could be you. Ask yourself, 'Am I ready?' If you can answer yes today, what will your answer be tomorrow?

"The end is near whether you wish to believe it or not. Repent and God's kingdom will be open to you. Salvation awaits those who accept Jesus into their lives. Amazing grace can be yours, and it won't cost money. Black Hills gold can't buy it, all your credit cards won't get it for you, but it's yours for the asking ... Can I get an amen here brothers and sisters?"

"Amen!" they shouted.

"Simply let Jesus lead you to the Father. Change your ways, repent of your sins, and God's grace shall save you from eternal damnation in the fires of hell. Isn't that truly *amazing*?"

They stood as one when the organ began again. Soldier dropped a fifty when the baskets were passed and felt good about it. The music stopped, and they recited the Lord's Prayer. The preacher led the congregation out the front and positioned himself to thank each person as the congregation exited.

"How are you this fine day, Dora?"

"Happy to be here, Pastor," she said. "This is my friend Jason."

Soldier offered his hand.

Taking Soldier's hand, the pastor said, "May you find the Lord. I sense your burden is heavy. Let Him show you the way." He released Soldier's hand and turned to his next congregant.

Screw you, Soldier thought, walking quickly away, Dora clinging to his arm.

"What's the matter, baby?"

"Who's he to tell me to find the Lord? What does he know about my burden?" he asked, wondering why the preacher had ticked him off so. "The end is near, my ass."

He cooled off on their walk to a small coffee shop that featured fresh-baked pastries. They enjoyed some huckleberry muffins, fresh melon, and grande cups of good coffee. *Maybe it's the water.*

Dora tried steering Jason into revealing some personal information with questions.

Occupation? Sales. Married? No. To Dora's relief, it finally morphed into sentences in which Soldier truthfully revealed things about himself. His parents were dead. He'd been raised in New York by his grandparents. He'd served in the army. But when Deputy Bill Carpenter came into the coffee shop, the conversation stopped. Again, Soldier went on alert. And that time, Dora sensed it.

The deputy went straight to the counter and picked up two coffees; his partner was waiting in the cruiser just outside. He turned, smiled, and asked, "Howdy do, Dora?" but gave his hard look to Soldier. Soldier wanted to slap him but instead gave the deputy a nod. Dora waved, and they watched Bill get into the cruiser and drive slowly away.

"You sure got a thing for Bill," Dora said.

"He's a jerk." Soldier bristled.

She looked deeply into Soldier's eyes, squeezed his hand, and smiled. That made all Soldier's thoughts of Deputy Bill vanish.

They drove to Deadwood and walked the main drag checking out the little gift shops and historical buildings. He led her into a jewelry store that featured Black Hills gold. When a pair of hoop earrings caught Dora's eye, he bought them for her in spite of her protests. Gold mining, mostly played out, was the reason Deadwood had gotten its start. Casino gambling kept it going. Soldier thought gambling a sucker's play and pointed out a drifter by the entrance to the Lone Star hitting up a passerby for a buck.

"There are ten of them for every winner," he told Dora.

Dora bought some flowers from a sidewalk vendor, and they continued their walk. At the edge of town, they entered the Deadwood Cemetery. They walked halfway up the hill and stopped at the grave where Wild Bill Hickok had been laid to rest. Next to him lay Calamity Jane. Dora told the story of Jane being reburied next to Hickok as a practical joke on Bill many years after his death. During Wild Bill's brief time in Deadwood, Calamity Jane's infatuation with his fame caused the man all kinds of grief.

Dora walked Soldier to another area of the cemetery. A family plot of two graves marked with tiny headstones read, "Ramon Agapito Cruz, August 7, 1976–February 11, 2009" and "Felicia

Ramona Cruz, September 2, 2003–February 11, 2009." Dora placed the flowers between the two markers. "My husband and daughter."

Soldier saw a tear on her cheek. He took her hand in his and kissed it. He couldn't remember feeling sorry for anyone ever until right then. They walked hand in hand to where they had parked not saying a word.

On the drive back to the cabin, Dora broke the silence. "Would you like to see Mount Rushmore, Jason?"

"The place where the presidents are carved into the mountain?"

"Yes. It's not too far from here. I'll fix us up a picnic. What do you say?"

Her enthusiasm broke through the gloom of sadness.

"Sounds like a plan to me," Soldier responded, grateful for the mood change.

Back at the cabin, Dora busied herself getting things together for their picnic. Soldier was looking at a framed photo collage on the living room wall. A picture of a younger Dora holding a baby, another of a toddler, one of a burly young man holding a four-year-old by the hand. A larger picture took up the rest of the frame. It showed a smiling Dora, the man, and the child posed in front of the cabin. They looked so happy. He felt the sadness coming back and turned away.

Her kitchen phone rang. “Hello?” She put the call on speaker so she could continue filling the picnic basket.

“Hello Dora, Seth Bullock here. Sorry to bother you on Sunday, but I’m in the middle of that shooting case. There’s a good chance the shooter might have touched your car when it was parked in the city garage. We’d like to check it for prints if you could bring it in today. You haven’t washed it, have you?”

“No Seth, I haven’t. Will it take long? I was planning a Sunday drive to Rushmore. I guess we could bring it by on the way out of town, maybe in an hour or so.”

“We’ll be here,” Bullock replied.

Soldier was alarmed by the nature of Sheriff Bullock’s call but hid his concern with a smile. On the pretext of getting the instruction booklet for his new phone from the glovebox of his rental, he went outside and let the air out of a tire on Dora's car while Dora gathered up their picnic lunch. They would go in Soldier's rental, and he would fake a call to the sheriff's office to tell Bullock where Dora's car was.

Chapter 40

Hearts Break

On the drive to Mount Rushmore, Soldier was amazed by the scenery, the wildlife, and the natural beauty of the land and wondered why he hadn't noticed any of it earlier in the day. He wondered if he'd ever taken the time to look at much of anything. He also wondered about the police hunt for him and thought that sooner or later, Michaels was sure to recognize him. Soldier was not one to be pushing his luck like that. He wondered why he was willing to take this gamble just to be with Dora. *Am I losing my edge, or is this what love is?*

Their enjoyment of Dora's little picnic under the gaze of Washington, Jefferson, Roosevelt, and Lincoln was interrupted by the inevitable. Soldier, ever looking for threats in his surroundings, happened to catch sight of Michaels, Bullock, and Monroe getting out of a sheriff's cruiser. Another cruiser pulled up to the entrance followed by a Park Service jeep and four rangers.

"Come with me," Soldier said, casually masking his high-alert status.

Taking her hand, Soldier led Dora into the souvenir shop, leaving their picnic remains on the bench. While the sheriff huddled with his posse, Dora looked at the array of souvenir snow globes. Soldier bought a cap, windbreaker, and sunglasses and put them on. Dora saw that Soldier was busy making a purchase and decided she'd add one of the globes to her collection. She shook a globe and held it up to the window to examine it in the light. Looking past the snow swirling around the miniature Mount Rushmore, she saw Deputy Bill handing out photos as Sheriff Bullock conversed with six park rangers at the viewing area entrance. She turned back to look at the man she'd met two days earlier and had thought might be her future. But when the crushing realization of what was really happening washed over her, the globe she was holding crashed to the floor and, like her dreams, shattered into a thousand pieces.

Soldier saw tears well up in her eyes. His heart was breaking. He watched Dora's world coming to a standstill and rushed to wrap her in his arms. She was having none of it; she pushed him away.

"I'm so sorry, baby. I'll call when I can. Please don't go outside till I'm gone," he said, handing her the car keys. He turned away to hide his tears and headed out the door using all he had to put thoughts of Dora to that other part of his mind.

Fight or flight? Totally outgunned, he knew flight was his only option. But if push came to shove, Deputy Bill would be his first target though he knew Bullock posed the bigger threat. He exited the shop and joined a group of Vietnam vets who were leaving a commemorative ceremony for fallen members of their old unit, the Third Recon Battalion, USMC. He fell into step with them heading for the buses that had pulled up to the entrance. He engaged one of the weathered men in conversation, adding a limp to his gait as they walked past two park rangers. A commotion broke out in the area of the restrooms, and the two rangers ran toward the ruckus, one of them dropping a flycr. Soldier picked up the fairly good likeness of himself and put it in his pocket as four of the park rangers wrestled a man to the ground. The military procession never broke ranks, continuing on to their buses unaware they had been infiltrated. After all, who could blame them? He wasn't called Soldier without reason.

On the bus, it seemed that time stood still while the passengers waited for the rest of their fellow warriors. But finally, the trips to the latrine and quick stops for souvenirs were completed, the last-minute selfies were taken, and the buses got underway.

Soldier Boy Mahan never looked back or he would have seen Sheriff Bullock and Agent Monroe take Dora into custody as Rollo Michaels stood by staring at the buses pulling from the curb. Soldier knew in his heart that he wouldn't be calling Dora. As hard as he was, he knew he just couldn't take that kind of pain ever again.

Chapter 41

Beware the Feds

Soldier Boy Mahan needed to avoid the airport and feared using the Jason Morton New Jersey ID he had shown the deputies, assuming an APB was already out for him in that name. He simply went to Smiling Jack's apartment to retrieve the things he knew a guy like Jack would always have hidden. He found a coroner's seal on the door and smiled as he broke it, wondering if the seal would stop anybody. Knowing what to look for, it didn't take Soldier long to find Jack's bugout bag stuffed in the sofa's back springs. He had to give Jack credit for its completeness: a New York driver's license, a Colt two-inch .38, six hundred in traveling cash, and keys to Jack's Harley. Soldier emptied his wallet of everything but two anonymous debit cards and the folding money. He used a pan on the stove to burn his fake Jersey ID and flushed the ashes in the toilet.

He checked the medicine chest above the sink and discovered the hair dye Jack used in his new life and thought, "Why not? Maybe blonds do have more fun." When done, he looked at himself in the mirror. Satisfied, he was ready to saddle up. The helmet was a little tight, the gloves didn't quite fit, but you do what you have to.

Glad night had fallen, he followed the beam of the Harley Iron 883's headlight southbound hoping to put Deadwood four hundred miles behind him by dawn. But he knew his encounter with Dora Cruz had caused him to screw up big time, almost getting caught twice. Even worse, he had left his prints, DNA, and travel bag at Dora's cabin. Once the authorities put it together it would be over for him.

Knowing what had to be done, he went to Dora's cabin first, hoping she was not there. She wasn't. He went in through a window, retrieved his travel bag, let out the cat, and set Dora's home on fire.

As he rode away he wondered what he would have done if Dora had been home? Such doubts made him vow to avoid similar encounters ever again

He was headed to Sparks, Nevada, where Big Vinnie's "rat-bastard" cousin Dominic Frattalli was hiding out in witness protection. There'd be no hanging around to see the sights. In, get it done, out, and on to the next. No entanglements. His work for Big Vinnie would continue to take him many places like Deadwood and beyond. Of this he was sure.

That night while Rene Monroe and I dined at separate tables in our hotel's restaurant, Sheriff Bullock and his detectives issued an APB after securing an arrest warrant for Jason Morton, Monroe having had the FBI put out a BOLO for Sean Mahan, earlier in the day. Evidence linking the two had yet to be found. The room had been cleaned and rented that afternoon, causing grief for the new guests when the search warrant was served. They ran the information Morton had provided on the car rental papers and were told by New Jersey authorities that the ID used was bogus. Thc car was dusted for prints also, but the only usable prints belonged to Dora Cruz. I assumed a state forensic team from Pierre would arrive Monday to see if they could find anything.

Monroe and I were headed to the airport in the morning, her flight to DC and mine to LA. She had declined my offer to join me for dinner but sat at my table when she had finished her dinner. bringing her glass of wine with her. It had been almost two years since the last time our paths had crossed.

"What did you and the sheriff wind up doing with Ms. Cruz?" I said.

"We released her about an hour ago to a friend. She's a mess, couldn't stop crying, to the point of hysteria. Bullock's detectives will try talking to her again in the morning."

"Didn't want to hold her?"

"She's just another victim, don't you think?"

"I do."

"Your name came up in an investigation of ours. How is it you know Vincenzo Costello, again?" she asked.

"Like I told you, we met once at a wedding in New York more than a year and a half ago. I was a guest of the groom. Why ask me again?"

"Wasn't Charlie Michaels your father and a known associate of Vincenzo Costello?" hitting me with her best shot.

"We don't get to choose our parents," I said, trying for calm.

"Don't try to bullshit me, Michaels. You know who Costello is, a New York crime boss who had you find Jack Cochran so he could be executed by Soldier Boy Mahan." A vein on her forehead pulsated.

"I was hired by Susan Cochran to find her brother, that's it."

"So you haven't been in contact with Costello recently?"

"I never said that. Let me ask you, Agent Monroe, is this conversation being recorded?" I asked with a smile while thinking maybe it was.

"Always the wiseass. You know, that shit gets old quick. When we first met in LA, I thought you were kind of cool, but now I know you're just another tool in Costello's toolbox."

“Phillips screwdriver or hammer?” I asked, assuming she took me for a simple tool.

“You’ll be hearing from the bureau soon, and they’ll be wanting some answers,” she said and rose, not picking up the check this time. “You’ve gotten yourself into some serious business here, and the bureau’s heavy hitters will be all over you and your operation. It’s like a colonoscopy without anesthesia. I hope you come out clean. Goodbye, Rollo.”

As I stood and watched her walk away, in walks the sheriff of Deadwood. My dinner wrestled with my angst as Bullock called her back to my table.

“We just got a call Dora Cruz’s house is on fire,” he announced. “We don’t know if she’s in it or not.”

Chapter 42

Bad News

Before checking in for my 10:20 a.m. flight from Rapid City to LA, I called Bullock's office to find out the status of Dora Cruz. Thankfully, she was alive and well at a friend's house. The fire was listed "suspicious origin," the home a "total loss." We had spent three hours at the scene last night with Bullock until it was determined no one was in the house.

My flight's departure was delayed fifteen minutes; the copilot being a late arrival according to the gate attendant. He showed up to a chorus of boos, resulting in free refreshments and extra pretzels on the first leg of our underbooked flight. At least I was spared the vagaries of the seating gods. Agent Monroe's warning of what lay ahead for me and Michaels & Associates kept me awake most of last night as I worked out a plan to cover my ass from a fed probe sans anesthesia. My hopes of catching a few winks turned to fantasy because of stops in Chicago and Phoenix. Keep your free refreshments, American Airlines.

My partner Clancy meeting me when I landed was a surprise, but he had volunteered for a reason. We had to talk. What he had to say I wasn't ready for. He had a problem. That meant we had a problem. When he was off those three days a week earlier, Sylvia had a lumpectomy. The biopsy found she has a virulent breast cancer. A double mastectomy had been scheduled at Cedars the coming Monday, and he'd need some serious time off.

"Oh shit, partner, I'm so sorry. Tell me what we can do."

"Pray that we caught this in time and it isn't spreading right now as we speak."

He lost it. He pulled to the curb on Century Boulevard. "You have to drive, Rollo."

We did the Chinese fire drill, him around the back, me around the front. Holding up traffic for some twenty or so seconds is considered a felony by many LA drivers.

Two hours' sleep in the last twenty-four didn't improve my driving any, and a few fellow travelers used their horns to tell me so. I used my middle finger to tell them I didn't agree. The thirty-minute drive was further complicated by a fender bender on Wilshire Boulevard. Clancy took the time to prep me for a case he'd inked on Friday.

"My actor friend's neighbor, a businessman named Phillipe Patek, is having trust issues with his business partner. He believes the partner and Mrs. Patek are having an affair, but that's only the half of it. Mr. Patek thinks they're also siphoning funds from the business, Sten-Tek Incorporated."

"You know we don't do divorce cases," I said.

"This is way beyond that, partner. Patek thinks they're planning on killing him. There are million-dollar policies on each partner."

"What have you done so far?"

"I knew with my being off for a while, you'd be short on manpower. So I contacted your buddy, Peter Gunn Electronics, and rented some equipment. Saturday, I installed two GPS transmitters on the partner's and Mrs. Patek's cars. I also bugged the partner's office so our client can record the calls, but I haven't done anything with the second bug," he said, admitting to a criminal act or two. Fortunately, none of Gunn's stuff was traceable.

Clancy had enough on his plate, so I didn't tell him of the FBI shit storm headed our way. It wouldn't surprise me if a couple of agents weren't waiting in my office right that minute. I probably should have given everyone a heads-up before I'd left Deadwood.

Once we arrived at Wilshire and La Brea, I drove around the block looking for the obvious black SUV with US government plates, the vehicle preferred by the feds for its ominous appearance. Seeing none, I parked Clancy's car in the underground parking lot. No fed car there either. After transferring my suitcase to my car, we went to our offices on the fourth floor.

"I'm going to the head," I told Clancy as we got off the elevator. "Call me if the FBI's there."

"What?"

I was washing my hands when my cell went off. Caller ID told me it was from the office. "Are they there?"

"Nobody here but us chickens," Linda said. "What's this FBI stuff? You have Clancy more confused than ever."

"If the coast is clear, I'll be right there to fill everybody in."

I entered and was greeted by the whole crew all wanting the complete rundown on my Deadwood experience. I obliged with the highlights of the shootout and my two arrests. But the involvement of the feds was the real eyebrow-raiser.

The Q&A was interrupted by a call from my BFF Bob Howser. "Hey Bob, how's it hanging?"

"Ringling Brothers Circus Museum was a wealth of information. Sis and I spent two days in the archive section, found all kinds of stuff. My mother actually married a clown, can you believe it? I also have another sister!"

"That's great news, Bob. I'm happy for you. Reminds me of something your sister said about your brother saying you were adopted. Can Phyllis come to the phone?"

"Yeah sure."

"Hello, Rollo. What do you need?" she asked.

"Remember telling me about Paul teasing Bobby about being adopted?"

"I do."

"Go to the local county hall of records, see if you can find any adoption or custody records under your father's or Bob's biological mother's name. It would be nice to let Uncle Meyer off his guilt trip thinking he was a kidnapper."

"Great idea. I'm on it, chief," she said, obviously in high spirits.

"Now that I've had my great idea for the day, I think I'll call it quits. Give me back to Bob, please. Hope to see you here in LA soon."

"What's got her so excited?" Bob asked.

"She'll tell you. When will you be back in Los Angeles?"

"I don't know, Rollo, maybe a week. I just wanted you and the gang to know how grateful I am. I never knew how smart my sister was, is—oh, you know what I mean. She really found all kinds of personal information in that twelve-thousand-square-foot treasure trove of records. I think we made copies of most of it. Let me speak with Ruth if she can."

"Sure thing, Bob. I hope to see you when you get back."

"I think Sis will be coming with me. Which reminds me, that lawyer guy who's your partner—does he do wills, powers of attorney, trusts, things like that?"

"Sure. He did some of those same things for me. I don't see myself dying of old age," I said and transferred his call to Ruth. I had some calls to make myself. The first was to my ex, the former Mrs. Michaels.

"You're not canceling your weekend with the kids, are you?" was her greeting. Caller ID might make a simple hello obsolete.

"No, Marie, I'll pick them up Saturday morning usual time. The reason I'm calling is I need your Cousin Angela's cell number. I had dinner with her and Vinnie a week ago, and she wanted me to find out something for her. Now I can't find the paper I wrote the info and her number on."

"I'll call you back. I have to look it up."

She was lying.

Twenty minutes later, Ruth told me Angela Costello was on line two.

"Your wife told me you were trying to call me but didn't have my cell number. What's this about?" she said, concern in her tone.

"You mean my *ex*-wife. You on your cell?"

"No. Don't own one. Vinnie doesn't trust them. I'll ask again, what's this about?"

"Go buy one right now and call me on it. It's very important. And make sure it can take, send, and receive pictures. Tell whoever sells it to you to show you how it works."

"You're not sending me anything weird, are you?"

"Maybe, Aunt Angie. Please hurry on this. I'll explain later when you call me. Goodbye."

The FBI wiretap logged the call on 04/26/17 1628hrs.

Vincenzo Costello was a big boy. That was why they called him Big Vinnie. But the wiretap on his phones could be used against me, and my contribution to the demise of Smiling Jack Cochran could have been misconstrued by some overzealous federal prosecutor looking to advance his or her career.

Forty-five hundred and a roll under the covers with Susan Cochran wasn't enough compensation for a serious stretch in a federal prison. Two nights in the Deadwood calaboose had already stretched my limits in the realm of incarceration.

Art came into my office with Clancy. They weren't there for coffee. They wanted more info on a possible FBI investigation into our business. Linda soon joined them, leaving Ruth and Nerd to take care of business. Art was first.

"Did you violate any federal laws?"

"No. At least not that I know of."

"Then why the heat?" Clancy asked.

"Guilt by association. A business partner of my deceased father probably paid the bill for my search for John Cochran. It turns out he was hiding out in South Dakota under the auspices of the witness protection program. Seems I was the finger man for Cochran's assassin."

"Your uncle Vinnie?" Linda asked.

"Gets worse. The FBI agent I ducked out my apartment window to avoid a year or so ago, another case, remember?" That got me just puzzled looks and shakes of heads. "Well, she catches the Cochran case. Flies in from DC and lets slip they have a wiretap on Big Vinnie, supposedly got him conversing with the shooter, kind of mentioning me in the conversation. Well, I've had a few conversations with Big Vinnie this past month and a few other times over the past five years. So it will all come down to what I knew and when I knew it."

"Did you know you were searching for Cochran so someone could pop him?" Art asked.

"No, I was working for the sister. Trouble with that, Vinnie sent her to me and paid most of the freight." I was looking at three rather glum faces. "Agent Monroe, who I think really doesn't believe me, warned me in no uncertain terms that the FBI would be up our asses for sure." I raised my hands to fend off further questions. "Guys, I'm running on empty. I need to go to my apartment, catch up on some sleep." I dismissed the assembly.

"We won't let them fuck with us," Art said, going for conviction with the f-bomb. "We won't cooperate. As your lawyer, Rollo, I'm advising you not to answer any queries and refer any federal investigators to your attorney, and that goes for the rest of you too."

I didn't know if Art's pep talk made any of us feel better, but I really appreciated his effort. *Thanks, partner.*

Chapter 43

Love Rekindled

One of the highlights of any trip at least for me is getting home. My landlady, housekeeper, and cat sitter all rolled into one sweet apartment manager had done her usual great job. In fact, she may have been too nice to my cat. His mass almost knocked me over when he jumped into my arms to greet me. A pot of newly sprouted wheat stood next to his water fountain indicating Mrs. Johnson had once again gone the extra mile to keep El Gato happy. But he refused to let me get to the stack of mail on the table by the door until he received the requisite number of belly rubs and ear scratches.

We curled up on the couch with him on my chest. I wanted to fall asleep listening to his purrs of contentment and almost made it there when my cell rang. It was Clancy. *Now what?*

"I just heard from our new client, Patek. Listening to his partner's phone calls has already paid off big time. Tillman has rented a weekend stay up the coast near San Simeon. Mr. and Mrs. Tillman are supposed to check in Friday night, check out Monday. Thing is, Mrs. Tillman is in Puerta Vallarta, due back a week from tomorrow. Mrs. Patek told our client she'd be visiting her sister for the weekend. So he wants us up there Saturday, get some photos, tail them around the clock, the kind of crap you hate, Rollo. Sorry, pard, but the money's good. He also wants a heads-up if they start back to LA early. Seems he has a team of accountants coming in to go over the books."

I didn't have the heart to tell Clancy it was my weekend with the kids rescheduled from the last weekend because of the Deadwood fiasco from which I'd just returned. *But tomorrow's another day*. Right then, a catnap was in order.

That evening after showering, shampooing, and donning my pajamas, I plopped in front of the TV to continue decompressing, maybe watch the Dodgers game or more likely have Vin Scully's replacement sing me to sleep with a Clayton Kershaw lullaby. *Dodger games will never be the same without Scully.* It was also decision time: *Delivery or try another frozen Red Baron?*

The *rat, tat-tat, rat, tat-tat-tat* on the door said Linda was there. My roommate, El Gato, knew the knock too and was all over it. I looked out the peep just in case the FBI had broken our secret code. They hadn't. It was Sweet Linda bearing gifts. No longer sleepy or feeling sorry for myself, I opened the door.

"You didn't eat yet, did you?" she asked, deftly stepping around the cat and handing me the bag.

"No" was all I could muster while caught between exhaustion and an adrenaline rush. My nose told me Japanese. My eyes confirmed that when I saw the receipt stapled to the bag. I took it to the kitchen counter, put my bottle of Jack Daniels away, and tore open the paper bag Linda had paid an extra quarter for, California never at a loss on how to spend other people's money. Done with the greeting ritual El Gato always put her through, she washed up at the sink then kissed my cheek.

"Welcome home," she said and took out a couple of plates. "Kabuki was pretty busy for a Monday. I got us some sushi, tempura, rice, and a couple of Kirin beers. Coffee table?"

"Sure. The game's about to start."

She set us up, and we sat. El Gato was squeezed between us. The little cup of wasabi was enough to keep him there and away from our food. The cilantro albacore rolls were to die for, and the tempura shrimp were always part of every order we got from Kabuki on Vine. Linda made sure one was put aside for her best buddy.

We cleaned it all up, fed the shrimp to the cat, and left the dishes in the sink. Linda went to the bathroom while I grabbed the mail from the entry table and reassumed my position in front of the TV. The score was 0–0, one out, bottom of the third. El Gato sat on the coffee table watching me go through my mail while he cleaned his whiskers and mush. Joe Davis sang Dodger praises, making them sound better than they were. All seemed right with the world, especially if you could avoid cable news.

Then Linda came out wearing the Japanese pearls I'd bought her at New York's Kennedy over a week ago. The pearls went extremely well with what she was wearing, which was nothing at all. El Gato stopped grooming. I dropped the mail and hit the off button, starting to rise.

"Lay back down there, big boy. Make room for your homecoming queen."

.

It was great to be home. The mail could wait another day. Or two.

Chapter 44

Disappointment

Telling my ex I wouldn't be able to take the kids for the weekend even two days before I was supposed to pick them up was always unpleasant. Always. But it was time to face the music. I closed my office door and made the call.

"You cannot do this to me again two weekends in a row, Rollo! Rex and I have plans for the weekend!" Marie shouted. "I'm supposed to have a life too, you know, but you get to traipse all over the country while I do all the parenting for Melissa and Brandon."

"I'm sorry, Marie, but it's not like I work a nine-to-five job. We have a bunch of cases going right now, and Clancy can't pull a weekend because Sylvia's having surgery."

I told her of the nightmare all women fear. Her anger diffused, she sought to change the subject.

"Listen, Rollo, the kids were upset you didn't call them last weekend, especially your daughter. You better call them. I won't do your dirty work for you again this weekend."

"I couldn't call. I was in jail last weekend," I said, immediately wishing I hadn't.

"In jail? For what?"

"Murder."

Of course that just complicated matters.

"That's not funny, you jerk," she yelled and hung up.

I hit redial and got a busy signal. *Sometimes the truth does set you free.*

I used my cell to call my daughter and got her voice mail. I pressed five and then called my son. Same result. *It's a school day, stupid!* I would await their calls, being a convenient dad and all. My ability to disappoint knew no bounds. My shortcomings were quickly filling my office, making me feel claustrophobic. I opened the door for some air. Fortunately, Linda walked into the outer office, keeping me from visiting all those dark places in my head. She shook water off her raincoat and hung it up. Obviously, sitting in front of a window I never looked out of left me clueless.

"Good afternoon. Judging from your glow, last night was very good for you," I said as she followed me to my office.

"It's probably the very long hot shower I took before I came in this afternoon," she said, pouring us some coffee. "Who ate all the doughnuts?"

"Like you don't know. Listen—I'm really glad you decided to come in. I need your help on this Patek case Clancy dropped on me. You need to tell Ruth you have to pass on that Phoenix trip this weekend. You and I'll be taking our act on the road to San Simeon."

I ran it down for her and asked her to get us booked into the Motel California for Friday, Saturday, and Sunday nights. I was just about to say something sexy and witty when I was interrupted.

"Your Aunt Angela on line two for you," Ruth announced over the intercom, allowing my homecoming queen to leave my office before she swooned.

"Hello, Angie. Are you at home right now, new phone in hand?" I asked, picturing Linda in her pearls.

"Yes. Now tell me what's going on," she demanded, her voice a bit strained.

"Walk outside to the sidewalk. See if you can play Pokémon."

"Can you hear me now? I don't know how to work this damn thing."

"Loud and clear. Tell my uncle his phones are tapped, the Hideaway is bugged for sure, and the house and home phone are probably wired too. The safest way for him to communicate with me is to send pictures. Got it?"

"Jesus, this is bad, Rollo. If it can happen to Trump ... How'd you find out?"

"Long story. Short version is somebody made a mistake. Have Uncle call me on your new phone, and don't give out the number to anybody, and don't call the fort or the house on this phone. Get a different phone for the everyday stuff like Hillary Clinton did. What phone did you buy?"

"It's an iPhone 6. Almost four hundred bucks."

"Uncle will thank me, don't you worry. Now that I have your cell number, I'll send Uncle a picture. Ciao, Aunt Angie." I took a Peter Gunn Electronics business card from my rolodex, shot a pic on my cell, and sent it to Angie's new phone. I called Gunn and filled him in. He'd be at the Fort Salonga Hideaway in two days.

Linda came in with a FedEx package overnighted from Deadwood. Judging from the weight, I was pretty sure it was my Walther. It was. The package also contained a note from Sheriff Bullock scribbled on the back of my booking slip that read, "Michaels—Next time you come to South Dakota you better be on vacation—Seth." I showed the note to Linda so she could share in my laughter.

I got some ammo out of the safe, loaded the empty magazine, and slid it into the butt. I chambered a round before holstering my best friend and clipped him inside my belt. Preparing to leave, I picked up my cell, and it rang in my hand. I almost dropped my daughter returning my call.

"Hey Mel, how ya doin'?"

"It's all good, Dad. What did you do to get Mom all upset?"

"Told her I'd need to pass on picking you and Brandon up again this weekend. I'm so sorry, Mel, but things are just crazy around here. Clancy's wife is going in the hospital, and I have to cover for him. Promise I'll make it up to you and Brando."

"Not a problem. Did you really get arrested last weekend?"

"Yes, but it was all just a big misunderstanding. I was in jail for only a few hours the first time. The second was even shorter."

"Twice?"

"It's a great story. I'll tell you the story next time we hook up. I love you, sweetness."

"You too."

"You too what?"

"You know."

"I know what?"

"I love you too," she whispered, obviously not alone.

"Put Jake on the phone."

That wasn't a total shot in the dark.

"Uh, hello, Mr. Michaels."

"Hello, Jake. You know I'll kick your ass if you don't treat my daughter right. Say goodbye, Jake."

"Yes, sir! Goodbye, sir."

Chapter 45

Cliff-Hanger

Rode hard and put up wet, I was awakened by the sounds of screeching gulls and crashing surf and sat up to get my bearings. An onshore breeze laden with the freshness of sea air came through the open balcony doors, billowing sheer curtains as if they were sails. The syncopated breathing of the beauty that lay beside me brought a smile to my face. Our love, an on-again-off-again affair of the heart, was currently in its on-again stage. Surely, this was the paradise of my dreams. *I hope I don't screw this up again.*

Though seemingly away from all the cares of a busy world, that was not the case. We were at this Motel California hanging from a cliff overlooking the Pacific because a client had hired us to monitor his business partner. Chances were the ability to mix business with pleasure was one of the reasons I'd chosen this profession. Or maybe one of my character defects had made the choice for me.

I quietly slid from beneath the covers so as not to awaken Sleeping Beauty. I felt the cold air rush over my nakedness, pulled my pajama bottoms from the top of the bedside lamp, and put them on. Once the coffee maker was figured out, I hit the shower. When I came out, the smell of fresh coffee overcame my aftershave. I donned my PJs over clean underwear and took a cup and Linda's laptop to the balcony while Linda still slept. I checked the laptop for any activity in the Tillman room just down the hall. The time stamp on the last sounds our mic picked up read 04:23. The objects of our surveillance were still sleeping.

The resident cliff-dwelling raccoons that had entertained us the night before had cleaned up the leftovers of our delivery pizza along with some of the box it had come in. I wondered if ignoring the "Don't Feed the Raccoons" warning conspicuously posted on the balcony railing could have gotten us evicted.

I sat enjoying the sea air. My cup of motel-room coffee not so much. I contemplated how the case was unfolding. Our client was a cuckold whose wife he suspected was having an affair with his business partner. As if that weren't egregious enough, he suspected the partner of embezzling millions from their company and of the pair plotting to take his life. A team of forensic accountants was scheduled to go over the books while his partner was away on a fake business trip. Millions were at stake, and I was to keep tabs on the partner and sound the alarm if he came anywhere near the business. Turns out the partner's business thing was a tryst at this Motel California with our client's wife.

Electronic surveillance got us a stay at the beachfront hideaway just two doors down from where "Mr. and Mrs. Sten Tillman" were booked for the weekend. We had placed a bug in the Tillman's room concealed in a floral arrangement. A five-dollar bill had a housekeeper do our work an hour before our laptop told us "Mr. and Mrs." had arrived in separate vehicles. Our partner Clancy, having lojacked both cars the past Saturday, made keeping track of the subjects easy up to that point.

Sleeping Beauty had awakened and joined me with the rest of the coffee. The view, the ocean breeze, and each other's company combined to make the coffee better. I reached for Linda's hand when a scream shattered the moment.

"That can't be good," Linda said as I jumped to my feet.

More screams and louder. I ran inside, grabbed my automatic from the nightstand, and rushed out into the hall. A housekeeping cart was parked in the hallway two doors down. The maid was slumped against the wall next to the opened door sobbing hysterically. Other guests were stepping into the hallway from their rooms.

A "He's got a gun!" had them retreating.

I went past the cart to the open door and entered room 108. The room was laid out just like ours. I checked the bathroom, the first door on my right. It was empty, the shower curtain pulled back. I gave the shallow closet a glance; it contained only clothes. Five paces in, I saw what the maid had seen—bloody footprints tracked from the bed to the opened balcony. Sten Tillman lay face up on the floor by the bed, his unseeing eyes half opened, blood pooled about his head and upper torso. His throat had been slashed. A box cutter lay atop a bloodied pillow on that side of the bed. My client's wife was missing.

The bugged bouquet sat on the table by the opened balcony door. An empty wine bottle and two wineglasses stood next to the vase. I maneuvered around the bloody footprints and retrieved our bug from the flowers while eyeballing the balcony for any trace of the missing Mrs. Patek.

"F-fr-freeze!" said a shaky voice, almost pleading.

"I am an officer," I said, raising my hands weapon pointed up. "I am going to turn around." I faced a double-barreled shotgun in the hands of a hotel employee whose name tag read, "Asst. Mgr. Estevez." "Let me see your badge"

"Estevez, I'm wearing my pajamas. Stop pointing that thing at me. Have you made the 911 call?"

"Si, policia. They are coming."

"Okay. We are going back into the hallway without touching anything in this room. You take your housekeeper to your office and keep her there until the police arrive, comprende?" I said, slowly backing him out the door while gently pushing the business end of his shotgun toward the floor. "I'm going to my room to put on some clothes." I closed the door to 108 behind us. "Nobody checks out until after the police arrive," I said to the back of his head as he led the maid away. *What the hell is Estevez doing with a shotgun?*

Linda was standing outside our room waiting for an explanation. Once in our room, I handed her the bug and told her Tillman was dead and Mrs. Patek was gone, sparing her the gory details of what I'd seen in 108. We dressed, packed our gear, and gave our room the once-over to be sure nothing would be left behind. The inevitable pounding on our door announced the law's arrival.

"Police! Come out with your hands up."

I removed my retired police ID and HR 218 concealed weapon permit from my wallet and slid them under the door. I whispered to Linda to lock the door behind me.

"I'm coming out unarmed," I announced and stepped out. The door closed behind me, and I was soon facedown on the hall carpet. The weight of a 190-pound deputy was focused on the middle of my back, and handcuffs were tightly applied. I was frisked for weapons and roughly hoisted to my feet. I remained cuffed to await the detectives' arrival from their respective homes, it being a Saturday, their normal day off. We filled the time by me telling the deputies of my observations and that they might want to secure the balcony and surrounding grounds on the ocean side. To their credit, they requested another unit to assist in securing the scene. A sergeant and lieutenant arrived, and I repeated what I had already told the deputies. The lieutenant dispatched one of the deputies to search the grounds below the balcony as if he had thought of it.

Finally, the arrival of the homicide detectives required yet a third telling. About then, the other deputy reported the discovery of a female body on the rocks below the balcony of 108. I assumed my client's wife was no longer missing.

The assembled posse conferred with the lieutenant and concluded that I probably hadn't cut the victim's throat with my Walther. My ID recorded, I was freed of the cuffs, dusted off, and kicked loose. I retrieved Linda and our bags and was heading down the hall when a Detective Zimmerman shouted, "Hey Michaels, hold on a minute. Who's that with you?"

"My secretary," I replied, causing Linda to redden and tighten her jaw, obviously pissed about the "my secretary" reference. *Oops!*

He took her name and a quick statement. Linda told him we'd been having coffee on our balcony when we'd heard the scream. I went to the hallway to check it out. Satisfied, the detective gave me a knowing wink and said we were free to go. We went to the front desk to check out, but the long line of guests wanting to leave meant our client was stuck for the full three days. More brass and the press showed up as we got into our car for the drive home. I wondered if the investigators would find the tracking devices Clancy had installed on each victim's car.

I phoned my client's home. No one answered, so I tried his cell and got his voice mail.

"Mr. Patek, Rollo Michaels here. Call me. Very important." I couldn't bring myself to say, "Your wife and partner are both dead."

After a three-hour drive back down the coast interrupted by a very late breakfast stop in Morro Bay, I dropped Linda off at her apartment in Santa Monica. We had hoped to enjoy the amenities and surrounding environs while monitoring the subjects, but murder has a way of screwing things up.

I took Pico Boulevard back to the Wilshire district and was surprised to find Clancy at Michaels & Associates. He was also surprised to see me.

"What are you doing here? Aren't you supposed to be in San Simeon?" he asked.

"Tillman and Patek's wife are both dead."

That got the conversation rolling. I didn't have the heart to remind him every domestic case is fraught with shit; that's why we didn't take them. I took a time-out to try the client's cell and home numbers again. Still no response. I left another "Call me" on his cell. His house phone rang nine times before I gave up. I was starting to get real worried.

"Isn't he going over the books with a bunch of accountants today?" was Clancy questioning where my head was at.

"Damn. I completely forgot. Thanks, pard." I called Patek's office at Sten-Tek, a dot.com selling electronics equipment, parts, and accessories to over a million online customers. The company was getting ready to go public. It was like the old

Radio Shack without the stores. It was after four in the afternoon.

"Sten-Tek Systems, how may I direct your call?" the receptionist asked, sounding bored and ready to go home.

"This is Roland Michaels. I need to speak to Philippe Patek. This is an emergency."

"He's in a meeting right now. May I have him call you when he gets out?" she said, sounding annoyed by my intrusion.

"What part of emergency don't you understand? Get him now!"

Two minutes later, Patek was on the line.

"Michaels, what the hell's the big deal? You have our receptionist in a panic," Patek complained.

"Your wife and partner have been murdered," I said. Nothing but silence. And I waited. Finally, I shouted, "Mr. Patek?" And the line went dead.

"What did he say?" Clancy asked.

"Nothing. Not a word. I expected questions. I guess the homicide team hasn't reached out to him yet either. Maybe they don't know where he is. Of course, if he did it, he wouldn't have questions."

"He would be suspect number one in anybody's playbook. I'd have him in the box right now" was Clancy's take.

"I think they're looking at it as a murder-suicide. She cuts Tillman's throat and dives off the balcony," I said. "But the box cutter? Doesn't seem right."

"Hey, she could be some kind of crazy bitch. Patek told me he was scared of her, says he sleeps in a separate bedroom with the door locked. Shit, Rollo, I'm sorry about this. It looked like a good payday for us."

"And I thought Linda and I were going to have a nice weekend in San Simeon. You know we got back together again, right?"

"No, but glad to hear it. Sylvia said it was only a matter of time. Speaking of Sylvia and time, I gotta get going. I'm taking her to one of your favorite spots for dinner, Paradise Cove, and I gots to be goin'," he said with a smile.

"How's she holding up?"

"I think she's scared shitless, but she won't show it. She's my rock, ya know?"

"That's our Sylvia, pard, but now it's your turn. Give her my love, and tell her I said to stay strong."

Left alone on a Saturday night usually led me to feeling sorry for myself and calling on my friend, Jack Daniels. Instead, I called Linda.

"You want to hang out?" I asked.

"Ruth and I are going to Harvelle's Blues Club on Fourth Street tonight, drink some alcohol for medicinal purposes. We could all meet there if you want to hook up."

"I'd be the meat in that sandwich?"

"No, but you could pick up the tab while you fantasize."

"What time?"

We met in the line that wouldn't start moving until reserved seating had been filled. We got in a little past eight thirty. Since the girls walked from their apartment building, I was elected the designated driver, leaving Linda and Ruth to enforce a one-drink-per-hour limit on my Jack

Daniels. Halfway into my first drink, my dates were ordering their second round of girly drinks. Afraid the pineapple and orange slices would limit the alcohol's effects, I told our waitress to bring two additional shooters of 151 for my dates and one of the Jack for me.

"Linda tells me you really know how to show a girl a good time," Ruth said, probably spurred on by the somber mood Linda and I were in. *I'll play*.

"I had to make two trips to the car around midnight, first for my handcuffs and the second for the leather lingerie I had bought her for my birthday," I said.

"You bought Linda leather lingerie for *your* birthday?"

"Well, duh."

"He did a nice job matching the color with my whip" was Linda's contribution to avoid going to where Ruth's question could have taken us.

We downed our shots in unison, toasting all the good that leather lingerie had done for the world. The couple at the next table added a hearty "Hear, hear!" and the party was on.

I danced with both women, causing a number of brave souls to assume I had my hands full and volunteer to help a guy out. This was great for the ladies' egos but not for mine. The music was a good mix of bluesy rock and occasional jazz numbers on request. But by eleven, Ruth and Linda were a little drunk and I was getting sleepy. Then the unexpected happened.

"We can't leave yet," Ruth announced, getting to her feet. She boldly walked up to the band's front man, and after a brief exchange, she was led onstage. A chair was quickly provided center stage as Ruth conferred with the piano player and drummer as if she knew what she was doing.

"What *is* she doing?" I asked Linda.

"You'll see."

The guitar player handed Ruth his acoustic eight-string as the front man adjusted the mic and announced, "Ladies and gentlemen, Miss Ruth Girardi."

The house lights dimmed. A baby spot focused on her to a smattering of applause, and she began, "Them that's got shall have, them that's not shall lose, so the Bible says, and it still is news, Mama may have, Papa may have, but God bless the child that got his own, that got his own," Ruth sang. The base kicked in, the drummer brushed the skin on his snare, and the piano player lightly touched some keys. We were all treated to a soulful rendition of the Billie Holiday classic. Ruth left them wanting more.

"Who knew?" I asked.

"Goes to show you," Linda said.

"Show what?"

"Rollo Michaels doesn't know everything."

"I never said that."

"But you sure act like it a lot of the time."

Chapter 46

Marvelous Marvin

By Monday morning's associates' meeting, the news about a murder-suicide at a San Simeon motel had had a weekend to smolder. A prominent businessman had been found brutally murdered in his room. The wife of his business partner was found on the rocks below the cliffside motel. This is the type of story that the media love to lead with. I filled the crew in with the facts behind the headlines and the nature of our involvement in the case. The detectives had Linda and I down as witnesses but didn't know of our true purpose for being at the motel.

Press speculation went for the obvious, but Detective Zimmerman and his partner followed facts. They drove to Beverly Hills Saturday evening intending to interview our client, Philippe Patek, the first twenty-four hours being critical to most homicide investigations, but the Southland's biggest legal shark, "Marvelous" Marvin Crippen,

Defender of Hollywood's elite, was already on the case and put a stop to that.

Starting with Saturday's news at eleven, Crippen could be seen on all the TV channels telling every one of his client's "shock" and "grief" and his desire to help the San Luis Obispo sheriff's office get to the bottom of the San Simeon "tragedy," saving "double murder" and "murder-suicide" for talking heads and headline writers.

"Marvin Crippen on line one," Linda announced over the intercom.

"Mr. Crippen," I said, "how may I help you?"

"Please call me Marvin. May I call you Rollo?"

"That would be marvelous, Marvin," I said, wondering if he appreciated my wit.

"Our client would like a meeting this afternoon. You in?" Right to the point.

"You still billing five hundred an hour?"

"Seven fifty on this one." He laughed.

"Tell him I'll be there but my price has gone up."

"Be at his house at two. Gate guard will have your name. See you there." The line went dead before I could hit him with another witticism.

I spent the next two hours explaining the Cochran/Deadwood case to my partner and legal adviser, Art. We decided to circle the wagons against what I believed was coming. That meant Art would need a little history of our firm's involvement with Vincenzo Big Vinnie Costello.

"You're saying your father was a member of organized crime?" Art asked, locking eyes for effect.

"He was a complicated man."

"And we've done work on behalf of mobsters?"

"They like to think of themselves as businessmen who employ extraordinary means to accomplish their goals."

"How many cases have we handled for these extraordinary businessmen?"

"Directly? One. Indirectly, maybe six."

That put furrows in the creases in Art's brow.

"And what is *indirectly* supposed to mean?"

The pitch of Art's voice rising with each question caused Linda to come into my office to see if we needed a referee.

"Referrals. The ones who paid by check are in the files. Cash went into our slush fund, no case file."

"We have a slush fund?"

"Time for you to go meet with Marvelous Marvin and our mutual client," Linda said, ending the inquisition. "I'll explain the fund to Art."

No wonder I love her. I love her?

Half an acre of Beverly Hills had been sacrificed to the Patek's driveway and parking area. A Corniche and two Mercedes were snuggled up in the shade of the portico. A uniformed chauffeur sat in the Rolls with a Bluetooth stuck in his ear. He was also Marvin's personal protection, an ex-cop I knew from another life. His nod as I drove past said he remembered me too. I parked my Lincoln next to another proud American, a GMC SUV also unafraid of the California sun. Marvin met me at the door.

"Rollo, I've heard nothing but good things about you."

He was probably lying. He offered his hand with a practiced smile.

"You're not struggling in anonymity yourself, counselor," I replied, putting the squeeze on the limp fish he'd handed me. "So why am I really here?"

I didn't let go until he squeezed back a little.

"Our client needs all the help we can give him. Mr. Patek refuses to believe his wife was a murderer and is in shock over her loss."

"Save that for the press. San Luis Obispo homicide dicks are working their butts off to put a case on him as we speak. I don't think they're buying the murder-suicide theory."

"We need you to stay on this case until the killer or killers are caught," he said, leading me into the kitchen of the Patek mansion. Our client was seated on a stool at the kitchen bar, a tall glass of ice and a half-empty bottle of eighteen-year-old Laphroaig within his reach. A suit was stationed by the kitchen door that led to a rear deck. Another suit appeared to be in charge of the deck and surrounding environs. A third suit came up behind me and placed a hand on my shoulder, tightening his grip as Crippen announced, "But first, we'll need some answers to a few ques—"

"Hold that son of a bitch so I can slap him," Patek barked.

I grabbed the hand on my shoulder and hip-rolled him into the suit rushing me from his post by the door. I drew my Walther and stuck it in Crippen's face, watching him go pale. "First one's for you, Marv."

The outside guy was looking in, grinning at the clowns as they untangled from the floor.

"They're his security, not mine," Crippen squealed. "Tell your people to stand down," he shouted to Patek. He did. They did. "I'm sorry, Rollo. Please. This was none of my doing. He's had too much to drink."

"I'm not d-d-drunk," Patek stuttered, his speech thick with booze. Rising from his stool, he slipped to the floor. "You ... you were supposed to protect her, my wife ... you're fired! Fired!" he said, his unsteady finger pointing at me for emphasis.

"And you're drunk on your ass," I said and headed for the door as the two wrinkled suits helped their boss to his feet. Crippen followed me outside.

"Can we meet at my office sometime later today?" he asked.

"You're kidding, right? What the hell was that in there, anyhow?" I asked, mustering up my best look of incredulity.

"Hey, the guy is out of his mind with shock and booze. I have no idea what he told those rent-a-cops. His man Rasheed hired them. Listen, Rollo, cut him some slack. We really need to talk."

"I'll be in my office till five, counselor. I'll make some time for you there. He's trying to lay this off on me. I think your client has all the motive and wherewithal to have done this, and it won't be long before the homicide detectives you're keeping from interviewing your client come knocking again."

"I'll need all you have on this case. Expect to hear from me," he said. "That's the first time I've had a gun stuck in my face. You wouldn't really have shot me, would you?"

"Depends on how scared I was."

"You didn't look scared to me, Michaels."

"Was that your two-hundred-dollar single malt being wasted in there?"

"No, that was our client's. You a scotch enthusiast?"

"Not the pretentious kind, in case you were thinking of a Christmas gift for me."

That made Crippen shake his head and go back into the Patek home.

I waved a goodbye to his driver and drove through the community guard station just as Detective Zimmerman and his partner were driving in. What I read on his lips did not bode well for me. The posse behind them included more deputies and a sheriff's CSI van. Curiosity got the better of me. I did a U-turn and went back in.

People lie. Some lie even when the truth would better serve them. Anyone tells you they don't lie is lying, which proves the point. Facts don't lie, but they're not as simple as plain black and white. They're subject to nuance, ambiguity, and interpretation. Lies are often easier to believe. Good lies are complicated, coming in all sorts of colors. Good liars use the whole palette to paint their pictures of deceit. The best liars dab on whiter shades of pale, using razzle-dazzle to further obscure the facts. Sifting through the bullshit is the investigator's main chore.

Patek found out there was a price to pay for lying to the man. The homicide dicks had shot all kinds of holes in his alibi in less than a day. This provided all the probable cause Judge "Hanging Harry" Reed needed to issue search warrants for just about anything Philippe Patek.

Rightly or wrongly, judges, especially those in the criminal justice system, earn their sobriquets in the courthouse. Prosecutors, police personnel, and defense attorneys soon learn which way a judge leans, so most jurists are tagged, and many of them are proud of their monikers.

"Got it!" Zimmerman shouted, holding up a blood-stained glove retrieved from the trunk of one of the Mercedes. Then CSI techs found trace evidence on the driver's seat and steering wheel when spraying luminal. Philippe Patek was arrested; he'd be transported to San Luis Obispo and be booked that evening for double homicide. His attorney wouldn't be visiting my humble office at Michaels & Associates. It was time to leave Patek's mansion before Zimmerman found time to get around to me.

Back at my office, Ruth informed me Clancy had phoned in a progress report on his wife's surgery. The surgeon said he was confident he had removed all the cancerous cells and had done all they could to minimize muscle damage. They also took some lymph nodes for testing. The results would determine if chemo and radiation might be needed.

Sylvia was in no shape for visitors, but Linda and Ruth were going to Cedars after work to check on Clancy and give him some moral support. I sent word with the ladies, and Art sent flowers. We all knew life could be inexplicably cruel, all of us having seen examples of that while doing what we do. But when it hit that close to home, our vulnerabilities were glaringly exposed. We all prayed for the best for Sylvia and Clancy. What else could we really do?

My cell rang. Caller ID said it was my son.

"Hey Brando, how ya doin'?"

"It's me. Where's my check?" my ex Marie barked.

I looked at my desk calendar. May 1, 2017. *Oh shit.*

"Hello? You there?"

"Yes, Marie. I'll drop it off this evening."

"Listen, your son needs some money for his class trip to Sacramento. They leave next Monday, and Mother's Day is the weekend after that. So forget about taking the kids that weekend. We'll be taking my mother to dinner."

"Will the kids be there when I drop off the check? Maybe take them for pizza or something? You could come with us to Pizza Hut maybe. Say around six?"

"Better make it seven. Brandon has baseball practice."

"See everybody then," I said, ending the call and not letting her have the last word. *These kinds of games helped end our marriage.*

Chapter 47

Equal Justice

During Phillipe Patek's bail hearing the following day, the Honorable "Don't Let 'Em Out" Stout refused to set bail even at $5 million hoping to impress the governor, who had a state Supreme Court vacancy to fill. Since bail was refused, the defense reciprocated by refusing to waive time, forcing the judge to set the preliminary hearing for the following Monday. This put added pressure on the prosecution and Lead Detective Peter Zimmerman, a twenty-three-year veteran of the force.

Marvelous Marv continued his client's "innocence campaign" with a not-so-impromptu press conference on the San Luis Obispo courthouse steps after the bail hearing. He cited the constitution, the right to reasonable bail, dropped the $5 million figure on the press, then rode off in his chauffeured Rolls, the California vanity plate on the rear reading "MARVLUS" telling all the world to kiss it.

The wheels of justice can be made to move quickly depending on who's pushing. Judge Stout obviously didn't know the governor was a friend of Marvin Crippen and an acquaintance of Phillipe Patek. That very afternoon, the defense waived time and another judge reaffirmed the bail at $5 million as had been suggested by Crippen earlier in the day. And "Don't Let 'Em Out" Stout's Supreme Court fantasy was vanquished.

Patek put his house up for collateral along with a million of his own cash, had an ankle bracelet locked on over his cashmere sock, and quietly bailed. He was home for supper, once again proving the inequality of the law. *Can he handle the 24-7 media stationed at his gate or will Rasheed try to scare them away?*

I didn't hear from Marvelous Marv again until Wednesday when he sent an associate counsel to see if I might have anything Patek's defense could use or more likely anything the prosecution could use. I should have been insulted that he hadn't come himself, but Miss Alicia Carter was not hard on the eyes, a fact I'm sure Marv had thoroughly considered. Every year, he hired a beautiful young lawyer right out of law school. Rumor had it these young ladies, known as the Marvelettes, were hired to *let* Marv. I was pretty sure he was too smart for that. She handed me her card and got right to it.

"Have you completed a final report for your work on behalf of Philippe Patek?"

"No. He fired me. I'm done with him. Coffee?" I asked, filling my cup.

"No thanks. Have you any work product, photographs, surveillance logs, recordings, or anything covering the time you were retained by Mr. Patek?"

"Patek paid a twenty-five hundred retainer that was all used up two days before the murders. I couldn't possibly round up all these materials until Patek squares up his account, about thirty-five hundred more."

"You and your secretary were interviewed at the scene. Have the detectives followed up with you since?" she asked, scribbling notes in her leather-bound folio.

"No, but I'm sure they'll get around to us soon."

"Marvin says you utilize the services of an electronic surveillance expert by the name of Peter Gunn. Did you bug—"

"I won't be going into details about how I do what I do, counselor. Your question surprises me, and I find your officious manner offensive. Is Marvin billing Patek seven-fifty for your time too?"

She reddened and blinked and I think bit on her lip to regain her composure.

"I'm sorry, Mr. Michaels. I don't mean to be."

"This is not an adversarial situation. I prefer to be called Rollo, Miss Carter. You came to my office to elicit my cooperation and start out by refusing my hospitality."

"I don't drink coffee."

"Perhaps some Evian or Pellegrino then?"

"The water would be fine, Rollo. Please call me Alicia. Again, I'm sorry for getting off on the wrong foot here," she said as I placed a cocktail napkin on my desk with a bottle of Evian I fetched from the credenza's mini fridge.

She unscrewed the top and offered a toast. "To new beginnings. Mr. Crippen suggests we hire you, catch up on Mr. Patek's bill, and make you our lead investigator for the duration. Would such an arrangement interest you?"

"Are you aware that Patek had his security people attack me yesterday?" I was curious to see if Marvin had sent the kid out blind. Her surprised expression said he had.

"Really? I had no idea. Mr. Crippen told me our client fired you because you failed to protect his wife," she said, probably in the dark about most of the case. "Were you injured?"

"No. Neither was your boss." That only further confused her, so I let up. "I'll give his offer some serious thought. Have Marvin call me tomorrow for an answer," I said, walking her to the door. Watching her walk to the elevators with the bottle of Evian clutched in her hand, I could see Marvin had an eye for the legal talent he hired to carry his water. I could also feel Linda glaring a hole in my back.

Marvin actually called a little later that afternoon and asked to meet at Patek's that evening. The promise of a Patek check got me to agree, at least to talk over Crippen's offer. But I was sure all he really wanted was what I knew; his in-house investigative team consisted of highly capable people.

I was listening to the recording from the bug in 108. Five minutes after checking into their room, Sten Tillman popped the champagne cork and Felicia Patek proposed a toast to the pending service of divorce papers on their spouses. They commented on the romantic view of the Pacific Ocean the balcony afforded and then went at it. Showers were followed by conversation about the California's dinner menu.

The recording program we were using was sound activated, and each activation was date and time stamped. About two hours in, Tillman received a call on his cell.

"What now?" Mrs. Patek asked.

"It's Laura, I've got to take this," Tillman said. "Hi, honey. How are things in Mexico?"

I heard a door close, probably the bathroom for privacy. Four minutes of silence ended with a door opening.

"Ready for some dinner?" Tillman asked.

"What did she want?"

"Just checking in is all. She said she'll be back on Wednesday."

They left the room.

Linda interrupted to remind me that the Sten Tillman funeral was set for two thirty at Forest Lawn Cemetery in Burbank. I needed to go. Felicia Martin Patek's obit in the *Los Angeles Times* said her funeral would be a private affair, omitting any other details.

"You get a chance, have Ruth transcribe this," I said, referring to the computer recording from our bug.

"You really want another person involved with this? I don't think that's a good idea, Rollo."

"You're right. You'll have to do it."

I went to my apartment, put on the black suit, and got to the graveside ceremony at three o'clock. The widow, Laura Tillman, had cut her vacation short and had returned Sunday. She and her two adult sons bravely sat through the proceedings.

About fifty mourners stood silently as a priest said a few words. Philippe Patek was not in attendance, but Detective Zimmerman was. His partner was in the parking lot taking down license plate numbers. I also spotted Alicia Carter in the crowd and walked over to her.

"You following me?" she asked softly.

"I was going to ask you the same. You know the deceased?"

"Stop following me," she said with a smile and walked away to join the line to console the widow, heads turning as she walked by.

I was heading to my car when I was braced by the two detectives.

"Long way from San Luis Obispo," I said.

"We need to talk," Zimmerman replied.

"There's a Starbucks a couple blocks from here. Follow me over."

I picked up the tab for Zimmerman's tea, his partner's water, and a double-shot espresso dropped into a grande mocha latte for me. We took an outside table, letting the freeway traffic noise keep our conversation private.

"Okay, Michaels, we don't like being sandbagged, so let's hear it or we're going after you for obstruction," the partner said. My buying the tea and bottled water wasn't getting me any slack.

I laid it out for them, telling everything except bugging the murder scene, because you never want to cop to a felony. I also spotted attorney Alicia Carter getting something other than coffee at the Starbucks counter.

Zimmerman proceeded to tell me they had big problems with the case. Forensics matched all the blood from the Mercedes to Mrs. Patek. So now they had nothing tying Mr. Patek to the murders, other than opportunity and possible motive. That she had apparently died from a broken neck and her lacerations were attributed to a hard landing on the rocks below the balcony better fit the murder-suicide theory. But her prints weren't on the box cutter and the Tillman blood was only on her feet. If she was going to kill her lover and then herself, why wipe the prints and wash her hands?

Because time had been waived at the second bail hearing, the district attorney gave the detectives three weeks to make a case or drop all charges. That they didn't have a case was the problem. "So now we're back at the beginning with you our only live lead. Who do you think killed our victims?" Zimmerman asked.

"Philippe Patek. The guy's wound up tighter than a two-dollar watch." That went right over their heads. "Jealousy, greed, revenge. Pick a motive. And where was he?"

"He doesn't have an alibi, but no one shows up on Motel California security cameras that we haven't identified. We did find a shoeprint on the ledge of the balcony that doesn't belong to either victim. What size shoes do you wear?" his partner asked.

"Elevens. I wasn't on their balcony."

Whether hoping for someone to share their burden or just to get even, the detectives sandbagged me. "We need to talk to your girlfriend," the partner said.

"Why is that?" I asked, sensing something was up. "You think she did it? Maybe I can help. She has an alibi." *He knows I'm holding something back.*

"Flowers," Zimmerman said.

"Flowers?"

"How did Linda's prints get in the room, on the vase, slick?" the partner sniped.

Ouch!

"We talked the maid into putting the flowers in their room before they arrived so we would know what room they were in," I said, directing my answer to Zimmerman, his partner's tone pissing me off. "Linda was never in the room. If I'd thought there was going to be a murder, I would have been slicker."

"Actually, the only prints we found on the vase were the maid's." Bozo kept firing. "You know, partner, this isn't so tough." He was on a roll.

"Did you tell your client where his wife and partner were staying?" Zimmerman asked.

"Patek told me Tillman booked a three-night stay at the California the day before but didn't have a room number. I confirmed their arrival and room number with Mr. Patek shortly after they checked in."

I realized security cameras would have recorded Linda carrying the bouquet.

"Why don't you take a ride with us to your office so we can verify this with your secretary Linda," Zimmerman said.

Realizing they wanted to play her against me, I took out my cell. "I don't think so, but I'll tell her you'd like to speak with her."

"We have to insist," the partner said, jumping to his feet and grabbing my hand holding the phone.

Aikido teaches us to redirect an aggressor's force against him. I turned in my seat with him holding on. The table went over, him with it, spilling my latte on Zimmerman's lap. Just when testosterone was about to overcome reason, Alicia Carter intervened.

"Stop!" Carter shouted.

By identifying herself as my lawyer, handing out business cards, and demanding badge numbers,

Carter defused the situation. When Burbank PD showed up, I empathized with Zimmerman having to stand there looking like he'd pissed his pants. Thankfully, reason prevailed. Starbucks management was mollified by us all just leaving. The detectives' interview of Linda would have to wait until the next day since one of them needed to change his pants. Carter and I went to our cars.

"So it's *you* who's following *me*," I said to Carter. "Something on your mind?"

"Dinner?" She smiled. "I recognized the detectives, and when they caught up with you in the parking lot, I got curious."

"Your boss must really want to see me tonight, no?"

"Yes, he does, and he usually gets what he wants."

"Buy you a drink?"

That got us two stools at the nearly empty bar of the Beverly Hilton, about fifteen minutes from our six-thirty rendezvous with Philippe and Marvelous Marv. I wondered how far she would go to be sure I made the meeting. The barkeep delivered her French white and my Jack rocks and asked if he should charge it to our room. She looked at me inquisitively as I smiled, dropping a twenty on the mahogany, and told him to keep the two-dollar change. It was still happy hour.

"Hope you're not thirsty," I said.

"I can expense account this if you'd like."

"Maybe next time," I said with a smile.

"Next time?"

We continued to fence a bit—thrust, parry, a double entendre now and then as I maneuvered for a corps-a-corps. She feigned an interest in what I did, attempting an ego massage. She let me know she was unattached, had an apartment in Playa del Rey she shared with her cat. Like any good attorney, she asked questions she already knew the answers to. She had obviously either googled me or was privy to the workup Crippen's investigators had probably done. She seemed disappointed when I declined another drink by pointing at my watch to remind her Marvin was waiting.

I was a little wary returning to the scene of my attempted mugging, so I held my Walther in my pants pocket as Alicia and I entered the Patek manse. Marvin and his lead investigator were waiting for us in the study, enjoying libations. Patek and his security people were nowhere to be seen.

"Alicia tells me you had a little run-in with San Luis Obispo homicide detectives," Marvin said. "Drink?"

"No thanks," I said. "They told me their case was going sideways and wanted my opinion on who did the deed."

"And you said ...?"

"Your client of course."

With that, Philippe Patek rushed into the room.

"Judas bastard!" he said, spittle flying rushing toward me until Marvin's investigator saved him from further humiliation and led him out of the room.

"Take this check for five thousand. It should cover what my client owes you. I'll need you to get together with Alicia and complete your report on what you did on behalf of Mr. Patek." He handed me an envelope marked "Michaels." It contained more than a check. I put it in my pocket.

Linda tickled my fancy via my vibrating smartphone. "I have to take this." I stepped outside.

"Yes?"

"Where are you?" she asked.

"The hills of Beverly, wha'sup?"

"You have to hear the recording from room one-oh-eight. We got the whole thing. It's all on there, Rollo."

Chapter 48

Revelations

A sudden movement from my right caused me to flinch. It was one of Patek's security suits, the outside guy I hadn't tossed on my first visit. His smile said he found pleasure in surprising me.

"You not allowed in the house?" I cracked. His smile faded, a hard look taking its place. "Tell your boss I was unexpectedly called away." An added "Please" got him to nod.

Marvin's man was leaning against the Rolls taking in the refined air of Beverly Hills mixed with hits on a cigarette.

"How ya doin', Michaels," he said, punctuating that with a flick of ash.

"I'm good, Frank. Keeping Marvin out of trouble must be a full-time job, judging from the company he keeps."

"Pay's good, dog. He asked me what I knew 'bout ya. I said guys on the job figured you an arrogant SOB." He laughed.

"So that's why he wants to hire me. Who's the silent brother over there?"

"The others call him Rasheed. Don't say much to any of 'em. Sneaks around kind of scary like. I make him as an ex-con."

"Stay good, Frank" was my goodbye. The two security guys I had had the run-in with Saturday had been relegated to gate duty. They wanted to talk. I rolled down my window.

"We were just trying to do our job," the one I had flipped said.

"None of that's on you," I said. "It's on your boss."

"Well, I don't appreciate what you did. Next time you won't be so lucky."

"You're joking, right?" I said.

"Yeah, he is," his partner said, pressing the button to open the gate. "Good night, sir."

It was eight when I got back to Michaels & Associates. The door was locked, but the lights were on. I tapped out the code: *rat, tat-tat, rat, tat-tat-tat*, and Linda's silhouette appeared on the wire-reinforced, frosted security glass.

"Rollo?" she whispered through the door.

"The one and only." That got me in.

"The recording creeped me out, so I locked the place up. Wait till you hear this," she said. She was shaking. I took her in my arms, and we embraced for a long time until her shaking stopped.

"Any coffee?" I asked.

"I could use something stronger. There's a bottle of Crown Royal in Art's desk."

"I'm in."

I got two paper cups out of the credenza while Linda retrieved Art's booze. She poured us each a double and went to her desk. I pulled up a chair beside her. She arrowed the play icon. The voiceprint graphics came alive on the computer screen, the date/time read 04/30/17 0411. Linda said, "Listen."

I heard a toilet flush followed by the click of a light switch.

"Rasheed? Oh God! What ... What have you done? ... Oh God, Rasheed ... Oh God ... No! ... Please no! ... no."

A woman's voice and struggling sounds.

"Sorry, Mrs. Patek, boss says ..."

Male voice followed by a muffled scream and choking sounds. Linda moved the cursor to pause.

"Who the hell is Rasheed?" Linda asked.

"One of Patek's security people. I was talking to him twenty-five minutes ago."

"Was that his voice?"

"Don't know. I've never heard him speak."

"You just said you were talking with him."

"He didn't talk back."

"You have that effect on people."

"I don't think he thought I was worth the breath it would take to speak to me."

"What's our play, Rollo? We should call Detective Zimmerman and fill him in. I have his cell," she said, fishing out his card from her desk and picking up the phone.

"Whoa, girl, that could put us out of business and me in jail. Let's talk this over, figure out our options. You hungry?"

"How could you think of eating after hearing that?"

"Feed the body, nourish the soul? I think that's how that goes."

We walked to the Gen Hwa Korean BBQ and had the pul kogi with vegetables and sides of steamed rice and kimchi. We washed it down with cold Korean beer straight from the bottle. Linda picked at her food, but I scarfed the grilled beef and vegetables right off the little charcoal grill centered in our table. Listening to the murders of two people was never supposed to be part of Linda's job description. I could see she was really having a tough time dealing with it and chopsticks too.

"I don't think I can be alone tonight, Rollo. Can I stay at your place?"

"Of course, but I thought you have a roomie?"

"Remember I told you Ruth moved into her new apartment over the weekend? A little bachelorette in the same building as me. She has some furniture at her mom's in Phoenix we were supposed to pick up. We postponed until this weekend, rent a trailer, and bring it back. We'll need to cut out early this Friday afternoon."

I summoned our server, knocked some of the rust off my Korean language skills, and paid the check. We spent the night at my place watching old movies on AMC, munching popcorn, and sipping lemonade. We fell asleep a couple of hours before dawn.

I awoke at my usual circadian rhythmic seven in the morning with a plan I fleshed out in the shower. While I dressed for action, Linda phoned Ruth and had her open up shop while she went back to sleep. I fed the cat, cleaned out his litterbox, and threw him on the bed with Linda. With no protest from either, I quietly made it out the door.

I was never much good at putting my trust in others, preferring to trust my own instincts above all. At least, when things went bad, I'd have only myself to blame. However, Linda's advice had never gotten me in trouble in any of those rare instances I had chosen to take it. Her first instinct was to call Detective Zimmerman and tell him what we knew. I dialed Zimmerman's cell.

"What do you want?"

"Help you close the case. Did you pull my phone records yet?"

"No comment."

"I called Patek on his cell 1-818-555-1790 at 8:20 the night of the murders. Gave him the room number and told him his wife and his partner had checked in. You got that cell record?"

I got another "No comment."

"You do record checks on Patek's employees? One of them looks like an ex-con to me. Name's Rasheed. I'd check his cell records too."

"Why's that?"

"Patek paid him to do them both. Did the ME find any DNA on Patek's wife, say around her neck?"

"How'd you know she was strangled, Michaels?"

"Lucky guess?"

"You bugged the room, didn't you? We found the GPS devices you had on both victims' rides. I want the recordings you made or I'll make life hell for you, pull your ticket ... put you out of business ... you'll wind up a school crossing guard, I'll—"

"What? You forget about jail, Zimmerman? I solve your case for you and you're gonna abuse me like this? I can't believe it. I didn't figure you to be that kind of guy ... Maybe the bozo you work with who's made me the object of his erection ... but you?"

"I want the tapes, Michaels, or else." He was ignoring my rhetoric.

"There are no tapes, Zimmerman, but here's what I'm willing to do for a brother of the badge. I'll tell Patek I wired the room and Rasheed gave him up on the tape."

"No deals, Michaels. At the very least, you're guilty of obstruction. For all I know, you could be an accomplice to a double homicide. I don't know what kind of PD you were on, but the San Luis Obispo sheriff's department doesn't make deals with criminals."

"Are you that stupid, really?" I said and hung up. Boy was Linda wrong.

While contemplating my next move, I opened the envelope Marvelous Marvin Crippen had handed me last evening. A check for $5,000 drawn on an account marked "Patek Defense Fund" accompanied a contract with highlight marks for my signature, binding me to Crippen for the duration of the case. I didn't see any stipulation that I couldn't cash the check without signing the contract.

Linda showed up for work shortly after I failed to get on a first-name basis with Detective Zimmerman. She carried a box of doughnuts from the coffee shop downstairs, placed them on my credenza, and began to make coffee.

"Last time I take advice from you," I said, skipping hello or good morning.

"What are you talking about now?"

"Zimmerman. I laid the whole case out for him and all I got was threats. Jail, license, he'd probably throw in waterboarding if he wasn't such a nice guy. I think I lost him when I told him I'd solved his case for him. Made him feel inadequate pointing out his shortcomings ... It's a guy thing."

"Nice going, Rollo. Now what?"

"Plan B naturally."

"You and your plan Bs," she said, shaking her head. "I seem to remember—"

My raised hands stopped the rest of it as I handed her the check. "Take this check to Crippen's bank and cash it. Bring me the cash."

"Wow, five thou. What's he want?"

"My soul."

"Wait. It's made out to you. You have to do it. Why not just deposit it in our account?"

"It might not be good that long. I'll go with you."

Chapter 49

Plan B

It was a comfortable quarter to eleven Friday morning when I arrived at Michaels & Associates and was met by Linda, Art, and Ruth. When the girls had come in to open up in the morning, they found the two San Luis Obispo detectives waiting in the hallway anxious to interview Linda. Not just another pretty face, she told them she'd be glad to as soon as her attorney arrived. She had them wait in the conference room while Ruth offered the detectives coffee and doughnuts.

Our partner-attorney arrived, never late to court but always late for everything else. After Linda told him what was going on, she and Art joined the detectives. Once the preliminary questions were asked and answered, Zimmerman broached the subject of us bugging the Tillman room at the California. Art, no slouch when it came to criminal law, jumped right in to plead the fifth and effectively put an end to the interview.

Zimmerman had to calm his partner down when Linda raised the "altercation" they had had with "her boss" the previous day. As they left, Zimmerman requested they tell me he wished to talk with me.

After I was told all this, Art asked some clarification questions and did his lawyerly duty again, advising both of us not to cooperate with the detectives. He cited concealing-evidence and destroying-evidence statutes to drive his point home. This made implementing plan B an imperative.

"Ruth, will you get hold of Manny and tell him I need him in here as soon as possible?" I asked, glad to be going into action mode but not without a cup of coffee and a couple of maple glazed. "Hey, what happened to my doughnuts?"

"The detectives ate them," Ruth said, adding insult to injury.

I settled for a French vanilla cruller and opened the safe. I'd been carrying the fifty Benjamins since the previous day because they felt good. I put the banded stack of bills in and took out a throwaway phone. I plugged it into the charger and told Linda, "Tonight we make Rasheed and his boss famous."

We ate doughnuts and drank coffee until Manny the Nerd arrived. Linda left the two of us alone, not wishing to be part of a conspiracy. I handed him Linda's laptop and an Amazon tablet and told him what I needed. Nerd said he needed to get some equipment from home including an old MP3 auxiliary speaker and a mini video camera. He was back at a quarter after two to show me the steps needed to make the equipment do what I'd asked.

"Rollo, that's some heavy shit you have there. The San Simeon murders?"

"Forget you ever heard it."

"I doubt I'll live that long, boss."

He hooked Linda's laptop to the auxiliary speaker and said, "On my way home, I'm going to fill my script for medicinal weed and smoke the whole damn bag." Before he left to smoke his medicine, he installed the additional camera on our CCTV security system and showed me how to access it on my too-smart-for-me phone.

The burner phone was fully charged. I took it and the tablet, which at that point contained the incriminating horror copied from Linda's laptop for a ride to Mulholland Drive. A lot of what I did was await further developments. Being impatient, I sometimes gave people a nudge to get things rolling. My first call was to the guy who had gotten me caught up in this mess.

"Patek residence, this is Rosa. May I help you?"

"This is Detective Zimmerman. I must speak with Mr. Patek. There's been a new development in his wife's murder case." I was lying and oozing with urgency.

"Yes sir, right away. Please hold."

A minute and a few ticks passed.

"Yes, Detective?" Patek asked.

"Actually it's me, Michaels. Listen to this."

I played it for him. I waited for a reaction. A half-dozen heartbeats later, he screamed. I heard the phone hit the floor. I heard Rosa rush in.

"Mr. Patek, what is it?" she yelled.

"Get out!" he yelled and was back on the phone.

"What do you want, you bastard?"

"What everybody wants, Phillippe. Money."

"How much?"

"A hundred grand cash. I'll call you with instructions."

I called Zimmerman, whispered, "Listen," and played the twenty-nine-second recording that could put Patek and his hired killer in prison for the rest of their lives.

Zimmerman's first reaction was predictable: "Who is this? Michaels?"

That was my cue to hang up. He had the ball, and I hoped he would run with it. Caller ID said he tried calling back three times.

I called the office to be sure Linda and Ruth got a head start on their weekend trip to Phoenix no arguments. She feigned reluctance but said she and Ruth were headed out the door when I called. They planned to return Sunday. I'd see them Monday. I called Patek back to give him a prod, piss him off into action.

"Bring the money to my office tonight. I'll give you the recording for the cash," I said.

"Tonight? I need time to raise the cash."

"Banks close late on Fridays. Be at my office by seven or I turn the recording over to Detective Zimmerman."

I hit the off button, opened up the phone, removed the battery, and smashed the phone on the pavement. My personal cell rang as I drove west on Mulholland. I committed another crime by answering when I saw it was Detective Zimmerman.

"I didn't know if we were still speaking or not," I said.

"I know you called me with that recording, Michaels. I need it to convict Patek and his errand boy, Rasheed Dupree."

"You know, Detective, if I *did* have a tape that incriminated Patek and Dupree, I'd bc sclling it to them for a hundred grand at my office tonight around seven o'clock. A good detective would probably wait until about seven fifteen before barging in to make the arrests and recover the evidence. Know a good detective?"

"Don't do this, Rollo."

"Later, Zim."

By that time, I had assumed we were on a first-name basis.

I continued along the crest of the Santa Monica Mountains, got off Mulholland at Getty Drive, and went up to the Getty Museum. If I'd wanted to get in, I would've had to have bought my ticket weeks earlier. I pulled to the side of the road and looked back down the pass at the early afternoon traffic starting to build on the northbound 405 Freeway. Westwood and Century City stood out in the haze. Old-timers were telling us that forty years ago, the smog would have obstructed the view.

The coffee and maple glazed I'd had at the office weren't going to get me through until seven, so I headed out to Cantor's Deli on Fairfax for a sandwich. You could live for a couple of days on one of their pastrami on ryes with a kosher dill and potato salad side.

By six thirty, I was ready and parked on a side street a block past my office. I donned a Rasta wig, ball cap, shades, and a tattered navy peacoat with my Walther in the pocket. I had just passed my building entrance when I spotted Detective Zimmerman in front of the theater on the other side of La Brea. I determined the lobby to our building was clear. I went around the corner and entered through the coffee shop. I rode the elevator one floor past mine, took the stairs down one, and entered my office through the back hallway. Inside, I checked that Linda had turned on our security system then made a pot of coffee.

I brought up the quad view on my computer to see the newly added hall, stairwell, outer office, and restroom cameras. According to Manny the Nerd, we were recording both audio and video. I then went to the safe and swapped my Walther for a .357 Magnum revolver and unlocked the door. Michaels & Associates was open and ready for business.

I was on my second cup when our security cameras picked up Rasheed Dupree as he exited the elevator, a jacket draped on his arm concealing his right hand. No Philippe Patek. The time on the computer screen said 7:03. He looked up and down the hallway and entered the restroom. I flipped the channel on the screen as he stuck his head out the door for another hall check. Back inside, he looked in the two stalls. Satisfied he was alone, he placed the Glock 10 his jacket concealed on the counter next to the sink. He splashed water on his face and dried himself with paper towels. He snorted two spoons of blow and broke a vial of amyl nitrate as a chaser. He picked up his Glock, screwed on a silencer, and said to the mirror, "Let's get ready to rumble."

Is Zimmerman going to make it to the show?

Chapter 50

And Beyond

A slight breeze was forming kaleidoscopic patterns on the water's surface as a mother goose guided her brood around the cypress sentries standing guard knee-deep in the lake. The sun kept peeking from behind cotton-ball clouds to be sure all was well. The breeze was but a fleeting thing, and soon, the water turned to glass, mirroring the beauty of the surrounding shore. Songbirds sang and doves cooed.

We were perched on a bench at the base of a wood trestle footbridge that led to the lake's small island. We took it all in as if a Monet has come to life there at southern Alabama's Lucky Lake Resort. We had arrived but an hour earlier after a two-thousand-mile drive that took most of three days for Linda to make. I had no idea she was capable of going on the lam in stealth mode—no traceable phones, credit cards, or vehicle having had Ruth rent us a car using her Arizona driver's license.

I was there to let my body heal from two broken ribs and a lacerated liver. Near-death experiences often lead to somber reflection. Maybe I could also find time to exorcise the demons haunting my psyche. I was sure my psychiatrist would want me to have dealt with the hubris that had gotten me shot. The generosity of a friend had provided this beautiful venue for me to do it.

This was also the perfect place to temporarily hide out while the FBI and the homicide units of three separate jurisdictions figured out why five people I'd recently come in contact with had died violent deaths. Well, maybe the FBI was after a little more, and even I was smart enough to know they weren't going to quit looking.

The past Monday morning, Marie and the kids had showed up at the hospital with flowers and a box of chocolates from See's. I wanted to save some for Linda but couldn't help myself. While I did my best to reassure Brandon and Melissa I was fine and expected to be out in a day or so, two FBI agents showed up at Michaels & Associates to interview me regarding the Cochran case.

When told by Art that I wasn't available, they got pissed off. Art informed them that he was corporate counsel and would be glad to assist. They requested to see our phone records and all work product relating to the Cochran case.

Art told them he would be happy to do that once served with a valid search warrant and/or subpoena. When he added he'd also need a waiver signed by any client involved releasing us from the confidentiality clause of our contract, the agents just got further pissed. They left with a promise to up the ante. It would be only a matter of time before they came to the hospital and threatened to confiscate my lime Jell-O to make me talk. But before that could happen, Linda took charge.

That afternoon, I left the hospital against doctor's orders. Linda took five grand in cash and a burner phone from my safe, and we began our "Escape from Los Angeles." She drove us to Lucky Lake so she could help me sort it all out without further help from well-meaning associates or the organized harassment of thc FBI.

As I recalled the events of six days earlier, Rasheed Dupree came out of the restroom, looked up and down the hall once more, then headed straight to the entrance of Michaels & Associates. He had again placed his jacket over the hand that held his silenced Glock. He entered the outer office without knocking and cautiously looked around. I pressed the play button on Linda's laptop and the remote speakers blared away.

"Rasheed? Oh God! What ... What have you done? ... Oh God, Rasheed ... Oh God ... No! ... Please no! ... no."

A woman's voice and struggling sounds.

"Sorry, Mrs. Patek, boss says ..."

Male voice followed by a muffled scream and choking sounds.

"Michaels?" he called out over the recorded last sounds Felicia Martin Patek ever made.

"Back here," I said, closing the laptop, the recording automatically erasing per Nerd's program. Dupree peeked around the doorjamb and entered my office. I feigned nonchalance, confident the .357 Magnum in my right hand was up to the challenge.

"Where's your boss?" seemed appropriate.

"He didn't have the balls, so he sent me to negotiate. Where's the recording?"

"You bring my money?" I said, patting the laptop with my left hand.

"I brought this instead," he said, swinging his jacketed arm in my direction and squeezing off two as I dove to my left, returning fire with my .357 through the kneehole of my metal desk, my ears ringing with the explosion of my magnum rounds. Or was it the banging of my head on the credenza as I sought cover?

I should have spent more on my Kevlar vest, but I thought the complete wraparound body armor made me look fat. A 10 mm round from his Glock had gone through the metal desktop and a drawer to find an opening between the breast plate and back plate of my vest, breaking two ribs before screwing up the leather on my chair. The walls were spinning. *More shots?* I passed out.

I came to on a gurney as it was being loaded into an ambulance. An LAPD newbie was assigned to ride with me to the hospital. My left hand being handcuffed to the rail of the gurney seemed very unnecessary.

"What's goin' on?" I asked, shaking the cuffs.

"You've been shot," the officer said with serious concern on a face better suited for a smile.

"I get that part. Why the cuffs?"

"They're for your own protection, sir." She was mouthing the company line and hinting at a smile.

"From what?" I asked. That got the medic to jab an IV into my right arm and give me something to keep me calm. Whatever was in the drip, it sure made the siren and yelping horn all I could remember of the rest of our ride to the hospital. Any other comments made by any of us would forever remain beyond my ability to recall.

If you're going to be shot, you couldn't be in a better place than Los Angeles. The ER team at LA County Hospital is one of the best anywhere this side of Afghanistan. They got this good because of practice, practice, and more practice, thanks to a never-ending supply of gunshot victims from South Central and the barrios of East LA. They also have a lockup ward there, and that's where I thought I was going. Whatever was in the IV made a five-minute run seem more like an hour.

They took me to Cedars, policy dictating I go to the closer ER. Because of Cedars' proximity to the rich and famous in Beverly Hills and Hollywood, some of the best doctors in the world worked there. It was going to cost our insurance a lot more, but I was in good hands.

I awoke in a recovery room with my arm still hooked up to happy juice but the handcuffs forgotten. Linda sat by the side of my bed while an LAPD homicide guy I knew from the old days stood at the foot. Detective Zimmerman stood by the door looking somber. *Am I dying?*

"What time is it?" I asked as if it made a difference.

"Two thirty. The bars are already closed," Van Cotright said with a smile. "Looks like Zimmerman here saved your bacon. You never could shoot straight. I'll be by to see you in a day or two, finish up the paperwork. I have to hook up with the San Luis Obispo shooting team at HQ. You should be there too, Detective," he said to Zimmerman. He said his goodbyes, gave Linda his card and a hug. That left Zim to fill in the blanks.

"Water," I croaked. Linda put a straw to my lips as Zimmerman stepped to the side of my bed.

"I spotted Rasheed Dupree enter your building right at seven," he began. "I waited five minutes to go in after him. The elevator was shut down, so I took the stairs. I'm just coming out the stairwell and hear shots as I head to your door. In I go, there's your buddy, gun in hand. I shout a 'Drop it,' he spins on me, and I fire.

"I tried to stop all this ... came by at six, but nobody was at your office ... doors locked ... your office phones rang, went to answer machine ... left three or four voice mails on your cell ... called Linda, said she was heading to Phoenix, didn't know where you were," he said.

"I didn't, Detective, only that he was probably up to no good," Linda explained.

"I staked out across the street hoping this wouldn't go down. I never saw you go into your building. Were you already there?" Zimmerman asked me.

"No ... got there ... six thirty," I think I said.

"My partner is still with Beverly Hills homicide at Patek's house. He went there with a Beverly Hills patrol unit to arrest your client, found him on the kitchen floor. His throat had been slit, kind of like you found his business partner, Tillman. We're betting Rasheed Dupree did it then went to your place to clean up loose ends," is what Zimmerman might have said to make the room spin around.

"You get the money?" I maybe asked as the lights were dimming and the walls moved.

"What mon—"

And the lights went out.

I opened my eyes again hoping I wasn't really where I thought I was. I wasn't. It was daylight, and I was in another room. Linda was curled up in a chair with a blanket and pillow fast asleep.

Turning on my side caused me to grunt and wake her up. "I thought you were going to Phoenix."

"We were halfway there when Zimmerman called, said you'd been injured and someone would have to lock up the office. He said you were going to Cedars by ambulance. I gave him Art's number.

Ruth drove us straight here." Linda stopped when the nurse entered the room.

"Why am I hooked up to a catheter?" figuring out the source of my other discomfort.

"Your doctor doesn't want you getting out of bed just yet," the nurse replied, holding up the half-filled bag. "Everything seems to be working."

Linda gave me a smile and a kiss on the cheek. "I'll be back this afternoon."

"I love you and want to marry you. What do you say?" I whispered.

"You're delirious. Go back to sleep." Another kiss. "Sweet dreams." She left.

After the orange juice, oatmeal, and one cup of a blackish brown liquid they said was coffee, I did what Linda had told me and went back to sleep to dream sweet dreams.

We stand on a beach under a trellis covered with blue irises. A preacher stands before us Bible in hand. "Do you, Linda, take Rollo to be—"

"I do," she says.

"Did you really say yes?"

"Well, duh! Of course I did, Rollo."

"Look, everyone is here, Linda. There's Susan Cochran talking to Agent Monroe, and there's Alicia Carter with Marvelous Marvin. Hi, Ruth! Thanks for bringing Bob and his sister. Isn't that Sheriff Bullock with Dora Cruz? Hey, Uncle Vinnie, Aunt Angie, whatsamaddayou?"

The offshore breeze shifts to an onshore wind. I feel cold ...

"Wake up, Mr. Michaels. It's time to pull that catheter out."

Epilogue

Of course, life goes on. Two weeks after fleeing, Linda and I returned to Los Angeles, unmarried but engaged, with no date set for nuptials. We picked out the ring in a Jared's jewelry store in Mobile, the small marquise diamond with six tiny baguettes, her choice, not mine. We made the announcement at the Monday associates' meeting. Our new commitment had us go house hunting, renting a three bedroom in Reseda by adding five hundred to the rents we were paying for our separate digs, the pool and hot tub sealing the deal.

Without the recording of the Motel California murders, Rasheed Dupree was left to carry the bag for all the murders to his grave. Since Detective Zimmerman had put one in Rasheed's ten-ring, who could argue otherwise? The beneficiary to all of this was Mrs. Tillman. The million-dollar life insurance policies on each partner were paid to the business, which she inherited from her cheating husband. But it wasn't long before lawyers, for who knows why, descended upon Sten-Tek for a piece of the pie. I guessed the partners' dream to take their company public died with them.

Then there was the mystery of the hundred-thousand cash withdrawal Phillippe Patek had made only a few hours before his death. It has yet to be found.

Clancy was only out for a week, coming back part-time to get us into the personal security business. The Morrow case continued to pay dividends, causing Clancy to sign up a very prominent Santa Monica plastic surgeon for our company to provide armed security for his home and surgery center. Enjoying his CEO status, he also brought Lucien Preston on board as Art's go-to guy on subpoena and process service. That little something in the mail Bob Howser promised turned out to be a check for $25,000. Michaels & Associates was certainly doing its part to make America great again.

Art was left to handle the FBI's search warrant of our case files and financials, winding up before a federal judge to change the warrant to a *subpoena duces tecum*. An acquaintance of Art's at the federal courts building tipped him off that the warrant had been issued. Being a former federal prosecutor, Art got right in to see the judge and worked out a deal whereby the judge would decide which files and records the FBI could have access to.

Two more weeks passed before Linda and Ruth were able to get the required records to the court. A few days later, we received notice of an IRS audit. *Coincidence? Yeah, right.* But our ability to parry the FBI pokes didn't stop their pressure.

I was called before a not-so-secret federal grand jury in New York in late June. The US attorney's gracious transportation proviso was a coach seat on the red-eye with a return to LA that evening. It took me four days to recover from the jet lag. My testimony took all of twenty minutes and established who I was, what I did, that I was an acquaintance of Vincenzo Costello, and I'd been present when John Cochran was murdered.

The highlight of my ten-hour visit to New York was running into Susan Cochran. She was with her mother in the hallway when I came out of the courtroom. Susan looked great; Mom looked sedated. Susan took out a ten-dollar bill from her purse and without saying a word tucked it into the hanky pocket of my suit jacket.

"Susan, it was a tip for the housekeeper."

"Why didn't you wake me up?" she asked.

"I would never have gotten back to California" got me a smile I'll always remember.

They went into the courtroom, and I went out to the Fort Salonga Hideaway to give my uncle Vinnie a heads-up about my testimony. He already knew all about it, as did most of New York's crime bosses. The feds were putting a target on Vincenzo Costello's back. The day after I returned to Los Angeles, Agent Monroe showed up at Michaels & Associates with a postscript to our little adventure in Deadwood.

"Did you know Dominic Frattalli?" she asked. "He was your uncle Vinnie's cousin."

"He's not my uncle, and I don't know Big Vinnie's extended family. Does your use of past tense imply Dominic is no longer with us?"

"Frattalli was executed just like Cochran, two to the back of the head. And just like Cochran, he was in witness protection. The bureau thinks Costello has penetrated the program and has assigned Soldier Boy Mahan to take these people out."

"So you're here to find out if I'm somehow involved in Fratalli's death too? You guys should be conducting an internal investigation instead of screwing over me and my associates. That phony secret grand jury bullshit can only get Costello killed, and you know it."

"And how is that a bad thing?"

"I'm losing a lot of respect for you, Rene."

"It's Special Agent Monroe now. I'll call off the dogs if you can help me out with this, Michaels. Talk it over with your lawyer. He worked my side of the fence before. He probably knows a lot about RICO prosecutions. And don't think I haven't figured out why Costello went dark, nipote mio. I'll be in touch," she said, putting the reason for her visit on the table and leaving. *Another woman pissed at me?*

On July Fourth, Linda and I hosted a company barbecue and pool party at our new place in Reseda. We all wore something pink in celebration of Sylvia's being pronounced cancer-free. My BFF, Bob Howser, was driven to the party by Ruth. His illness continued to take a physical toll, but his spirit had already bought him an extra two months. We all wished we could celebrate his recovery someday too.

Nerd showed up with his date, Lucien. They had become a couple. Art brought along his latest love, Tanya, a paralegal from Scott Mathew's office. They chose this occasion to announce their engagement, big ring and all, making me feel sorry for both of them.

I pointed to the pile of illegal fireworks I'd transported across state lines and asked Art, "You think the FBI will add those to my transgressions list?"

"I wouldn't put it past Monroe. What did you do to piss her off?"

"Just being me does that to some people."

The caterer arrived right on time. Six full racks of Tony Roma's ribs, baked beans, slaw, potato salad, roasted corn on the cob all combined for a great buffet. Three kinds of beer and ten bottles of California reds and whites promised to keep us all going past the ten o'clock pyrotechnics.

"Hey, Ruth, did you remember your guitar?" I yelled from the hot tub.

"In the car, hoping for a paying gig."

"Sing for your supper," Linda said, showing she still had my back.

I sipped a few brews and reveled in the camaraderie of friends. We were ten people not wanting to face life alone and believing business should never come before friendship.

My phone rang.

"Hi, Mel. You and Brando are coming over for the fireworks, right?"

"You bet. Save us some ribs. Can I bring Jake?"

"Sure, but you better hurry before the beer runs out."

"Oh, Dad!"

Acknowledgments

First, I wish to thank all of you who served as the models for each of the characters in this novel. You know who you are. I'll neither confirm nor deny your identity.

Second, a shout-out to all my friends out there facing their personal battles with cancer. Your courage and strength inspired two of my characters. May God keep you in His grace. You are in my prayers.

Finally, thank you, Linda, for being my proofreader, critic, and conscience. Keeping me chained to my computer when just plain encouragement wasn't quite enough may have been a bit over the top. Can you bring me another cup of coffee ... *please?*

Warm and fuzzy

Printed in the United States
By Bookmasters